NEVER FORGET

ROBERT W. KIRBY

INKUBATOR
BOOKS

Published by Inkubator Books
www.inkubatorbooks.com

ISBN (eBook): 978-1-83756-380-7
ISBN (Paperback): 978-1-83756-381-4
ISBN (Hardback): 978-1-83756-382-1

1

People would often ask her, 'So, what's it like to be a Fincher?'

She'd say something silly and sarcastic, like, 'Isn't that some type of pretty bird?'

When she'd been around seventeen, two lads had approached her in the street, and she'd truly learned what it *was* like to be a Fincher in North Sutton. Even now, all these years later, their horrible faces were etched on her mind. She'd guessed they were yobs from the Eden estate. Those two boys were part of a larger mob, which stood watching eagerly from the other side of the road. Those faces were less clear, but there had been a few girls with them; she remembered their cruel, cackle-like laughs.

The younger boy had told her Ernest was a sicko who deserved to die. The other one, older and stockier, had prodded her hard in the chest with his chunky finger and said, 'You're his granddaughter, which means you have that murderer's blood pumping in your veins.'

The prod had really hurt her right boob, but she'd kept a brave face and hadn't let the pain show.

'How's it feel to have killer's blood?' the younger boy had said with a wicked grin. 'Do you think you'll kill someone one day? I bet you will. I bet you'd like to kill me! You would, right?'

'My dad reckons Ernest is innocent, and someone in his family is the real killer. Is that true?' the stocky boy had said. 'Did you do it?'

She'd held her head high, keeping her mouth firmly shut.

'Oi, you rude slag, don't ignore him,' the other boy had barked.

They'd thrown bits of rubbish at her. Splashed some fizzy drink in her face.

'Drop dead, you losers!' she'd yelled.

'Bitch,' they'd shouted in unison.

She'd shook her head, turned away, and decided she wouldn't entertain the pair of horrible delinquents. Why should she? They had no right to demand answers from her.

Groups of noisy teenagers were gathering everywhere at that point. Gaping, unkind faces, eager to watch the thrilling exchange, revel in her misery, and hopefully witness an altercation.

She'd strutted off, muttering, 'I wouldn't waste my energy on you pair of pathetic pricks.'

One of the boys had shoved her from behind, and she'd fallen into the road to a chorus of jeers and hoots. Before she'd been able to rise to her feet, she was kicked in the face several times. At least one girl had joined in the attack; she knew that because she remembered her shrill shriek as she punched, slapped and clawed at her.

The beating was more humiliating than painful. Well, at the time, anyway. Later that day, when she'd rinsed her bloodied face in the sink, she'd almost passed out. She'd held onto the taps, eyeing herself in the mirror, scrutinising that waxy reflection gaping back at her. Saw the fresh streak of blood streaming out of nostrils that were caked in dry gore, and the several raised grazes on her cheeks that were hot, red and raw.

'What's it like to be a Fincher?' she'd whispered to herself through gritted teeth.

She'd answered her own question with a scream, so high-pitched and intense that, even to this day, she's surprised the glass in that mirror didn't shatter into a trillion pieces.

Now the bleak memory sickened her more than ever.

If only she possessed the ability to morph into a deft finch or perhaps a graceful jaybird. Because then she'd fly far away from this hostile town.

And she'd never come back.

2

Jennifer stared at the page on her laptop for a long time, gripping her hedgehog stress ball tightly in her right hand. She'd been working on this scene all day. Working on this instead of chipping away at the ever-growing pile of legal documents she *should* be editing.

She dropped the hedgehog, peeled a tangerine, shoved the entire thing into her mouth. Then she snatched off her glasses, gave them a good clean with a microfibre cloth and slid them back on. As she read the piece for the third time, she drummed her fingers on the desk.

The Jeopardy of Love
Jennifer Fincher
Act 1 / Scene 1: Clearing in the Forest

The curtains open on a small clearing bathed in a moody, dark-blue moonlight. We hear the sounds of nature at night. The lonely hoot of a distant owl. The raspy croak of frogs and acute chirps of crickets. A small fire burns at the centre, and huddled around it are two figures swathed in heavy blankets.

Everett – Will you not just let me look upon your face one more time?

Isla – I told you to stay away.

Everett – You ask the impossible of me. Let me embrace you. Let us survive this bitterly cold night... together, Isla, my love.

Isla – I am not cold.

Everett – But your heart is cold, and mine is even colder without you in my life. My every waking moment is utter torturous misery without you. Meaningless and empty. Like a once-flourishing rose, now abandoned in a darkened room, where it's left to fade, wilt and die.

Isla – I cannot leave my husband.

Everett – Your husband is a miscreant and does not deserve you.

Isla – I can never leave him. He'd hunt me to the edges of the world and beyond. My fate is sealed. I must stay with him.

Everett – Your fate is your own, Isla. You should decide your path, not that monster.

Isla – Words. These are just words.

Everett – No! Not just words. I mean to take action.

The wind picks up, and the fire is suddenly extinguished. The sounds of the forest cease in that moment. A brief pause, then Everett throws his blanket aside, and we see he is a well-built man in his early thirties, with a pencil moustache.

[Everett stands and breaks out into song.]

Jennifer let out a deflating sigh and muttered, 'Meh,' before selecting the entire block of text on her laptop. As her finger hovered over the delete button, the doorbell sounded, and she stopped. She pulled up the feed to her doorbell camera and studied the screen. The wiry man who stood there was haggard and hollow-eyed. His scraggly beard and attire gave him the appearance of an ageing guitarist from some naff heavy metal tribute band. He eyed the camera with small, light grey eyes that were both dull and shrewd.

Howard Fincher. She hardly recognised the scruffy sod.

Jennifer made her way to the door, took a deep intake of air, then opened it. 'Hello, Dad.'

'Hi, Jen. All right?' he asked in a quiet voice.

Jennifer caught a whiff of him. A mixture of musty clothes, stale booze and grease. 'Yep.'

'You busy? It's only... I need to talk. It's important.'

'You'd better come in. I was just taking a ten-minute break.' Jennifer led him into the living area. 'Sorry, I'd have tidied up a bit if I'd known I was having company.'

He gazed around the small space as if taking things in for the first time. 'It's spotless in here, Jen.'

Jennifer wanted to correct him and say, *My name is Jennifer*. Instead, she tidied up the pens and books that sat on her workstation, which dominated the room. She didn't like having visits sprung upon her like this. She couldn't stand other people seeing her in a shambles, even if it was just her dad, who no doubt hadn't picked up a bottle of bleach in the last two decades.

'Take a seat, Dad. I'll make you a drink.'

'Did you buy this place?' He plonked down on her freshly made sofa.

She screamed inside. She'd have to wipe that clean throw off and wash it again this afternoon. The cushions, too. 'I rent it from the elderly couple next door. It's just a self-contained annexe. Small, but very cosy, and perfect for little old me.'

'It's nice. Very modern.'

'So, I have peppermint tea or some nice strong Colombian coffee. Instant, but very good.'

'Any beer?'

'No, but I opened a bottle of Merlot on Friday, which I didn't make much of a dent in, so if you fancy finishing that off, you're more than welcome.'

'Cheers.'

Jennifer went into the kitchen area and retrieved the chilled wine and a bottle of water for herself.

'Are you still working from home?' he asked.

Jennifer grabbed a glass from the cupboard. 'Yes, that's right.'

'What is it you do again?'

Jennifer rinsed the glass under the hot tap. 'I proofread

and analyse documents for several law firms.' She poured a generous helping of wine into the glass and took the drinks back into the living area, where she found that her dad had moved from the sofa and was now examining her laptop's screen. She almost dropped the drinks. 'Wine!'

'Oh, ta.' He accepted the glass and took a sip. 'So you're writing a new play for the theatre group? Still into all that, I see.'

Jennifer smiled stiffly, trying not to show her indignation at the liberty he'd taken by reading her work without her consent. She pushed down the laptop's lid, switched off her main PC monitor, and suffered in silence. Nobody, but nobody, got to read her work until she had a finished piece to present.

'What's that group called again?'

'The Flair Play Drama Group.'

'Is that funny little bloke with the bald head still in charge?'

'Dale Appleton. Yes, he's the theatre director.'

'Didn't you date him?'

'No, I didn't. He's just my friend.'

He poked a finger at her hedgehog and grinned. 'Still like hedgehogs?'

'That's my Stress-Hog,' said Jennifer, scooping him up and placing him on a shelf next to her elegant white orchid.

'Do you remember Reggie-Hedgy? You still have him?'

'Huh, yes, I do remember Reggie. No, I have no clue where he ended up. Guess I must've lost him.'

'You and Reggie were inseparable.' He shuffled back over to the sofa and slumped down. She noticed he'd kept his clumpy walking boots on, which meant the floor would need a good spray and a vigorous mop once he'd left.

'Is it a mystery? The play?'

'Dale's asked me to write a musical drama with elements including love, murder and betrayal. But I need some fresh inspiration. I'm struggling to get out of the starting blocks with this one. It's about a love triangle set in eighteenth-century Dorset. A mistreated woman who tries to leave her ruthless husband, who's also the head of a smuggling ring on the Isle of Purbeck.'

'Oh, interesting stuff,' he said, sounding unenthusiastic. 'You not having wine?'

Jennifer sipped her water and perched herself on the arm of the sofa. 'I must get back to work soon. Plus, I only drink on Fridays and Sundays. It's my little rule not to touch the stuff on any other days. Save special occasions, of course.'

He took another sip, and his face clouded with sadness.

Jennifer felt a tad mean. She'd not seen the man in over four months, so perhaps he considered this to be a 'special occasion'.

'I'm here about your grandad. I'm here about Ernest.'

A sudden icy shiver shot down Jennifer's back, and she clapped her hand about the bottle of water, making it crumple.

'The Probation Service contacted me about his upcoming release. He'll be out on licence, which basically means they'll be keeping an eye on him; he'll have strict rules to adhere to, but he'll be a free man.'

'I see. Right. OK. I appreciate you coming to tell me this,' she said.

'This is big. It's going to be hard for all of us.'

She nodded.

'Twenty-five years. Well, that's hardly life, is it? Bah, it's sickening, isn't it?'

Jennifer stayed silent as she processed this news.

'There's more,' her dad said, gulping down his wine. 'Ernest has written to me as well. He's told me he intends to move back into Barren's Lodge, which means he is planning to stay here.'

'Can he do that?'

'He still owns the old place, so yeah, he can, and there's nothing we can do to stop him.'

'Will you go and see him?'

His disgruntled expression confirmed his answer was a resounding no.

'He must be old now,' she pointed out. 'In his eighties.'

'So?'

'We don't need to be afraid of him, do we?'

'No. *We* don't need to be afraid of him,' he said with an edge of venom in his tone.

3

Breathe in deeply... exhale. *Hand on heart,* she told herself as she ran her hand over the newspaper nestled inside the plastic folder, its aged edges frayed and crumpled. Without removing the page, she read the article while sipping a black coffee.

The residents of North Sutton have never forgotten the murder of Katherine Fincher, who was killed by her own father at his residence on the outskirts of the town. She was just thirty-eight when she died, leaving behind three children. Ava, sixteen at the time, Stacey, fourteen, and Jennifer, nine. But even to this day, her father, Ernest Moorby, has desperately pleaded his innocence despite the overwhelming evidence against him. Ernest was incarcerated when he was fifty-seven. At the time of her murder, Katherine and her children were temporarily living at Barren's Lodge because of marital issues.

This heinous crime still haunts the town. It clings to it like a dark, melancholy cloud that refuses to dissipate despite the passing of time. So, ten years on, we ask ourselves these questions: Just who was Katherine Fincher? Why did her own father take her life that fateful day? And will Ernest ever speak the truth, accept the blame and give Katherine's tormented family the answers they desperately seek?

She put down the article and decided she couldn't face any of this today. She shoved the page inside the pink ring binder and tossed it back into the storage box.

Annoyed with herself, she sipped the coffee again and winced at the horrid taste. It tasted sour and foul. Three days without sugar. Only three. She just couldn't adapt to drinking coffee without it. *Zero discipline, that's my problem,* she told herself.

She tried to close the lid back on the storage box, and the plastic clip snapped off in her hand. She viewed the broken clip in her open palm for a good ten seconds before she lost her temper and tossed the entire box of papers across the kitchen worktop.

As she tried to steady her nerves and lower her racing heartbeat, she decided she would have a nice big brown sugar in her coffee, and once she'd had that much-needed sugary caffeine boost, she'd grab the folding camping fire, a few logs and burn her entire bloody box of morbid historical news reports.

4

Jennifer tried to keep other things at the forefront of her mind and forget about Ernest. It had been three weeks since her dad dropped the bombshell news. Luckily, with the new play and the piles of work she had to deal with, it had been easy for her to lose herself in other things. Then she'd spotted that post on social media earlier. A link to a webpage that was dedicated to outing Ernest. And since seeing it, she could not get her grandad and his recent release from prison out of her head.

Now, some six hours after glimpsing the site, she grabbed her Stress-Hog, squeezed him until his eyes bulged, opened the webpage and forced herself to view it again.

Make Moorby Move

Is twenty-five years long enough for such a heinous crime? Do you think this is justice? Do you want this man back in our peaceful community, freely roaming the streets with every chance of re-offending?

Ernest may well be an old man now, but he's still a cold-blooded killer, and if you believe this is unfair, join the thousands who agree by signing our petition today.

There are approximately eighty thousand residents in our town, and we want every single one of you to add your name to our list. Make your signature count. Have your say.

We will be heard. We will force the authorities to take action.

Act now... Make Ernest Moorby, the beast who killed his own daughter, move out of our town. We don't want him here. We do not accept murderers into our community.

By clicking the link below, YOU can put things right.

Keep North Sutton safe.

Jennifer realised she'd clamped her Stress-Hog so hard that his eyes were now larger than his body, so she eased the pressure.

Under the webpage's *Sign the petition now* button was a photo of Ernest, which she guessed must have been taken at the time of the murder. In the shot he had unkempt steely-grey hair, and his strong face carried a sad, distant look, like he'd been desperately trying to cast his mind away elsewhere. Anywhere that wasn't outside a packed Crown Court, where a drove of media-hungry journalists fought like vultures to grab that perfect shot of the condemned man.

The photo generated a thousand memories, and, oddly

enough, many of these were very happy ones, which confused her somewhat. How could someone she hated with a passion generate such warm and fuzzy memories within her?

And she *did* hate him.

Didn't she?

Jennifer knew one thing – and that was she wasn't afraid of the old man. But her grandad, and these conflicting emotions, intrigued her. She wondered if her sisters, Ava and Stacey, were having the same thoughts about the man. She'd expected at least one of them to have reached out and discussed the recent state of affairs, but she'd not heard a peep out of them.

Maybe I should reach out to them, she mused, before dismissing that idea.

Jennifer put down her Stress-Hog and pulled up Google maps on her PC. She wanted to refresh her memory. She wanted to see where Barren's Lodge was located.

Tomorrow afternoon, she'd speak to her grandad in person, decide how she felt; then she'd take appropriate action.

5

J ennifer had butterflies in her stomach as she rode her scooter down the single-track lane towards the enormous willow tree, which marked the entrance to the property.

She'd forgotten all about that tree. The willow's overhanging branches dominated the entire lane. They dangled down so far, they touched the road. She would giggle as her mum drove the car through them, while singing, 'Here we go again. Through the magical carwash.' Those spindly branches would dance over the roof and rub across the windows as the vehicle moved under the tree. Once the windscreen was clear of brush, and they'd left the tree's veil, it felt like they'd entered a new world as Barren's Lodge appeared ahead of them.

Jennifer eased up her speed as she made for the curtain of branches. As she entered, the tree seemed to come alive, grabbing at her arms and scraping past her visor. It didn't seem like the magical experience she recalled as a child; instead, it generated a growing sense of dread. A sense that she was heading to a woeful place where she was no longer welcome. A place where *nobody* was welcome. As she rode out of the other side, she became aware of how much noise her trusty Honda PCX was making.

She rode up to the small courtyard that led to the main gate, then brought the bike to a stop.

Jennifer killed the Honda's engine, kicked up the stand and yanked off her helmet.

It was so quiet here, and the eerie silence made her uneasy as she viewed the entrance. The wooden barn gate that sat between two grey outbuildings held the faded Barren's Lodge sign.

Jennifer dismounted the Honda and scanned the area. Tall silver birches ringed the courtyard, and a tangle of untidy green vines was creeping over the roof of one of the outbuildings, where a swarm of noisy wasps massed. She tried the gate, but it was locked with a steel padlock, so she clumsily clambered over it, the crash helmet hindering her efforts.

Once inside, the noise of the wasps intensified, and she swatted a mob of them away as she made her way up the snaking driveway away from the little winged terrors. She glanced back as she went, noticing that part of the outbuilding's roof had collapsed in, and a vast cloud of wasps swarmed there. During the absence of people, the busy insects had no doubt reigned supreme over the empty property.

Jennifer wondered what else had set up home at Barren's Lodge. She visualised nests of adders in the woodshed, beady-eyed crows occupying the loft space, and hordes of giant rats scurrying through a network of intricate tunnels under the main house. The house that she could now see just ahead of her.

Barren's Lodge was a dirty-white building with a grey slate roof that was patched with light green lichen. It had four chimneys, two of which were tall and in awful shape. One appeared to be tilting, and she reckoned a good gust of wind would topple it. Sections of broken guttering hung precariously, and those few pipes still clinging onto the property were overflowing with clumps of pulpy moss.

Jennifer had always remembered the old house as a rustic, charming home, but now the words that came to mind for this place were ominous, decrepit and depressing, yet it still evoked a slight nostalgia deep down inside her somewhere.

As Jennifer approached the building, her heart rate quickened, and she almost spun around and ran. She stopped and held her helmet against her chest as she studied that little courtyard where the flowerpots once sat. This was the spot where guests would be greeted and offered refreshments before they'd be led to their holiday cabins. It was also the spot where her mum would sit and smoke.

The courtyard looked a state now. Weeds poked from broken slabs, smashed flowerpots scattered the ground, and an array of stagnant water holes were dotted here and there, with clouds of tiny gnats clustered around the puddles. The green round table still sat there, with its two matching chairs.

Jennifer placed the helmet on the table and rubbed a finger over the peeling green paint. She'd seen her mum at this very table on the day she died. She pictured her now, sitting here in the sun, smoking, her face set in a sullen grimace. There'd been a breeze that day, and she could remember her mum's long brunette hair flapping in her face as she puffed away, not bothering to remove the strands.

When she'd spotted Jennifer, she had eyed her carefully for several moments, frown lines crinkling her brow, as if she wasn't sure who was watching her. Then she thumbed out the cigarette against the table, removed the hair from her face and offered her a tired but affectionate smile. 'Hello, my little sweet pea.'

Was that the last time I saw my mum smile? Was that the last time she called me sweet pea?

Katherine Fincher had been gorgeous and kept her figure in fabulous shape despite her love of sugary drinks, cakes and all things sweet and naughty. She'd had the most amazing hazel eyes that could both sparkle with delight and drown you in a deep sadness. Jennifer often wished she'd inherited just a smidge of her mum's loveliness. Stacey and Ava both had. She'd somehow ended up with podgy cheeks, mousy brown hair and zero allure. The reality that Jennifer was different had been apparent from an early age, hence Ava often pointing out that she was indeed the ugly duckling of the family. Jennifer never bothered disputing this. It had been true then and still was now.

'Excuse me. Can I help you?' The man's voice cutting through the silence made Jennifer jump. Even though there'd been no menace in his tone, just curiosity.

Jennifer turned to face the man, offering him a peppy grin. 'Hello... Grandad.' Calling him 'Grandad' seemed strange and inappropriate. Like simply in doing so, she'd already been disloyal to her dead mum.

This man standing here gawping at her. This man she knew only *as* Grandad looked tired, frail, forlorn. His head was completely bald, and he wore large, square glasses. The most distinctive change was the bushy white beard that gave him the appearance of a grizzled sailor. He wore a baggy blue T-shirt, straight cargo shorts and white socks pulled up to his pale, knobbly knees. A pair of open-fronted sandals finished off his rather unstylish attire.

Not that she had fabulous dress sense herself. Nerdy, frumpy and boring were all words her sisters had used in the past to describe her fashion sense. At least she knew where she'd inherited her dodgy taste in clobber from now.

The pair gazed at each other for a while before the penny dropped, and he gasped, 'Jennifer? My word, it's you, isn't it?' His voice sounded broken and sad. His eyes clouded with tears, and he cracked an astonished grin. 'I can't believe my eyes.' He swallowed audibly and put a hand over his mouth as tears slipped down his wrinkled cheeks.

'I... I think you might have a wasp problem in that outhouse,' she said, her voice bright.

'I can't believe you've come. I just... Oh my. It's so wonderful to see you,' he croaked.

His sad happiness was genuine. There could be no doubting that.

He stepped closer to her, and for a moment she was sure that he was going to hug her, but instead he smiled through the tears, shaking his head in disbelief. As though he couldn't take any of this in.

Jennifer had lots of questions. Hundreds. She decided those could wait.

He peered over her shoulder as if checking to see if anybody else had come with her.

'Just me,' she said, wondering if he was disappointed it hadn't been one of her older sisters visiting.

'You haven't changed a bit, Jennifer. Well, obviously you look older, but you know what I mean.'

She kind of *did* know what he meant.

'Please come in for tea,' he said.

Jennifer nodded. 'I'd like that.'

'The house is a bit of a mess. It's all got damp and shabby over the years. Lots to do. Lots.' Ernest opened the front door and shuffled inside.

As Jennifer glanced into the darkened house, she struggled to take the first step to follow him. She forced her trembling legs to move.

Once in the hallway, her heart rate became irregular, and she needed to take a few sharp intakes of air as she glanced to her right, getting a full view of the vast room that once was the main lounge.

The high stone fireplace caught her eye, and she stared at it as she stepped into the airless room that was covered in dark wood panelling. Her palms were sweaty as she walked over to the fireplace and touched one of the lumpy stones that made up the centrepiece. The stones rose up to the ceiling, where they finished into a V-shape. Time had not touched those giant stones, although the fireplace inside was black and smeared with thick grime. Jennifer caught a whiff of something nasty. Something dead. A bird would be her best guess.

'Come through,' called Ernest, his voice distant as it echoed around the old building.

Jennifer walked over to the window and tugged back the heavy red curtains, which disturbed several years' worth of dust and dirt. As the intense sun rays speared through the window, dust particles danced and floated around the immense room like it was snowing indoors. So thick, it made her cough.

'A bit surreal being back here, right?' he said, now standing in the doorway, a shroud of particles drifting about his silhouette.

Jennifer nodded, running her finger through a layer of dust that had collected on a long oak display cabinet. On top sat an array of trinkets: a deer carved out of wood, a faded silver vase, a small globe on a brass meridian.

'Like a dream, I suppose,' he added ruefully.

Jennifer spun the old globe with one finger. 'Mm. Yes, it is.'

'You used to be obsessed with that globe when you were a little girl. You once told me you wanted to explore every single country in the world. Apart from the cold places. Do you remember that?'

Jennifer offered him a quick smile and nodded. But she didn't have any recollection of that. She thought it sounded more like something Ava would have said.

'Kettle should be boiled.' With that, he scuttled off.

As Jennifer made to follow him, her eyes dropped to the scuffed wooden floor, and a memory popped into her head that was so crystal clear, it scared her. On the day her mum died, Jennifer had seen broken glass on the floor of this room. Glass and blood... everywhere.

And with that graphic memory came something else – a potent smell that she could almost catch now. *Whisky*. It had been a smashed whisky bottle on the floor.

Her grandad's booze.

But her mum's blood.

6

———

She took out her favourite ballpoint pen and gave it a good hard shake. The pen with the smooth black ink that she used whenever she jotted her signature. She scribbled a few lines on a blank piece of paper, and happy that the pen was working adequately, she started to write down those jumbled thoughts whirling around inside her aching head. As she wrote, she spoke the words.

'I could never say these things to you in person. I wouldn't be able to. I often wonder what it's been like to be locked away for all those years. I try to imagine what went through your head the first time that cell door closed behind you and the reality of the situation dawned. Did you panic and make a lunge for freedom? Did you sob at the hopelessness of the situation? Perhaps it took several days, weeks or even months before it hit you. Before it fully sank in. Or did you just accept it?

'I once had a recurring dream where you were tunnelling out of your cell using an acid-like substance that you made in the prison kitchen. You could only make a small batch each week, but gradually the hole grew with each splash of the potent mix. It's so silly; to create the mix, you mashed up some potato peelings with white vinegar and purified broccoli. Like that would work. So daft. Dreams can be so ridiculous. Sometimes in my dreams that hole seemed huge. Big enough for the average person to stand in. Then another night it would be no more than a tiny crack, as if you'd been forced to start the process all over again, and I would assume this meant you had been transferred to another cell. I kept picturing this prison with holes in half of the cells, and guards scratching their heads, perplexed by the bizarre breaches throughout the complex.

'Then those dreams stopped for a while. And during one cold winter's night, I dreamed I woke up to find you in my room. Oh, boy, you looked super vexed. I woke up for real before I got to find out why you'd come. Before I got to find out *what* you'd planned to do to me.

'That was the last time I saw you in my dreams, and my mind hasn't returned to the prison during my sleep since. Although, to be honest, I suspect that's because I don't sleep anymore. Not properly. A few snatched hours here and there. Sometimes my body shuts down because I'm so exhausted, but my mind doesn't fully click off. It's safer that way. I manage to cope. I'm used to it now. Well, you did always say I had a wacky, overactive imagination. The truth is, my brain never stops. It's always ticking away... Always churning out thoughts and ideas.

'OK, I'll get to the point of this letter now. You need to leave North Sutton. If you stay in town, I promise bad things will happen. I'll make them happen. You probably don't have long left now, so don't waste your golden years hanging around here and making life difficult for everyone. Go far away. Leave town. Leave Kent. Or, preferably, leave the damn country.'

She stopped writing, stopped speaking, and laughed without humour. What was she thinking? She'd never actually send the stupid letter, so why the hell was she bothering with this? It was like she needed to rip the thoughts out of her scrambled brain. As if that would wipe them somehow.

Annoyed now, she scribbled over her words until the page resembled the crazy doodling of an overhyped toddler. Once the pen was empty of ink, she snatched up the paper, tore it into shreds and shoved it in the bin.

Breathe in deeply... exhale. Hand on heart. Eyes glued shut.

If she wanted that old bastard out of town, she'd need to be far more proactive and inventive because a stupid letter wouldn't cut it.

7

M aple Green was as lovely as ever. Jennifer liked this part of town. Quiet, safe, charming. The best part of North Sutton to live in if you had a family. But also the most expensive. She could see why Stacey and David had been so keen to move here all those years back.

She turned her scooter into Pine Close and slowed to a crawl. Took in all the attractive, semi-detached properties with wide drives and pristine gardens. Then she caught sight of a gunmetal grey BMW X5 go racing past her. Caught the serious expression fixed on the driver's uptight face.

Ava had arrived.

Jennifer watched as the bulky vehicle made an abrupt turn and zipped onto a driveway in front of her. She followed at a snail's pace, allowing time for Ava to get inside first. Thus avoiding any awkward one-to-one small talk with her eldest sister.

Jennifer pulled into the driveway and was surprised to see David. All he had on was a pair of tight swimming shorts and sliders. He was busy washing down his car, the make of which she was unable to decipher thanks to the amount of soapy bubbles covering it. He'd grown his facial hair since she'd last seen him. His little horseshoe-shaped beard suited him well, but she thought his mop of shaggy brown hair could do with a good trim. He wouldn't have looked out of place riding a surfboard on the Cornish coast.

David noticed her and flashed her a hearty grin as he wrung out the sponge with two hands. 'Long time no see. Welcome to North Sutton's sexiest carwash. Twenty for the bike.'

She clambered off her scooter and yanked off her helmet. 'Wow, that's quite expensive.'

He shook his wet hair and pointed to his naked chest. 'You get what you pay for here.'

'Is it cheaper if you put your shirt back on?'

David pretended to be offended and picked up his jet wash. 'What? Most certainly not.' He shot a jet of water up into the air, and a few droplets rained down on her. 'And how are you? It's been a while. I'd give you a hug to welcome you, but...'

Jennifer laughed. 'You can owe me a hug when you're less soggy and sudsy.'

'Deal. Ava went out the back to find Stacey. Your dad's here too. Good luck.'

'Hey?'

David pulled a mock serious expression. 'Ava had a face on her. I barely got a grunt out of her.'

'You didn't offer to wash *her* car?'

'I didn't, no. I'm staying well out of her way. It might take me a very, very long time to wash this.'

'OK. Off I go, then. Groovy beard, by the way, David. Makes you look younger.'

'Yeah, you reckon?'

'Oh, defo. And you missed a bit.'

David cracked a charming grin, clicked on his jet wash and fired a blast at his car.

Jennifer opened the side gate and made her way around the back and into the garden.

Into the lion's den.

'Time to grasp the nettle,' she muttered to herself as a ginger cat scurried past her legs.

Stacey and her dad sat around a large glass-topped table with a wide white canopy above them. Ava was pulling up a seat and chatting to Stacey in a low voice. They hadn't seen her yet as she watched from the gate.

Her dad had shaved off his facial hair, giving him a younger, yet more hostile appearance. The clean shave exposed his sunken cheeks, and his eyes seemed far more discernible on his naked, gaunt face. She certainly preferred him with the unruly beard.

Jennifer approached her family. Ava was the first to spot her, and she gave her a wave, accompanied by a luke-warm smile. She had on a pair of huge sunglasses and a long, flowing dress with a split that exposed one pale, slender leg. The black dress, though lovely, seemed total overkill for a family meet-up. Her eldest sister had lost some weight since their last get-together. A *lot* of weight. Her long face appeared sculpted, her sharp nose prominent.

'It's North Sutton's most prestigious playwright,' said Ava, in a tone so indifferent Jennifer wasn't sure if she'd meant this as a compliment or a less-than-subtle gibe.

Her dad's eyes flicked up from his phone. 'Hey, Jen,' he muttered before setting his eyes back on the phone.

'She hates being called Jen,' said Ava bluntly.

Jennifer approached, and Stacey got up from the table, a bubbly grin on her face. 'Jennifer, you're here,' she gushed.

Whereas Ava had lost weight, Stacey had gained it and looked rather buxom. A pudgy roll was noticeable under her low-cut white blouse, and she'd acquired what could only be described as a bubble butt and cankles.

Stacey hugged Jennifer. 'You look well, sis. Love the choppy pixie cut. I have never seen it so short. Suits you.'

'Thanks. You too,' said Jennifer. She meant it. OK, Stacey had put on a few pounds, but she carried it well. She still looked as pretty as ever, and her eyes, the colour of dark chocolate, sparkled brightly. The freckles on her nose, her slightly oily complexion and baby cheeks made her look like she could be in her late twenties, not clocking forty.

'Do you ever age, Stacey? You appear younger every time I see you,' said Jennifer.

'Flattery will get you everywhere in this house. Tea, coffee, wine? And would you like a slice of lemon cake? It's homemade.'

Ava flicked back her bouncy raven hair. 'Homemade by you or David?'

'David. He's quite the whizz in the kitchen,' said Stacey with a proud grin.

'Good culinary skills and he spends his weekends meticulously washing the car. What a guy,' said Ava.

Jennifer pulled up a seat. 'A cold drink and cake would be fab. Cheers. Not alcohol.'

'Where are the kids?' said Howard, still scanning his phone.

'With David's folks. They've gone down to Ramsgate for the afternoon,' said Stacey.

Ava rolled her eyes dramatically. 'Dad, has anyone ever told you that you're worse than a bloody fifteen-year-old schoolgirl with that phone of yours?'

'Mm, what's that?' he asked, distracted.

'Never mind,' said Ava.

'You sure you don't want cake, Ava?' asked Stacey.

Ava shook her head. 'Water will be fine. Ice and lemon if you have it.'

Stacey headed for the house. 'Sure. Be back in a tick, everybody. I'll grab you a fruit juice, Jennifer.'

Ava stretched out one long, bony arm across the table. Jennifer studied the thick mass of tattoos on it. A black sleeve of wild patterns, bands and symbols covered Ava's skin from her wrist to her shoulder. There were two new additions she'd not seen before. A rose twisting around her bicep and a lion with half its face covered in floral patterns. The latter most likely to express her love of being a Leo. Although Jennifer thought the inkings looked amazing, she had no desire to race off to get any of her own. If she liked a certain piece of artwork, she would just hang it on a canvas. That seemed less... permanent.

Ava caught her peeking at the new body art and grinned. 'What do you think?'

'Did it hurt?'

Ava nodded. 'In places. But a little pain was well worth the end result.'

Howard put down the phone. 'You getting the right arm done, Ava?'

'No.'

An uncomfortable silence grew for a few moments,

which Jennifer was tempted to fill. Only, she struggled to think of one thing to say to either of them. She willed Stacey to return, knowing she'd fill the stilted silence with no effort.

Her dad eyed his phone and scratched his neck. 'How's the play coming along, Jen?'

'Not great. I'm toying with a new idea. It might be a tad... provocative. It would be a thorny subject to cover.'

'Sounds intriguing. What's it about?' asked Ava.

'I'd rather not say. I tend to keep my ideas close to my chest. It's my funny way,' said Jennifer. She felt exhausted all of a sudden.

'Suit yourself,' said Ava, in a tone that suggested she hadn't been that bothered anyway.

Stacey returned with a tray of drinks and a long cake already sliced. 'Sorry, Ava, no lemons left. Is lime OK?'

Ava sighed through her nose. 'I prefer lemon. But don't worry if that's all you have.'

Stacey gave her a wry smile. 'Sorry.'

Howard made a grab for the cake and ate most of his slice in one bite. 'Oh, flippin' good that. You have lemon in your cake, so why do you need it in your bloody water, Ava? Fussy.'

'All the decorum of a gluttonous gibbon. And I'm not having any cake,' said Ava, as if the very idea of eating some would be preposterous.

'Yep, that's me,' he said, licking his fingers.

The heat today wasn't helping Jennifer's languid state. She tried and failed to suppress a long, gaping yawn.

On the rare occasions when Jennifer interacted with her family members, she would often view them as characters from an off-the-wall story.

Are all families this strange?

If Jennifer depicted Ava in a truthful light, the audience would see her as tactless, pretentious and temperamental. She'd fit the role of the villain of her tale rather well.

Hold up, is this how I really perceive my eldest sister? My antagonist? My arch-rival?

This idea generated a tiny smile. Jennifer imagined Ava's livid face as she witnessed her character coming alive on the theatre's stage. Not that Ava would *ever* bother attending one of her plays.

Jennifer brooded over her own preconception of herself. What qualities did she possess? She knew how Ava viewed her. The odd little ugly duckling. Annoying, withdrawn... obsessive.

'Are we actually going to talk about the reason we have been summoned?' said Ava.

Her sister's words snapped Jennifer out of her sleepy daze.

'Why spoil a pleasant afternoon? It is a lovely day,' said Stacey.

'Because we need to discuss this. It's important,' said Howard.

'Do we really have to go there at all?' said Stacey.

And Stacey. Nurturing, wholesome, tolerant.

Ava put down her glass and folded her arms. 'We can't pretend this isn't happening. It's all over social media. There's even a petition set up. I trust you've all signed it.'

'Yes,' Howard said, dusting off cake crumbs from his hands.

'I'm going to,' said Stacey meekly.

But also indecisive, timid and sometimes a tad needy.

Shut up, Jennifer. Stop characterising your family members, you bloody mad cow.

Stacey let out a sad sigh. 'I still can't get my head around all this.'

'I don't think he should be made to move. He's a frail old man. He can't hurt anybody,' said Jennifer.

The other three gawped at Jennifer like she'd admitted to some vile atrocity, such as firebombing a local orphanage. She knew she might as well just come out with it. No point in delaying any longer. 'I spoke to him the other day. I went to Barren's Lodge.'

Stacey's mouth dropped open.

Ava's face stayed deadpan, but her light grey eyes narrowed, like a wolf homing in on its unfortunate prey.

Her dad arched his eyebrows and grabbed another slice of cake.

'And I might go back there again,' said Jennifer.

Ava sipped a meagre amount of water through thin lips. 'How charitable of you.'

'Have you seen what they are saying online, Jennifer? They reckon he'll be targeted. You shouldn't go back there. It isn't safe to be around... Grandad.'

'Don't you dare call him that! You can't use *that* name,' snapped Ava.

Stacey's nostrils flared. 'OK. Sorry. Even if... *Ernest* is old and harmless—'

'Which he isn't,' interjected Howard.

'Even if he is, it doesn't matter, because that place is dangerous. And how can he even afford to stay there?' said Stacey.

'Gran's life insurance, probably,' said Ava. 'The old knobhead has loads of cash stashed away anyway. Not to mention his old timber yard business. He sold that and made a bomb when he was in his late forties.'

Stacey shook her head. 'How's it fair he comes out and still has everything?'

'He's a lonely old prick with nobody to share it with,' said Ava. 'What does he have now? Jack shit.'

'The house is a total mess. He needs help,' said Jennifer.

Ava glared at Jennifer. 'What? Are you serious? You have a bloody screw loose. Oh, sod this. I can't listen to this.' She stood up. 'This is so typical of her. She has to be the weirdo, as usual. She's only doing this to spite us all.'

'I just don't understand why you'd even want to see him,' said Stacey, her face a picture of sincerity.

Jennifer shrugged. 'What if... what if he has been telling the truth all these years? Can you imagine that?'

'He is lying,' said Ava, as if her word were final and not up for debate.

'But why? For what reason?' asked Jennifer.

'Because he doesn't want to admit to what he did. It was so messed up,' said Ava. 'Because by putting his hands up, he'd somehow make it all real. And he can't handle that fact.'

Jennifer nodded. 'So you're suggesting that he placed himself in some type of delusional realm in which he's *not* guilty? Never considered that. Our minds must work differently.'

Ava pursed her lips. 'There's a massive understatement. So, wait up. Are you saying you've always believed him to be innocent?'

'Oh, no. I'm not saying that at all,' said Jennifer.

'Sounds like you are,' said Ava.

'I meant that I've always assumed he lied for a different reason,' said Jennifer.

'And that is?' asked Ava.

It was Stacey who answered. 'Because he couldn't stand

the idea of being branded a monster for the rest of his life. So he injected an element of doubt. And he's still doing it. Even now, he's not prepared to say what he did.'

Jennifer picked up her fruit juice. 'But if he was innocent, hypothetically speaking here, then could you imagine what that would have been like? All those years in prison.'

Ava snorted. 'I don't like hypothetical discussions. They are pointless.'

Jennifer cleared her throat. 'Say it turned out he *was* innocent. What would you say to him?'

Ava shook her head. 'I am not hearing this. If you ever loved Mum, then I cannot comprehend how you can even stomach to spend a single second in that vile man's company. The jury made a unanimous decision. The evidence was irrefutable.'

'Ava, she was a bit too young to remember,' said Stacey.

'What do you think about this, Dad?' demanded Ava.

'Jennifer needs to make up her own mind about how she feels about that man,' he said coolly, then flicked some crumbs from his jean shorts.

'I need to be somewhere. I'm going,' said Ava. She stabbed a long finger at Jennifer. 'You need to drag your head out of the clouds, girl. This isn't one of your stupid theatre dramas. This is the real world. Try living in it. Act like an adult, for once. How about that?' With that, she stomped off.

Stacey grimaced. 'A bit rich, coming from her.'

David came through the patio doors and strolled over to them, whistling. He soon grasped he'd walked in on their conversation at a bad time. 'OK, so what did I miss?'

8

J ennifer followed a tractor hauling a trailer stacked high with hay. Every time the vehicle passed under low trees, it brushed off a cloud of hay bits, which floated about the lane like slow-falling rain. Her visor was up, and she felt bits of dry chaff hitting her cheeks. The noisy, lumbering vehicle took up the entire lane, so overtaking it wasn't an option.

She was in no real rush. In fact, she didn't even know why she was so compelled to return to Barren's Lodge. Ava's indignant face popped into her head. The veins in her elongated neck were taut as she pulled that bitter expression Jennifer had always hated when they were younger. Something between a surly pout and furious sniff, as though she'd smelled a terrible whiff and was intent on tracking down the culprit because she wanted to admonish them.

Jennifer had tried to bond with Ava, but her eldest sister never had much time for her. And she'd never forgotten the time when she'd made breakfast in bed for Ava. A little surprise for her fifteenth birthday. She'd got up early, snuck downstairs and prepared everything. Ava had screamed at Jennifer for waking her, and promptly told her to fuck off and die, before shoving the tray and sending the contents flying. Jennifer's pyjamas ended up covered in cranberry juice, scrambled eggs and baked beans. She'd sobbed all morning, and Ava had never said sorry for that moody outburst. Their dad had got involved and ordered Ava to apologise. She never did.

They hadn't clicked. Pieces from different puzzles left in the wrong box that could never connect, no matter how many angles you tried, or how hard you attempted to force them to slot into place.

Not like Ava and Stacey. They clicked together. They always had.

The tractor turned off and slowly drove into a rapeseed field. And she opened up the throttle and sped down the lane.

When Jennifer arrived at Barren's Lodge and stepped off her scooter, a cold shiver edged right through her bones. Taking off her helmet, she rubbed the hay bits from her face and gazed into the trees. Why did she have a sudden, horrible sensation that someone was out there in the woods spying on her?

She stood still and silent for a good minute and eyed the narrow spaces between the trees. She couldn't see anybody, so she guessed she was just getting the heebie-jeebies because of all the rumours floating around. All this nonsense that this place would be targeted by so-called vigilantes.

As before, Jennifer clambered over the gate and made her way onto the property. Past the irritated wasps and down to the main house.

She caught a nasty pong in the air. As she stepped closer to the house, the stench grew stronger, and she soon found the cause of the grim odour. The windows were covered in a thick brown substance. A fine breeze wafted more of the nasty smell her way, and she almost gagged. It reeked.

Ernest was on his hands and knees at the side of the property, fighting with an old yellow hose reel.

'Grandad, it's me,' she called.

'Hey, Jennifer. You... came back,' he said through a series of breathless grunts, sounding a bit surprised as he tried to dislodge the jammed hose.

Jennifer gazed up. The upstairs windows were all smeared with lumpy brown muck. 'Seems they got every one of your windows. Gross.'

'Yep. Didn't miss a single one. They didn't spread it so thickly up there as they did the downstairs ones, but there's enough to suggest the culprit used a ladder to nip up and apply a good layer of the crud to each window,' he said matter-of-factly.

'Mm. Can see that. Would you say that's human or animal excrement?'

As if that mattered.

'If I had to guess, I'd say human,' he said.

'Wow. That's really quite foul. Who'd do something so hideous?'

Ernest was sweating from the effort of yanking the hose. He'd pulled about a foot through, but it was jammed again. 'They left a letter. Pinned it to my front door. It's on the metal table. Just there.' He patted his bald, sweaty head with a piece of red cloth.

Jennifer pinched her nostrils between her thumb and index finger as she trotted over to the table to retrieve the note. 'When did this happen?' she asked, sounding like she was putting on a silly voice, but not wanting to release her nose because of the almost unbearably nasty stench. 'Were you home?'

'No. At a meeting with my supervising probation officer. When I came back... I found the place like this.'

Jennifer moved away from the house and studied the note.

Ernest Moorby, you are not welcome in North Sutton.
Leave now. If you fail to do what we are asking, then this
is just the start. Things will escalate. If you stay here, you
will be sorry. Very sorry indeed.

She read the words again. And then it struck her. The handwriting looked strangely familiar.

9

J ennifer spent most of the afternoon pitching in with the cleaning operation. After donning a pair of rubber gloves and some old overalls before helping her grandad hose off the muck, they took their tea and a plate of cheese sandwiches each into the rear courtyard. They sat on a rickety bench that creaked under their weight and enjoyed the quiet for a while. Ernest had insisted they must have a spot of lunch after their laborious effort, despite Jennifer declining the offer more than once. She struggled to comprehend how he could even think about food after such a foul task.

As they sat there, more and more childhood memories flooded her mind. There were three cabins on the premises that were once used as holiday lets. She remembered helping her gran, Sally, run chores about the place. Fetching firewood, collecting towels, refilling the tea bags and sugar sachets in the little kitchens.

Sometimes she would play with the children who would come here to stay on their holidays. There was a nice boy called Kenny who would come every summer, and he had a massive crush on her. He'd always show off when she was around, but she'd secretly liked that, because – as she recalled now – that made her feel rather special. Ava had spitefully said he probably had a learning disability, which was why he'd given her the time of day.

Jennifer had spent entire summers here, and those weeks were filled with fond memories. She started considering that those times were perhaps the best of her life. Idyllic, fun-filled days full of wide smiles, sunshine and people who cared about her.

Then that last summer, when they'd moved in here with their mum and left their real home, everything changed. Just like that.

After her mum's murder, she'd heard that Sally kept things running for a time, but Barren's Lodge was never the same again. Those cheerful families who used to come here all stayed away, and the only visitors would be those who were drawn to the place because of its macabre reputation.

As their gran aged and struggled to keep things in order, Ava had been left in charge of running the place, but after Sally passed away five years ago, Ava had refused to return, which was when the place fell into disrepair. Like Jennifer, Stacey had not come back here after that day, and Ava had once told them she would have happily burned the entire building to a cinder. She detested Barren's Lodge and had only come here to help their grandmother. Ava had loved her dearly. The two of them had shared an unbreakable bond.

Ernest cleared his throat. 'What are you thinking about?'

'Mm, sorry?'

'You look like you're a million miles away, dear girl.' He

had his plate perched on his knees, his sandwiches almost gone.

Jennifer grinned. He'd always called her that as a child. 'I wore gloves and washed my hands three times, but I'm still not confident touching my food.'

'You need to eat.'

'Yeah, but not after scrubbing poo off a load of windows.'

'Do you think people who clean sewage pipes or unclog city drains don't eat any lunch?'

Jennifer studied the sandwich and willed herself to take a quick bite. She didn't.

He popped the last piece of food into his mouth. 'Come now, I don't think that's the only thing on your mind.'

'Grandad, I don't think you should stay here. In town, I mean.'

'I don't have anywhere else to go. This place is all I have.'

'Sell it. Surely it will cost too much to run it by yourself.'

'Who'd want to buy this run-down old hovel?'

'Put it on the market at a cut price, then some out-of-town property tycoon will take it and do it up. I bet you'd get more than you expect. All this land. It will be worth a lot.'

'My memories are here. I belong here.'

'You could make new memories. Somewhere else.' She gestured at her own plate. 'Fancy another?'

Ernest eagerly picked up one of her sandwiches. 'So, tell me about your sisters. What are they up to these days?'

'Stacey's a stay-at-home mum now. Looks after her two, Harriet and Evan. Before that, she worked as a supply teacher. Her husband, David, works for a big pharmaceutical company. He was some sort of data analyst, but he's a head honcho now. He earns good money. They make a lovely couple. I bet you'd like him. They seem very happy.'

'And Ava?'

'Ava's a private German language teacher. She's got a bachelor's degree and is also a fully qualified translator. She lived in Frankfurt for five years; she was dating a guy out there called Omar, but things didn't work out, so she came home.'

'And your dad, what's he doing with himself these days?' he asked, an edge of disdain creeping into his voice.

'Not much. He's been out of work for a while.'

He nodded and pulled a sour face. 'A total bloody layabout, then?'

Jennifer didn't answer the question, assuming it was rhetorical. And she wouldn't sit here and bad-mouth her dad. If anything, she felt sorry for him. Plus, he got enough stick from her sisters without her slagging him off behind his back.

She watched Ernest from the corner of her eye as she pushed the sandwich around her plate with one finger. His mood had changed, and whatever he was now thinking about had brought about a sullenness to him that she didn't much like the look of.

10

Jennifer and Ernest stood by the gate. A few wasps buzzed around, though the swarm seemed calm at that moment.

'Pesky things. I guess that's one outbuilding I won't be using until I deal with them,' he said.

'You could leave them be. They could guard the entrance, like security. Might send those trespassers fleeing.'

'Good plan. You always did have the quirky ideas.' He swatted a few wasps away. 'I'm going to restore this place back to how it once was.'

'You're going to reopen the holiday cabins?'

'Oo, no. I'm way too old for all that malarkey. No, I mean the house. I want to make the building nice again. I had hoped you'd help me design the place.'

'I'm not sure I can come back.' She watched him. Saw the deep sadness in his eyes as his craggy face clouded with anguish.

'I understand,' he said in a dejected tone. 'Of course, I fully understand.'

'You won't find peace here. You must know that.'

'Are you trying to get rid of me, lady?'

'No. Well, yes. But not like that.'

He ambled over to the gate and leaned over the top, letting out a heavy sigh. 'This place has been in my family for three generations. Once I'm gone, it will pass on to you and your sisters. It's your legacy.'

'They won't want it. I'm not sure I do, either. My visits here have already caused a rift. Ava is really mad at me.'

'Not surprised. That girl was always so... tetchy. The queen of the eye roll,' he said with a disgruntled grin. 'You were different. You were always so peppy and bright. And you were never led by others. You had your own mind. An individual. You didn't care what the others thought.'

'But it doesn't feel right. Being here. I feel like I'm, I dunno, I'm...'

'Like you're being disrespectful to your mother's memory?'

Jennifer nodded.

'Yet you came. And I'm certain there's a good reason you did.'

She stood next to him and also leaned on the gate. 'I have so many fond memories of this place... before *that* day. I suppose I maybe want to find out how it shifted from a blissful haven to a dreadful nightmare in such a short space of time.'

'Ah, well, I'd say you are seeing things through rose-tinted glasses. There were plenty of problems boiling under the surface before your mother passed. *Plenty*. Your sisters were not always kind to you.'

Passed? Interesting way to phrase it, decided Jennifer.

'Aren't all sisters spiteful to their younger siblings? That's normal, isn't it? And I understood my parents were not always happy. I don't recall getting upset; after all, I accepted their unsettled relationship as normal. Parents didn't always get on, and I knew that. They just got on with things for the sake of their children.'

'I want to show you something. I'm sure if you see it, you will change your mind about coming back.' He moved away from the gate, stretched, then tried to hide a low groan. 'Will you come with me?'

Jennifer took a deep breath. 'OK. Go on. Show me.'

11

The grounds of Barren's Lodge resembled a jungle. Masses of ugly weeds, compact nettles and over-grown grass. The view that once greeted a person from this very spot was one of vast, neatly cut lawns, unspoiled hedges and stunning flowers arranged perfectly. The cobbled pathway that Jennifer now stood upon weaved through the entire three acres of land here.

They made their way deep into the grounds. Her grandad used a wooden walking stick to knock brambles and bracken from their route.

The silence unnerved Jennifer, and she wanted to say something to break it. She could not speak. It was as if speaking, or making any noise, wasn't permitted down here because it would disturb the spirits that inhabited the untamed garden.

They reached the centre where the path branched off three ways, and they both stopped.

The left path led to the observatory. Taking a right would

lead you to the ragstone grotto where the foxglove and white dead nettle grew in abundance.

And then there was the path that led straight ahead, which took you down to the dire place at the bottom of the grounds. The place she didn't care to think about. The route was foreboding and dark. It snaked through overhanging sycamore trees and wild, straw-like grass. The sight filled Jennifer with a strange unease that made her stomach lurch and legs quiver.

Surely not that way. I'm not ready to go down there.

Her grandad raised his walking stick and pointed left. Then he flashed her a nervous grin, his eyes flicked over to the centre path for a few seconds, then he shuffled on.

The building soon came into view. Well, what they could see of it under the mass of creeping buttercup, giant stinging nettles and blackberry bushes hugging the structure. The wooden building had several names. Jennifer had called it the observatory, their gran the summer house, Stacey the play-den, and, to their grandad, it was always the workshop. The unusual, hexagonal-shaped construction had huge windows and a roof with a viewing platform with a two-foot-high rope fence around it.

'You remember this place?' he asked softly.

'Are you serious? Can we go inside?'

Ernest jangled a ring of keys. 'I hope so.' He ambled over and slotted a big bronze-coloured key into the faded white door, which looked out of place because the rest of the building had been painted an umber colour. He fiddled and twisted the key, then nudged the door with his shoulder. It opened with a groan.

'First time lucky,' said Jennifer.

The pair went inside. Sunlight speared through the gaps

in the bushes, giving more than enough light to see inside. She took in the smells of paints and oils. 'It's not even damp in here. Not one bit.' From inside, you'd once been able to gaze out of the windows to the wheat field. Not now. Nature had taken over and blocked the view.

'I don't like to blow my own trumpet, but when I build something, I build it to last.'

'You built this? I never knew that. Impressive.'

He smiled wistfully and gestured to the big doll's house on a table at the centre of the room. 'I also built that for you girls.'

Jennifer walked over to the house and trailed her finger along the red dusty roof tiles. 'That I *do* remember. Stacey and I had been awestruck by all the intricate details. The working lights, the tiny boxes of cereals, the reclining sofas.' She kneeled and examined the inside of the house. Aside from swirls of dust, everything was in pristine condition. The colour wasn't quite the pink they'd always referred to it as. More like salmon. 'We played with this all the time. Entire afternoons.'

He laughed. 'It took me almost as long to build that model as it did this place.'

Jennifer stood up and scanned the walls between the windows where all the shelving units were fixed. Children's books, PVA glue, paints, brushes, bits of crafting wood and aerosol-paint sprays lined the rows of shelves. She picked up a tube of yellow acrylic paint and opened the lid. 'Uh-oh, paint looks dry.' She stuck her finger inside. 'Yep, dry as a box of old crackers.'

'Yellow is still your favourite colour, I see.'

Jennifer studied the paint bottle. 'I'm not sure I have a favourite colour.'

'You did as a child. Ava was black, Stacey purple, and you adored yellow. Because it reminded you of the sun.'

'Huh. Funny, I don't remember that,' she said. She was sure Stacey had been the one who loved yellow, but she didn't want to get picky. How good could his memory be at his age?

She replaced the bottle and stepped over to a bulky set of drawers under a scuffed window that was covered in droplets of red, green and orange paint. Her foot touched on something underneath the drawers. She glanced down to find a small wooden puppet, wearing a tatty red T-shirt, peering up at her. 'Ah, who are you?' She scooped up the vintage toy and studied its face. The toy was strangely sinister, and it had a black mark on its right cheek. It looked suspiciously like a cigarette burn.

'That queer old thing had strings once. You used to act out plays with it. Make it dance and sing,' said Ernest quietly. 'I never much liked him.'

'I think it's a girl,' said Jennifer, though she had no clue as to how she knew this fact.

As she continued to study the puppet, an anxious feeling washed over her. She couldn't explain it, but she knew this toy held unsettling memories.

'Huh, yes. I think you girls called her Polly Puppet,' he said. 'You ended up afraid of her, and you wouldn't allow the thing to come inside the house.'

Jennifer placed the toy back and nudged it with her fingers until it was out of sight. Then she rummaged about in a drawer that was tough to open. It was full of sheets of A4 paper, and most of them were colourful drawings. She sifted through the artwork and smiled. Many of them were her own scribbles; nearly all of them were pretty terrible. 'Oh, wow. These are our drawings,' she gushed.

So many memories flooded her mind as she flicked through the artwork. Stacey laughing with her as they played down here. Spending entire days just messing about and making pointless stuff. Their gran would bring them lunch, and she'd sometimes stick on some classical music and tell the girls stories. Jennifer thumbed through the papers. They were bone dry; none of them had decomposed or even got remotely damp over the long years, testimony to the fact that her grandad had done a top-class job on the construction of this place. Even if it did feel like a shrine to their youth.

The tomb that held the Fincher family's childhood memorabilia.

Ernest rubbed a smear from a hanging mirror decorated with small pink and white flowers. He gazed at his reflection for some time. As if he didn't seem too impressed with what he saw gawping back at him. 'I'm old, Jennifer, and I don't like it. My bones ache, and it's hard to accept the end is close.'

'We all have to get old, Grandad. I'm sure you have plenty left in the tank,' she said. Then cringed at her lame and clichéd reply.

But he kept staring at himself, rheumy eyes glistening, as if he'd not heard her speak.

Jennifer opened another drawer to a wonky set of chest of drawers. More arts and craft stuff. And more stacks of drawings. 'Ah, now this *was* a fine drawing,' she said with a smile, holding up a respectable sketch of a multicoloured hot air balloon. She spotted the two stick men hanging on for dear life. They had oversized heads and big Os for mouths to portray their terror at their ordeal. She frowned, her smile fading. 'I drew this when I spotted a balloon drifting over the field one afternoon. I was so certain it was going to crash, but they managed to save it at the last minute with a whooshing blast of hot air that sent it back up again.'

The depiction of the crew members plummeting from the basket, however, was an added feature not in her original piece. Affirmation that someone had sabotaged her fabulous drawing. She'd gone moaning to her mum on several occasions, claiming that one of her sisters kept ruining her cherished work. Stacey could be sneaky at times, but Ava would have been the obvious culprit, although she'd not come up here often.

Jennifer tried to picture if she'd ever seen Ava down here with them, but she seemed unable to conjure up one memory of her eldest sister in this place. Perhaps she'd been too grown-up for all that childish triviality. She imagined a younger Ava using those exact words. But Ava might well have come here during the night. After all, Jennifer had caught her smoking cigarettes in the grotto more than once.

She gazed at another drawing and tried to work out what exactly she was seeing. It appeared to be an illustration of a girl hanging from a rope attached to a tall, slender tree. On closer inspection, she noticed there was blood seeping from the girl's eyes, and her tongue, which was out of proportion to the rest of her body, was dark blue and lolling from her gaping mouth. There were even droplets of yellowish dribble at the corners of her lips.

'Jesus, who sketched this morbid piece?' She snapped a photo of the drawing on her phone. Then she noticed some tiny writing in the corner:

The swinging girl. JF.

I have no recollection of drawing that, she thought, wincing at what seemed to be the title. Was this subtle play on words deliberate? Or something written by an innocent, unworldly child?

They'd not been back here since... *it* happened. So this couldn't be a twisted interpretation of what had happened that day. Because this had been created before that awful incident.

That's surely not meant to be her. Is it?

'I didn't kill her.'

So quiet were those words, Jennifer thought she'd imagined her grandad speaking them.

'I didn't kill my Katherine. How could they even consider that I would have done that?'

He seemed to be addressing himself in the mirror and not speaking to Jennifer. When she saw the tears streaming down his wrinkled cheeks, she knew she had to say something. But what? How did you respond to something like that?

'I need someone to believe me. I really do,' he whispered. 'I have reconciled with the years spent in prison for a crime I didn't commit, but the idea of my entire family hating me for ever... it is too much to bear. It's torture. Pure torture.'

And the words slipped quietly out of Jennifer's mouth. 'I believe you, Grandad.' She slid the creepy drawing back inside the drawer and used her thigh to slam it shut.

He sobbed, shoulders shifting up and down, glasses slipping from his veiny nose. 'Then I can die peacefully tomorrow. Because that's all I need. Just one... *just* one of you.' He closed his teary eyes and placed his hands together as if praying. *Perhaps he was.*

Jennifer wiped her brow. She was sweating profusely. She noticed how close it was in there. 'Let's go up top and get some air, shall we?'

Twenty-five years.

How many days was that?

How many weeks?

How many hours?

She decided not to calculate the figures. They would be far too depressingly soul-destroying. Instead, she turned the words into a funny little song in her head.

Twenty-five years... duh, duh, duh.

How many days?

You don't want to know.

12

W alking up the steep steps and reaching the viewing platform of the observatory felt like stepping back in time. The wooden planks were slippery with moss, and the white metal bench and matching table looked well-weathered. Jennifer held onto the rope that sectioned off the entire top area and gazed out across the view. The vast wheat field. High and bright. A layer of July heat was just visible on its surface. A floating, translucid ripple of warmth.

She'd seen this crop grow tall during the many summers she'd spent here. She often recalled it that way. But she'd also seen it cut low in the late summer. Re-ploughed and spread with muck as autumn approached. They didn't come much during those times because the vulgar stench would be overwhelming.

The field was over a mile wide, stretching the length of Barren's Lodge and beyond. And in the other direction, it was twice that distance. Out where the small copse stood and continuing on to where the overgrown footpath snaked into Cobble Wood, where the view, a lush medley of tall birches, rounded elms and chunky oaks, finished.

What did they once call the copse? The Island? No. *The Forbidden Island*, that was it.

They'd gone there once, she recalled. The memory was somewhat vague. They'd walked there using the deep tractor tracks through the wheat. Boy, did they get into trouble for that little on-a-whim escapade. Was it Ava's idea or Stacey's? There'd been a big argument over it. Hadn't their mum come searching for them? Yes, she had come marching through that wheat field.

'Why would you take your little sister out here?' their mum had demanded to know.

One of her sisters found this funny and was subsequently scolded.

'You wouldn't be smirking if one of you had been chopped into pieces by a combine harvester.'

'If it was Jennifer, we might have,' one of them had retorted.

Which sister had that been?

'Have you two been boozing?' her mum had asked.

It was true, Jennifer recalled. Her sisters had been drinking some peculiar, red-coloured drink on their trek out there. She did have a hazy recollection of one of them making her swig from the bottle. Ava had discarded the empty bottle into the trees near the start of the copse with a brazen grin. Jennifer remembered being mad about this. Littering was one of her bugbears. Still is.

Jennifer searched her mind for memories of the copse itself. They must've explored it. Perhaps the visit had been so unremarkable, and there wasn't all that much to remember. Probably just a few old trees, lots of midges, plus a million bramble bushes to cut your ankles to ribbons.

Things were like that sometimes. When you viewed something from a distance for such a long time, once you got to see it up close, it didn't live up to your expectations. That was dispiriting. Jennifer couldn't help but think that this funny little island of compact trees held some significance. To what, though, she couldn't say. Had they gone there searching for something? Or someone?

A warm breeze hit, and with it came another memory of Stacey holding onto the viewing deck rope, dressed like a pirate. Makeshift patch covering one eye, bandana made from torn cloth, stuffed toy parrot, the works. They'd been up here on a gusty day and pretended they were on a pirate ship out on dangerous seas. As the wind whipped over the crop, they'd imagined that the fluttering wheat was a wild, uncharted ocean, and they were brave female buccaneers, ready to take on the world.

Stacey had been so animated and fun back in those days. OK, she would sometimes be a right moody cow when their big sister was around. Not always, but she had her moments. Especially during the final summer they'd spent here. When she'd started maturing, or 'blossoming', as their gran saw fit to phrase it.

'Turning into a stroppy little mare,' was how their mum had voiced her sister's rapid transfiguration from the cutesy, high-spirited girl she'd been, to the snappy, uncommunicative teenage nightmare she'd resembled that summer.

Jennifer felt bad for Stacey, because she understood how much regret she now harboured for the way she'd behaved during those last months. Those last months their mum had been with them. Alive.

Life is full of regrets.

'All OK up there?' her grandad asked.

'Yeah, it's quite a trip down memory lane.'

'I can imagine it is. I won't come up. My knees are not what they once were. I confess, I am struggling today.'

'I'll come down.'

Then another memory popped into Jennifer's mind as she took one last gaze across the field... a frightful one. That man she'd seen out there in the light grey boilersuit. The man with no face. Or a face she couldn't seem to conjure in her mind, anyway.

She'd seen him standing in the middle of that field. She'd been fixed in this very spot, clutching the same piece of coarse rope. It had been on a scorching hot summer's day when she'd first noticed him weaving through the crop in the far distance. Jennifer remembered thinking how angry the farmer would be if he'd caught this stranger blatantly making his own pathway with little regard to the damage he was doing. He'd then disappeared from her sight. She'd been very nervous and considered fleeing back to the house to tell, but her curiosity had forced her to stay where she was, keeping her eyes peeled. Staying vigilant.

Ten minutes later, she'd seen him again. But he'd no longer been moving. Just watching. Not close enough for her to make out his features, but close enough for her to discern what he was doing. He'd been staring right at her. Openly eyeing her and not moving at all. Fixed to the spot like some eerie scarecrow.

Now, despite the glorious sunshine on her face, a freezing cold tremor ran straight through her entire body, making her jolt like a bucket of ice had been thrown over her. Jennifer knew she'd seen that man in the boilersuit more than once during that summer.

During that summer when her grandad, Ernest Moorby, had allegedly murdered his own daughter.

A daughter he professed to loving more than life itself.

Jennifer took a few deep breaths. Tried to control her racing thoughts and thrumming heart.

The heat rose and danced on the crop. She turned away from the field. Eyes moving in the other direction. To the overgrown area that she was unable to see through the dense trees and tangled bushes blocking the way. She stepped forward, boots making the planks creak underfoot, and she was afforded a glimpse of a small clearing near to *that* spot. The place she couldn't go. Not yet. She wasn't ready for that. Might *never* be ready for that.

They'd all warned her not to come here. A tiny part of her now considered her family might have been right.

13

J ennifer viewed the menu and didn't see much on there that she fancied. The vegetarian options were lacklustre, but she didn't want to complain. Their dad had picked the venue. And he'd been the one who suggested this midweek family get-together. Seldom did they all socialise. Apart from those customary gatherings at Christmas or the occasional birthday bash.

Jennifer had nearly declined the offer to attend. She knew what this little shindig was all about. But she'd felt obliged to come along and hear what they had to say. Besides, she had some things to say herself. She flicked her wrist and checked her watch. Six minutes, she told herself. Six minutes before *she* would become the main topic of discussion.

'Gammon is top notch,' said Howard, scooping up a menu.

Jennifer would challenge the idea that anything served in here could really be described as 'top notch'.

David caught her eye and offered her a boyish smile as

he scanned his own menu. Then he pulled a face. An expression that said something along the lines of *You're in big trouble, lady.*

In response, Jennifer raised her eyebrows and mimicked bashing the menu against her face.

Ava must have caught the exchange as she scanned her own crumpled menu, because she gave them a teacher-like glower followed by an eye roll, as if she'd caught two students disrupting her class.

'How's the private tutoring going, Ava?' asked David.

'Fantastic. Busy,' said Ava, her face brightening for a split second.

'Are your students ever disappointed when they rock up to find their German teacher isn't German and is just your average townie?' asked David.

'Actually, yeah. One lady refused to have me teach her because she said, and I quote, "It is improper to be taught a foreign language by a non-native speaker,"' said Ava.

Stacey put down her menu. 'No way. What a cow.'

'I tried to point out that it is, in fact, easier to teach someone a language that you yourself have had to learn. There are benefits to that,' said Ava.

Stacey nodded in agreement. 'Of course. Makes sense.'

Ava shrugged. 'Not to sound too egotistical... But I'd say her loss. I'm a cracking tutor.'

'My French teacher was French, and she was awful. Very unpredictable and sometimes quite aggressive,' said David.

Stacey started cleaning her knife with a napkin. 'Mm, was she, though? Or were you just an annoying sod at school who refused to listen and drove her cuckoo?'

David poked a finger at his chest. 'Who, me? Top student in every single class.'

Stacey moved on to her fork. 'Yeah, sure. I can envisage you now. "Hey, miss, how do you say you massive dickhead in French?" That was you, right?'

Ava joined in. 'I bet he was one of those brattish boys who sat in the back, shouting out lewd comments, and exulted in irritating the hell out of the entire class.'

'I'm really insulted by that. Deeply insulted,' croaked David, unable to keep a straight face.

Jennifer chuckled and caught the cheeky grin David was giving her.

'So, Jen, we need to have a serious talk tonight.'

And their dad's words instantly ruined the playful ambiance in their little corner.

Jennifer checked her watch again. She'd been way too optimistic going for six minutes. A spirited waitress, with her hair tied up in a high topknot, attended their table, stopping any chance of her replying.

'Gammon and chips, no pineapple,' said Howard.

'Halloumi burger with sweet potato fries, please. Oh, and another Pepsi, cheers,' said Jennifer.

The waitress turned to Stacey, who said, 'Oo, um, I'll have the hot Mexican burger.'

David patted his belly. 'Ribeye for me. Nice and rare. With a corn on the cob and... blue cheese sauce.'

Ava quickly scanned the menu again. 'Mixed salad. And the crispy squid.'

The waitress beamed, took their menus and left.

David nudged Stacey. 'Squid. In here. Brave lady.' He made the sign of the cross over his chest.

Stacey poked him in the hand with the back of her fork. 'Stop being a doughnut.'

'Freshly caught from Ramsgate six weeks ago,' said Ava.

'Have you heard what's being said?' Howard cleared his throat, insisting on their attention. 'The rumours going around town?'

'About the squid?' said Ava flippantly.

David chuckled, but quickly fixed his face and removed the jovial grin. 'Right. Yeah. You mean about Barren's Lodge? People are chatting online. I don't want to dampen the mood, but there are some mad rumours doing the rounds. Ernest even has his own meme. We won't go there.'

'No, we won't,' snapped Stacey. 'Did you go back, Jennifer?'

Jennifer realised all eyes were suddenly fixed on her. She flattened out her napkin. 'I went to the observatory. Do you remember that place, Stacey?'

Stacey took a deep breath, snatched up her fork, began cleaning it once again. 'This is insane. Why are you doing this?'

'I'm fine,' said Jennifer in a calm voice. 'It's fine.'

'It's bloody not,' said Ava.

Jennifer offered her eldest sister a reassuring smile. 'You don't need to worry about me. I'm OK.'

Ava slumped in her seat and groaned. 'Give me strength. Someone, please give me strength.'

'Jen, if nothing else, Barren's Lodge will likely be targeted,' said Howard. 'You will be stuck in the middle of this, and we don't want you to get hurt.' He swigged back the dregs of his beer, and his eyes hunted the quiet restaurant, no doubt searching for the waitress so he could order a refill.

David sighed. 'Your dad's right. People are out to get that old guy, and you'd be very foolish to be hanging around his house. We're worried. That's all.'

'I'm fine. Really, you don't need to make a fuss,' said

Jennifer, recalling hearing her grandad dry heaving while they'd been scrubbing the filth from his windows.

Ava rubbed her eyes and let out a long moan. 'What is wrong with her?' she asked nobody in particular.

'I think she's just a bit muddled by all this,' said Stacey.

'She needs to see a therapist. She needs to have her head looked at. This is bloody bonkers,' said Ava, talking now like Jennifer was an irksome child whom she no longer had the patience or energy to deal with.

Jennifer couldn't help but be relieved when their food arrived, and they all sat and ate quietly. Aside from the odd knife scrape on a plate, their corner stayed silent for a good five minutes.

Still, Jennifer could stand it no longer. She put down her cutlery and sat up straight, composing herself. 'I remembered something. And I think it might be important.'

They all stopped eating and held her with sceptical stares.

Jennifer spoke evenly as she said, 'I saw someone *that* summer. A man standing in the field, watching the property. Watching me. He was wearing a light grey boilersuit. Not too dissimilar to the ones they wore in the *Ghostbusters* movie.'

Nobody at the table said a word for what seemed like a long time.

Jennifer's cheeks were suddenly hot.

David broke the uncomfortable silence. 'Cool film. "Weee *got* one!"'

'Shut up, David,' said Stacey.

David held up his hands. 'Sorry, it involuntarily slips out every time that movie is mentioned.'

'You loved all the eighties movies, Jen. I reckon you've

seen *ET* more times than anyone on this planet. But you did get a bit obsessed,' said Howard.

David went to speak, but Stacey elbowed him.

'Yep, you did like to act out scenes from those films,' said Stacey.

Jennifer sighed, wishing she'd not mentioned the movie reference.

'Never mind *Ghostbusters*,' said Ava. 'How old was this mysterious man in the field?'

'Not sure. His face seemed kind of... blurry in my memory,' Jennifer mused.

Her sisters shared a glance. Ava had a pained frown etched on her forehead, and Stacey appeared concerned.

Howard, elbows on the table and hands balled into fists, said, 'Why didn't you mention this before, Jen? Back then?'

'Maybe I did. I can't recall.'

'It was likely Dad you saw. Or Gran... Ernest,' suggested Stacey.

Ava nodded. 'It probably *was* Dad. He had those old mechanic's overalls.'

'Why would I have been standing in the field like some nutter? And my overalls were dark blue, not grey,' said Howard, an aggrieved note to his voice.

'I don't know, do I? I don't know why we're even discussing this. It's ridiculous,' said Ava.

'I don't think it is. And I remember seeing that man before. That boilersuit could be significant. It... it's so annoying that I can't quite piece my memories together, because it seems so important,' said Jennifer.

Ava closed her eyes and rubbed her temples with her index fingers. 'OK, I'm officially done. I have no clue as to what exactly you're playing at here, Jennifer, but please stop.

You have your head in the clouds. You're stuck in some weird bubble that we clearly cannot penetrate. And, quite frankly, I'm bored with trying.'

Jennifer steepled her fingers and squeezed them, wishing she had her Stress-Hog to hand.

Ava opened her eyes and made a wheezing sound as she breathed. As if desperately trying to calm herself and hold back the barrage of insults she wanted to unleash on her sister. 'I'm going to make this simple for you to grasp, Jennifer,' she declared. 'If you return to that place... if you even speak with that old shit-bag one more time... even if it's just to say howdy-fucking-do, then we are done. Understand? We will officially no longer be sisters, and I will refuse to speak with you ever again. Clear enough? Or would you like me to say it to you in German as well?'

'Ava!' gasped Stacey.

Jennifer didn't know why, but she had the urge to giggle at Ava. She imagined herself going from a giggle to a full-blown, tear-inducing belly laugh. She often did this. Found hilarity in situations that were anything but funny. Your big sister threatening to disown you wasn't exactly a laughing matter.

So, doing her best to keep a straight face, she shuffled around in her shoulder bag and withdrew thirty pounds. 'Nice meal,' she quipped. 'That should cover me. I'd better be off. Hectic day tomorrow.'

14

As Jennifer climbed onto her scooter, she noted Stacey in an ungainly jog across the carpark. 'Jennifer, wait up. Stay for dessert. Don't listen to Ava. You know what she's like sometimes.'

'I'm not much of a pudding lover. And I really do have to get back. I need to prepare some forms for tomorrow's schedule. Busy, busy, busy.'

'We're all worried about you, so please don't think we're ganging up on you.'

'I get it, but I'm not a child. It's a tad patronising.'

'I'm going to tell you something. It's important and might upset you a little, because I know how much you adored Mum.'

'I'm all ears.'

Stacey gazed back at the restaurant and slipped a packet of Silk Cut out of her bag. 'Don't tell David. I quit months ago.' She popped a cigarette between her lips and fired up her plastic lighter. 'I only have the odd one here and there.'

'Doesn't he smell smoke on you?'

'Mints, perfume and mouthwash seem to hide the smell.'

'Well, don't gurgle the perfume by accident. So, go on, what do you want to tell me?'

'Do you remember those sleep troubles you had?'

'I can't say that I do.'

'When you were around eight, the problems started. Staying at Barren's Lodge seemed to trigger them. Or certainly make them worse. Especially during the time Mum and Dad were having those issues.'

'When they split up, you mean?'

'You suffered from a sleepwalking disorder called somnambulism.'

'I did?'

Stacey checked no one was watching, then took a deep drag. 'You don't remember? Seriously?'

'I was a light sleeper. I struggled to nod off, though I have no memory of sleepwalking.' Jennifer crinkled her nose. 'You saw me sleepwalk?'

Stacey nodded. 'The first time freaked me out. I followed you downstairs and told you to get back into bed.'

'Where the hell was I going?'

'You were trying to go outside.'

'Huh. That's so... queer.'

'Do you still do it?'

Jennifer shrugged. 'Sleepwalk? If I do, then I have never even put a pen out of place during my twilight strolls.'

'I'm sure you'd have some idea. I once found you sleep-walking out on the front lawn, waving to the owls and making hooting sounds at them.'

'That's cute. Were they waving back?'

'Jennifer, please take this seriously.'

'I am... Ava's never mentioned this. Neither has Dad.'

'Well, they must have known something about it. Once, I witnessed Mum crushing up pills and mixing the powder into your hot chocolate, and when I questioned her, Mum told me she sometimes used a mild sedative to help you sleep. To help with your anxious, racing thoughts, which would get much worse during bedtime.'

'This sounds interesting.'

'No, it's disturbing. I strongly believe this medication had terrible side effects. I'm quite certain it caused you to have those severe night terrors; then in the daytime, you'd be left in a strange dreamlike state, where you'd waffle on about things that made little sense. You drove Ava and me nuts at times.' She paused, took another deep drag on her Silk Cut. 'Please don't mention the drugs-in-your-drink thing. Not to Ava or Dad.'

'Why?'

Stacey took a final tug on her smoke and rubbed it out on the ground. 'Oh, they'll think I'm bad-mouthing her. Dishonouring her memory and all that stuff. I loved Mum to bits, but sometimes... oh, it doesn't matter.'

Jennifer removed her phone from her bag and pulled up the shot she'd taken of the creepy artwork she'd found in the observatory. 'What do you make of this?'

Stacey studied the screen, an expression on her face like she'd just seen a fly land on her dinner plate. 'You've been going through all our old artwork. Oh, God.'

'Who drew this picture?'

'You did. It's even got your initials on. See.' Stacey used two fingers on the screen to zoom in on the photo. 'JF. I vividly remember you drawing that one.'

'The tree is mine. That vulgar image *is* not. Who defaced the picture like that? Is this meant to be... Mum?'

'No. How is it even similar, Jennifer? Mum didn't hang from a bloody tree.'

'No, but there is a similarity. You have to admit that. Right? Some sort of metaphor?'

'Jennifer, I am getting extremely concerned about you. Come on, you must remember this? The little girl you kept having nightmares about. You confided in me loads about her.'

'Who is she?'

'You said you met her in your dreams, and you were so convinced she was real. A girl from the travelling community who was left an orphan after her parents died in a caravan fire.'

'Seriously?'

'Yeah, you told us she'd been killed out there. She was talking to you in your sleep, begging you to go out to the Forbidden Island to find her body. So that she wasn't abandoned for ever or eaten by the foxes.'

'We walked out there, right? All three of us. Mum got super cross.'

'You remember going out there with us?'

'Sort of. I recall Mum getting mad, and I think I drank some booze.'

'Ava let you have a tiny swig, but only because you wouldn't stop pestering her.' Stacey shook her head. 'You were adamant we would find this orphan's body in the trees. It was a little weird, let me tell you. I mean, I knew the entire thing was nonsense, but traipsing about in that overgrown woodland, hunting for that strange girl you dreamed had been murdered out there... it was damn creepy.'

'Oh. OK. That is... Yeah, now you mention it. I guess this

is bringing up some more fuzzy memories. She had greenish eyes and raven hair. She was younger than me.'

'And she was frightened she'd spend eternity stuck out there, hanging from a branch. That's what you told us. You also said her siblings killed her because she was mega annoying. You'd say, "Polly talks to me every night. I can't leave the poor girl's body swinging from that deformed tree." Totally nuts, right?'

'Hold up. Polly? Isn't that also the name of the funny wooden puppet thing?'

Stacey frowned and pondered over this for a moment. Then she gave a quick shrug. 'Maybe. I think you named the puppet after the girl. Or perhaps it was the other way around.'

'Freaky.'

'Those pills, Jennifer. See what I'm getting at here?'

'Sounds like you might be right there.'

'Do you need to speak to someone about all this?'

'No. No. Don't be silly.'

'Look, going to Barren's Lodge always made you... act differently. I don't know how to explain it, but that place did something to you. Messed with your head. And I think it's still messing with your head.'

'We had some good times there. I'm sure we did.'

'Dead girls in trees, sleepwalking, seeing men in boiler-suits out in the field, it's all because of those pills Mum forced you to take. They weren't prescribed, and she had no right to give them to you. So don't trust those memories.'

Jennifer didn't say anything as she let this sink in.

'Stay away. That place is... wrong.'

Jennifer went to speak, but Stacey cut her off.

'Don't rebuff what I'm saying with some quirky counter.

I'm here. You can always talk to me. I get we only see each other on occasion. I do. I just need you to understand that if you need to talk about all this stuff, then you call me. I'll come. I promise.'

'I appreciate that. It means a lot.'

'But, Jennifer, listen to me carefully. I know you've always been distant with us. You're a lone wolf. But don't alienate yourself from your entire family. That would be awful. Please don't.'

'I'm not intending to.'

'If you keep going back, that's what will happen. You must realise that.'

'I have my reasons.'

'You reckon *he* has answers for you?'

'Stacey, being there... after all those years, it was so surreal. I started remembering things. Almost straight away. I visualised Mum sitting at that metal table. I haven't remembered her like that since... since...'

'This won't help.'

'But it was such a clear memory. Like a moving portrait. The colour of her eyes. The sadness in them. The last time that I recalled her smiling at me had somehow been brushed out of my mind, yet it had been there all along. I needed to be in the right place. She had hair blowing in her face, and she thumbed out her cigarette. No ashtray, just straight on the table.'

'Grandad would moan at her for doing that.'

'I really want to remember everything about what happened that day, but I can't. It's all so jumbled.'

'Why? Why are you doing this to yourself?'

'How do you unlock all the memories? Do you think there is a way? That somehow you can select a day in your past and… I dunno, relive it all. Run through the entire thing as if viewing a play or TV drama.'

'No. Only in science fiction movies. And why on earth would you want to replay the day Mum died? That would be horrible.'

'Grandad told me he's innocent.' Jennifer shuddered at the thought of it. 'The pain in his eyes was torment to witness.'

Stacey groaned. 'Don't let him suck you in.'

Jennifer shook her head, then in one decisive move, she tugged on her crash helmet.

A flash of images came. *Her mum's sad smile. The broken glass. The blood puddles on the floor. The sinister man in the boilersuit.*

'I will need to go back to Barren's Lodge. I'll make no secret of that,' she said, firing up the Honda's engine.

The harsh stench of whisky.

Stacey slapped down Jennifer's visor. 'You always were too obstinate for your own good. Ride safe, you.' She tapped her hand on top of the helmet. 'And be bloody careful. Please! Promise me.'

Jennifer nodded. And then whizzed off.

JENNIFER'S MIND WAS ELSEWHERE. Miles away. Her eyelids were so heavy. They were screaming at her to let them close. For a moment. *Just a moment.* Although very sleepy, this still frustrated her to no end. She'd desperately wanted to feel this tired at bedtime, but *now* her body wanted to shut down. While she was zipping along a narrow rural lane, doing forty on her scooter. Typical. The conversation she'd had with

Stacey after the meal yesterday evening had been playing on her mind all night. The birds had been outside her window, chirping, and the sun had been creeping up, yet she'd not slept for a minute.

The van racing along the lane snapped her awake. It was going some. Heading straight for her.

A series of rapid thoughts hit her.

The driver can't see me.

The driver is distracted.

They are aiming at me.

Jennifer swerved, and the van thundered past her without slowing. The single-track road had a little grass verge, which she was forced up onto. The scooter hit a bump, her body juddered, and the handlebars were snatched away from her. As she tumbled, she heard harsh brakes screeching.

Jennifer found herself sitting on her bum, a little dazed, angry, but more concerned about her beloved scooter than her own injuries. The fall from the bike, though scary, didn't end up being too dramatic. Her bottom and shoulder did smart, and she guessed there'd be a few grazes and bruises. She decided the softness of the grassy verge had saved her from any broken bones.

The sound of a vehicle reversing urgently pulled her attention back to the lane. She froze as the van charged backwards. Its course became all too clear in those perilous seconds. As it veered her way, steaming up on to the grass, powering right at her.

15

Jennifer scrambled to her feet, stumbled back and somehow scuttled away. What saved her was a sturdy road sign. She fell between its tall metal legs, and the van was forced to stop. It came within millimetres of smashing straight into it.

Jennifer lay there in the long grass, panting as the van revved fiercely, churning up mud and greenery in its bid to move back out of the verge. The exhaust belched out black, choking fumes. It roared forward, went back onto the lane, then came to a sudden halt.

Jennifer couldn't move. Fear gripped her, and she couldn't think straight.

The van's door opened with a noisy creak. The vehicle was an old grey Volkswagen Crafter with a high roof and a deep tear over the back wheel arch. Damage done long ago and left to rust.

Move, she urged herself, wondering where she could run to. Next to the verge lay impenetrable thorn bushes. High and no doubt deep. And she dared not sprint up the lane.

She caught the sound of another vehicle and scrambled desperately to get up.

A small red car crawled up the lane.

The van's door slammed shut. Tyres screeching, it raced off.

Jennifer watched the van speed into the distance, not managing to get a read on the plate.

The driver of the red car, undoubtedly her saviour, strode over. A short, portly man wearing big round spectacles, cargo shorts and a green anorak. 'Everything all right? Has there been an accident?'

'Did you... catch that van on your dash-cam?' she asked, hearing her voice waver. Her hands were trembling.

The man tapped his chin with his index finger. 'Oo, no, sorry. I don't have a camera. My wife's always telling me to get one. "Gordon, you'll come a cropper one day and have no proof. Then you'll be sorry." Alas, she's right. Again. When will I ever listen?'

Jennifer adjusted her specs and examined her scooter. 'Not to worry.'

He flashed her a sorry smile. 'Did that van force you off the road? Much damage?'

Jennifer removed a few handfuls of tufts of grass and mud from the scooter. She located some cracks and scratches on the bodywork. If she'd been alone, she would have spat out curses at the other driver's unjust transgression. What exactly had she done to warrant such fierce hostility? Then she spotted a split along her front wheel arch, and her outrage bubbled up inside her.

'OK? Need a hand?' asked the man, a quizzical expression on his round face.

If this kindly chap had not pulled up when he did, what

would the driver of that van done to her? Had they been trying to frighten her? If so, what had she done to annoy the driver so much? Maybe they'd taken offence because she was in the centre of the lane? Then another idea struck her. Did the driver target her on purpose? Could this be linked to her grandad? These thoughts made her feel quite light-headed, so she quickly tried to dismiss them in that moment.

'Need me to call somebody?' the man asked, head tilted to one side.

'Thank you for stopping. I'm OK.'

'Looks like that plonker should have been the one stopping. Honestly, some people shouldn't be on the road. You drive... or should I say *ride* safe now.'

'I will, thank you. Do you know what this road is called?'

'Bicknor Lane.'

Jennifer nodded her thanks, remounted her scooter, and gazed back to the sign that had possibly been what stopped her from being crushed under the wheels of that grey VW. It read 'Welcome to North Sutton'.

As Jennifer pulled into Barren's Lodge, she was still shaking. The five-minute ride from where the incident took place to her grandad's had been harrowing. She'd been watching out for that Volkswagen van the entire time, convinced it would come flying out of a side road or farm track and steam right at her again.

She'd not clocked the driver or registration, but the vehicle was distinctive. She'd recognise the van if it happened by her again. Or, God forbid, the driver tried to do her another mischief. Had that been out-of-control road rage or something far more nefarious? Running her off the lane was one thing, but reversing at her like that seemed like a deliberate act of violence. As if they'd wanted to hurt her. *Or worse.*

Jennifer flipped up her visor and gasped. 'What the...' She kicked down the scooter's stand and leaped off as she took in the scene. Piles and piles of rubbish greeted her. Sack loads of general waste, masses of battered pallets, broken chairs and even an old fridge-freezer that lay on its side with the door ajar. Some of the junk had been deposited outside the gate, but the majority had been thrown over and lay strewn all over the property's main driveway.

She climbed the gate and dropped down on top of a big pile of rubble and broken slabs. There were at least twelve clear cement bags in the midst of the junk and broken wood. It appeared as though someone had stood here and emptied them out for maximum mess and turmoil.

Jennifer tugged off her crash helmet. 'Grandad? You here?'

As she moved, the wasps started going wild, and she swatted them away as she tiptoed through the reeking carnage. Now flies and other insects were joining the gathering, no doubt drawn by the rank junk. She slipped on some stones and almost stood on a piece of broken pallet that had several rusty nails jutting out of it. Then she saw her grandad leaving the outbuilding. The one swarming with angry wasps. She saw him curse and slap his arm – one must have stung him.

'Grandad?'

'Two ticks,' he said, snapping a padlock on the door. 'I... I was searching for some shovels.' He sounded cagey.

'I don't think you should go in there. If that swarm attacks, they will really hurt you.'

'Come on,' he said, waving her away from the gate.

As they walked away, the wasps' anger seemed to grow, and they buzzed frenetically. It was as if they were sending a warning. *Last chance, humans. Off with you, or else.*

'When did this happen?' she asked, upping her pace and gesturing for him to do the same.

'Just now. Bastards.'

'You saw them? They blatantly did this while you were here? Insolent sods.'

'Yup. I was out the back when I heard a commotion. They'd already unloaded most of it by the time I got to the gate. My arrival didn't stop them either.'

'You get a good look at them?'

'Nope. They wore baseball caps and face masks. Like the surgical ones that doctors use.'

'How many? Did they say anything?'

'Two. Yes, one said, "Barren's Lodge is the town's new dump. Time to go, Moorby. Time to pack up and leave for good, or this never ends." They also used some more colourful words to reinforce that statement. I won't repeat those.'

'The van? Was the van grey? An old high-top VW?' After asking this question, she decided the timeframe didn't add up. Could they have raced here, unloaded in minutes, and somehow bolted off before she arrived? Seemed unlikely.

'I... I couldn't say. The entire thing took me by such surprise, I didn't even register details like that. I'm not sure I noticed a vehicle at all.'

'I'm calling the police.' She almost spilled the beans

about her own ordeal, but stopped herself. She didn't want to add to her grandad's stressful situation.

'There's no point.'

'You want them to get away with this?' She gestured in horror at the chaos around them. 'Look what they did. When will it end?'

'When they get bored. And they will.'

Jennifer breathed a long sigh. She had a strong feeling that the vindictive behaviour he'd so far been subjected to was just the beginning. 'Point or not,' she said, 'I'm calling the police.'

OUT OF THE corner of her eye, Jennifer spotted her grandad scowling at the two male officers as she led them away from the property and opened the gate up for them. They'd been friendly enough and taken plenty of details, clarifying that they should contact them immediately if there was even a sniff of more foul play out here. She'd also privately explained to the officers about what had happened on the lane, pointing out that she had no way to prove if the two incidents were connected, but she was giving way to the idea that they were. Although, with no evidence to back up her version of events, she got the sense that not much could realistically be done about the mystery driver.

'You really should get yourself a camera for your helmet,' one of the officers suggested. 'We may have been able to trace the driver and charge them with dangerous driving if you'd captured this incident.'

Jennifer nodded. 'Yes, I will do that.'

'We'll take a slow drive around the lanes now. See if we can spot this van,' the other officer confirmed.

'Thank you so much,' she said, waving the uniformed men off.

Jennifer marched back to her grandad. His face was all screwed up as he continued to give the two officers a dirty glare as they got into the marked car and drove under the willow tree.

'The police are not the enemy, Grandad.'

He snorted. 'Aren't they?'

'They were very helpful.'

'Sure they were.'

'You might have at least spoken to them. You made it rather awkward.'

'You think they'll help me?'

Jennifer tutted. 'Yes. Why wouldn't they?'

'They won't. I'll never put my faith in the justice system. Not ever. Understand? I clocked the look that brash bloke kept giving me. He was throwing me the evil eye.'

'You're being paranoid. Neither of them seemed brash to me.'

He shook his head, a moody expression on his face. 'I know what I saw.'

'Grandad, you can't let these people get away with it.'

He turned and shuffled away. 'Who said I was intending to?' he mumbled.

16

When she opened her eyes to complete blackness, a flutter of panic hit her. *Is it usually this dark?* Had there been a power cut?

She fumbled about for her phone, thumbed on the light and slipped out of bed. The small warm-white plug-in light wasn't on near her bedside. She left the bedroom and flicked on another light. Nothing. Definitely a power cut, then.

Using the torch on her phone, she made her way to the toilet. After using the loo, she flipped down the seat and sat back down, her mind racing. She checked her phone and let out a faint groan. Exactly 3.27 a.m. Although, that meant she'd nodded off for a good hour.

Maybe she should celebrate such a rare occasion with a nice, strong coffee. There'd be no point heading back to bed now. She'd never drift off at this hour. There'd be more chance of the Loch Ness Monster bobbing up from the bathtub and suggesting with a wink that they take a selfie together.

A sudden thought hit her. No electric – no hot water.

Bugger. She tried the bathroom light again. *Click.* No joy. *No joy...* A bit like how she felt. Like there was *no joy* to be found anymore. Everything depressed her. Everything seemed so impossible to deal with.

She kept telling herself that the wheels were now in motion. These things took time. To not be impatient. To take control. And to breathe... It was important to just breathe. She practised now.

Breathe in deeply... exhale. Hand on heart. Eyes glued shut. Breathe again. Empty my muddled mind. Relax. Let those crazy thoughts fizz away. Fizz and pop. Fizz and pop. That's right.

Fizz.

And.

Pop.

The light clicked on.

Ernest Moorby stood in the corner, rheumy eyes blazing with fury, lips curled back in a frightening snarl. He looked impossibly old and haggard. More like a bloated corpse than a doddery pensioner.

She closed her eyes and clasped a hand over her mouth to stop the scream slipping out. 'It's not real. It's not real. It's not real,' she muttered, her jaw locking in terror.

She opened her eyes. Gone. He'd gone. Of course. Like always.

Hands shaking like an alcoholic with severe delirium tremens. Breathing gone to the dogs. Harsh, rasping blasts of air emitting from her nostrils now. Like an angry dragon about to let fly a blast of fire.

Breathe in deeply... exhale. Hand on heart.

Eyes... glued... shut.

17

Today the weather had changed. Blue skies replaced with a blanket of steely clouds that would be impossible for the sun to dissolve before sundown. Ten days since her first visit here.

The atmosphere felt different today. The absence of the July sun and the bleakness of the skies cast a disheartening energy. A strange tension simmered here now. An unwelcoming aura that felt palpable. And rubbish was strewn everywhere. Bits of tatty fencing, coils of snapped piping, piles of mulched grass and torn builder's sacks full of dusty stones.

Jennifer nudged a torn black sack with her red Dr. Martens boot. Inside the sack was a plastic shopping bag filled with kids' shoes. Had this been destined for the charity shop? She saw an olive-green child's boot with a frog face. Little bulging eyes and a wide grin. She'd owned a similar pair as a child, and she grinned at the memory of her donning a pair and smiling joyfully at the idea of dashing through puddles.

That memory ebbed away. Replaced with another one. The little shoe. The dip. The movie *Who Framed Roger Rabbit*. She'd watched the film once and been left emotionally scarred. The sweet, squeaky cartoon shoe bouncing over to say hello to Judge Doom before the evil character snatched it up and plunged it slowly into the Dip, his concoction of toon-destroying acid. Seeing that innocent shoe dissolving into a pinkish oil had mortified Jennifer, and she'd sobbed for hours. It broke her young heart; she'd been left reeling.

Weeks later, her sisters had called her into the lounge and explained they had something cool for her to watch. They'd paused the screen on the scene when the poor shoe had registered its fate and its mouth fell open in horror. Played it for her just as she'd come skipping into the room. Her cheerful smile had been wiped from her face like a plaster being torn from a nasty, still-raw wound. They'd both found her distress and horror at revisiting that terrible scene hilarious.

'It's not real, you idiot. It's a stupid movie. Get a grip.' Ava had laughed.

'Come on, don't be such a wet blanket. You need to toughen up, Jennifer,' Stacey had teased.

Jennifer had fled straight to her mum, bawling her eyes out.

The smell of rancid burning snapped her back to the present. Coils of toxic black smoke rose into the air from behind the main house. Jennifer and her grandad had both contacted several waste disposal firms to come and collect the junk. Once they were given the address, they either hung up or said, 'No chance.' So her grandad was doing the job himself and polluting half of North Sutton in the process. He'd no doubt refuse to let her contact the police again.

When Jennifer found the fire, she stopped dead and observed in silence. The bonfire was massive. Thick, dark, choking smoke spewed into the gloomy sky.

And there stood Ernest Moorby. The eighty-two-year-old was chopping up wooden pallets with an axe. His ancient face was fixed in a stony grimace as he slammed that axe down. With evident aggression, he stomped on a long piece of wood, snapped it in two, then effortlessly hurled it into the dancing flames. Next, tugging his axe free from the mangled wood, he set about another large pallet. Hacked it like a madman. Like he hated that bit of wood so much he wanted to obliterate it.

She decided that Ernest wasn't quite the enfeebled geriatric he'd have her believe. He appeared every bit the seasoned prisoner her family had warned her about. She almost shouted over – *Hey, do you need your walking stick, Grandad?* But she didn't say a word.

Jennifer left him to it and carried on walking into the grounds. She moved fast and found herself at the centre. Although she'd been telling herself she wasn't ready for *that* middle path, she took it without considering the after-effects. Like she'd put herself on autopilot and her legs just kept moving.

She trudged down into the gloomy part of the grounds, where light didn't always shine. Even on bright, sun-soaked days, it would often stay gloomy here. Today, it almost seemed like night had arrived early as she trudged along the overgrown path to where the lines of sycamores towered. To the end of the grounds.

When she arrived at the old fishpond, her chest became tight, and an overwhelming sense of panic caused her to waver. The pond, encompassed by a high stone base and topped with spongy moss, was half filled with black, oily water. It stank of rotten eggs.

Her mum would come down here to read, relax and write short stories. It had looked – and smelled – different back then. Quaint and enchanting, with tall plants, vivid rose bushes, blue iris and stone figurines. The sun always seemed to break through the trees when her mum perched on the curved stone bench overlooking the water. Or that was how Jennifer remembered it.

Remnants of the statues were still here. Smashed and ruined. A marble depiction of Fortuna, the Roman goddess, crumbled on the ground, held down by weeds as if they were attempting to pull her through the earth itself. The striking figurine that had sat upon a square plinth, long hair flowing down to her knees, once smooth and white, now cracked and green with thick lichen. Sinking, lopsided, into the mud.

Jennifer climbed up onto the stone base and gazed into the blackness, remembering when the pond had been deep and full of large orange fish. She stood where the big white angel once stood, proud and tall.

Breathe... exhale.

The angel that one of her sisters had supposedly pushed into the water, killing two fish in the process. She remembered regarding her grandad with great interest as he'd hauled a heavy length of silver chain down here. Saw him donning fishing waders and hanging his legs over the side. He'd made what reminded her of a cowboy's lasso with one end of the chain, and he'd submerged himself in the greenish water to secure the looped end around the hefty statue.

Jennifer had studied the coiled bundle of chain left on the pond's edge as it moved and clanked while he'd been down there messing about with the statue. He'd been a while, and she'd become a little worried about him.

'Need a hand, Grandad?' she'd asked when he resurfaced, spluttering and coughing.

'Better stay back. I don't want you falling in here, missy,' he'd replied as he'd hauled himself out and grabbed hold of the other end of the chain. 'I have secured that end to her. Now it's time to use my huge muscles.'

'I can swim. Can't be that deep.'

'You'd be surprised at how deep it is. Look how much chain has disappeared down there. I can't even stand up in the water.'

'Does it hide a secret world? Could I wear a snorkel, dive under and take a peek?'

'No, no, no. There are lots of tangly reeds that might drag you under. Imagine getting stuck down there!'

Jennifer had stood gawping, hands on her hips, as he'd heaved the other end of the chain with all his might. Pulled it until he was red in the face. Like he'd been playing a game of tug of war on his own.

'I think it's a bit stuck, Grandad,' she'd pointed out as the chain crunched against the lip of the pond, breaking up the concrete base.

'Hmm, I think you're right. She's not budging at all, stubborn mare. Perhaps my muscles are not quite big enough, eh?' he'd said, wrapping the chain's end around a natural stone boulder. 'I'll get your daddy to help me tug her up later. I just hope her wings don't break off. She's my favourite statue.'

'Perhaps Dad could pull, and you could go under and free her from the water?' she'd suggested.

'Always such a helpful girl.' He'd nodded thoughtfully. 'That could work.'

She'd beamed at him. 'I didn't push it. I swear. I don't think I'm even strong enough!'

He'd laughed and, grinning, said, 'It doesn't matter. We'll sort it. Be careful of that chain. It's a real trip hazard.'

The memory of this exchange made Jennifer feel quite dizzy, so she took a step back away from the rank, uninviting water.

Her grandad had never returned to pull the angel free from the bed of the pond. He'd left that chain in place. Until later that night, when he'd supposedly used the same chain to snake around her mum's neck before shoving her into that water.

Jennifer sank to her haunches. *What if I've got this wrong?* she thought.

18

The jumbled memories kept coming, but there were still pieces missing. But Jennifer had a better understanding of things now. She'd need to take some of those memories with a pinch of salt because if she'd been routinely given sedatives, which had scrambled her young mind, then those memories might not be genuine.

The conversation with her grandad had been real, she was sure of that. But other things seemed less clear. The man in the field. The trip to the Forbidden Island. Those impressions were not so detailed. They resembled the sort of fuzzy images you'd see after removing your prescription glasses, or when you watched a scene through a rain-soaked window. Also, why did that spinning globe keep popping into her head?

Jennifer pulled her knees up to her chin. She didn't know how long she'd been slumped there, against a piece of broken statue, enjoying the silence. She'd managed to resist the urge to sob. She staved off some tiny mosquitoes intent on attacking her hands, and dragged herself up.

The air itself seemed thick and unnatural, and she realised how stuffy it was down there. The faint smell of the fire started drifting down, and her mind immediately went back to what she'd seen on her arrival. How different her grandad had looked. His enraged, determined snarl while he powered down that axe.

Jennifer decided that she'd sneak back out of the property without him spotting her. Tonight, there was research to do. She'd dig up every bit of information possible on her mum's murder and learn all there was to know.

Her phone buzzed in her jean shorts. She retrieved the device and was puzzled to see David's number up on the screen. 'Hello.'

'Hey, Jennifer. You doing OK?'

She gazed around and frowned. 'Yes, I guess. What's up?'

'I was wondering if we could meet up. For a chat.'

'About what?'

'Ah, well, about... stuff. Your sister. And everything. The stuff going on.'

He sounded strange. Drunk.

'Are you in the pub, David?'

'Yep, guilty. And I'd like some company. I could do with seeing a friendly face, to be honest.'

'Are you OK? You sound a tad weird.'

'I'm really knackered. Busy day. So? About our chat?'

'I'm a little tied up with stuff right now.' She didn't have any intentions of meeting David on his own. Even if he did want to discuss her sister. That didn't seem right.

'I'm concerned about Stacey. She's so upset. Even the kids have noticed.'

'But what's that got to do with me?'

No reply.

'David?'

He breathed a long, sad sigh. 'She's worried sick about you. Come on, Jennifer, don't act so naïve. You're putting everyone on edge by going to that place... Are you there now?'

'No,' she lied.

'Look, if you get a bit of free time, you message me. Yeah? You get in touch, and I'll meet you. We can talk about all this. Try to make sense of it.'

'That's nice of you to offer. Thanks, David. You take care. Bye.'

Jennifer ended the call, feeling deeply uneasy about David's offer.

As she made to leave, she stole one last glance at the oily water. She wondered if the angel had been left down there for all this time, or if the police had removed it as evidence. If they had, then where was it now? She envisioned the angel wrapped in plastic and standing in the far corner of some forgotten storeroom with an evidence tag on its broken wing.

19

The search online for information about Katherine Fincher's murder was like opening Pandora's box and stuffing your head right inside it. Forums, pictures, newspaper articles and videos filled the page. The murder had put the plain and unremarkable town of North Sutton on the map, for all the wrong reasons. And now, with her mum's convicted murderer free, all the old forgotten stuff was relevant again.

One of the top hits was a YouTube film called *The Case of Katherine Fincher*. The video had more than one hundred and twenty thousand views and over five hundred comments. It had been posted a decade ago.

With some trepidation, Jennifer clicked play, viewed an advert about credit-checking software, and waited for the film to begin.

A short intro with some rolling credits, then a pretty brunette in her late twenties came into view. She wore over-sized horn-rimmed glasses and had her hair tied back with a wide red headband. She flashed a warm, yet professional grin at the camera. 'Welcome to the Fanatic's Crime Channel. I'm Mabel Grice-Hutchinson. I'm the author of *The Demons Walk Among Us*, creator of the vodcast *I See Killers in the Windows*, and an avid crime aficionado. Just like you.'

Jennifer picked up her Stress-Hog. She had an inclination she'd need him.

Mabel continued talking about herself. California-born, now living in London, she devoted her life to investigating true crime mysteries.

Jennifer turned up the volume and the brightness on her PC.

Mabel patted her hands together. 'As always, I have to point out that everything mentioned in my video is obtained legally. Information gleaned from sources such as old interviews, articles and statements is accessible to anyone. I'm merely slotting all the pieces together in order to try to make sense of this bizarre crime. Now, there are lots of questions about this case, but the biggest among them are these: Just what would drive a man to kill his own daughter? And was the right person charged for her murder? Ernest Moorby fervently denied being responsible for this unthinkable deed and continues to do so. Let's see what we think as we delve into the murder of Katherine Fincher.'

Cut to Mabel in a beanie hat, thick purple scarf and parka. She gestured ahead and declared, 'Here we are in the grounds of Barren's Lodge. Standing here, it's hard to believe what took place here fifteen years ago. For those of you who don't know, Barren's Lodge is located on the border of a town called North Sutton, five miles northeast of Canterbury. I'm not trespassing. I have rented a wood cabin on the premises for the night. I have been transparent as to why I am here, and although Sally Moorby, Ernest's wife, is being very amiable with me, she has specifically asked not to be shown in the film, which I must respect.'

We get a long drawn-out shot of the main house. Jennifer was certain she could see a shape at the upstairs window.

The camera moved back to Mabel. 'Ava Fincher, Katherine's eldest daughter, is helping her grandmother today. Again, I don't have permission to include her in this footage, and she's declined to talk to me.'

Jennifer snorted. That would be an interview she'd liked to have seen. Then she sat up stiffly as she caught sight of where Mabel stood. She'd only gone snooping down at the pond.

Mabel scanned the area with a respectful expression. When she continued, there was genuine sadness in her voice. 'And so, this is the place. The spot where Katherine's life was snatched away from her. A devoted mother of three, with a zest for life. A young woman with a passion for poetry, nature, for living life.' The YouTuber slipped in some mud and flapped her arms to stop herself from plummeting. She then laughed it off.

There was an air of innocence to Mabel that Jennifer quite liked.

Mabel's self-effacing grin ebbed away when she reached the lip of the pond. 'Being here feels almost... wrong. Like I'm intruding. Like I'm violating the place.'

Jennifer tensed. She'd had a similar feeling today.

Mabel pointed to an empty area on the concrete base. 'On this spot stood a tall angel statue. For decades it had been here, proudly overseeing the giant carp that once swam here. Until the day Katherine died. So who pushed the statue into the water? And why? That morning, Ernest disclosed that he'd used a length of chain as some kind of pulley to try to tug the angel out of the pond. He'd not managed to do so.'

Mabel stepped over to a giant boulder and crouched beside it. 'He then wrapped the end of the chain around this very rock.' She placed her hand into a small gap underneath. 'Probably jamming it right under. See? He told police he intended to return with Howard, Katherine's husband, to haul it free. We'll discuss Howard Fincher in more detail later.'

Cut to Mabel in a cabin, boots off, slumped in front of a log fire. 'It's late now. I'm the only guest. They say that this place was once popular all year round with ramblers, nature lovers and families wanting to swap their bustling cities for some nice peaceful downtime. Away from it all. So what *did* happen here?'

The film cut to old TV footage of a sullen-faced Ernest being led away by uniformed officers.

Mabel continued to speak as more news footage played. 'The evidence was overwhelming. Or so it seems. First, let's talk about the witnesses... While on the last day of their holidays at one of the cabins here, Mr and Mrs Ragbourne, a couple enjoying a romantic getaway, witnessed two people having a heated argument in the garden outside the main house. As the middle-aged couple packed up their things late that afternoon, they were quite disturbed by how intense the quarrel was becoming. The pair claim they saw Ernest, drunk and shouting at Katherine, who'd then called him a drunken fool and told him in no uncertain terms to stay out of her business.'

Some still photos of Katherine now. A beautiful shot of her gazing dreamily at the camera.

Then back to Mabel in the cabin. 'In their statement,

Ernest was said to have bellowed, "That man is your husband! This is no way to act." They'd described him as being wobbly and belligerent. And he'd been clutching a bottle of booze. What looked like whisky. The pair had gone inside and resumed the argument. Later, the Ragbournes claim to have heard doors banging and glass smashing. Around this time, Katherine's daughter, Stacey, who was fourteen at the time, had come down to see what all the noise was about, but had been ordered back to bed by her mother. Stacey told detectives that her mother had a deep cut across her hand and was struggling to stem the blood flow with wads of kitchen roll. Her mother wouldn't let her help despite Stacey's best efforts to assist her.

'The next day, Sally Fincher had returned early from a short trip away, to find Ernest passed out in the armchair, reeking of whisky. There was glass and blood all over the lounge floor, and her husband's memory of the night before was hazy. Katherine was not in the house.' Mabel prodded at the fire with a poker, causing the logs to flame and spit. 'Now, according to Sally's statement, Ava, sixteen at the time, had spoken to her gran upstairs, and the girl had been bewildered and bruised, claiming that, the previous night, someone had driven a car straight at her and made her plummet into a rocky ditch. She'd been heading down the lane when lights burst on, and she was forced to dive from the vehicle's path.'

This last part intrigued Jennifer. How had she never heard anything about this?

'Later that morning, Sally made the shocking discovery while searching the grounds for Katherine,' Mabel continued, an urgency in her tone that had not been there before. 'She found her daughter in that pond. She had a chain wrapped around her neck; the other end was still firmly attached to the angel statue that Ernest had tried to pull free of the water the previous day – with that same chain. The police later discovered Ernest's gold watch in the pond. The strap torn as if ripped from his wrist. The post-mortem revealed the following... Drowning was the actual cause of death, not asphyxiation, and the whisky bottle Ernest was drinking from had been used to slice open Katherine's hand. It was confirmed that a small amount of his daughter's blood was also found on his clothes.

'When asked about the blood, Ernest said he'd also tried to help his daughter stem the flow of blood from her cut hand, but she'd shoved him away.'

Mabel poked the fire again and let that statement linger a few moments. 'The belief is that Katherine would have been alive and conscious in that water. Fighting to get to the surface, with the chain tightening about her neck. Coiling like a murderous snake. They say that if there had been a few more inches of chain, she'd have been able to emerge and take that much-needed gulp of air. The more she fought, the tighter that chain got. It was also revealed that part of the chain had hooked on the tip of the angel's wing, making her desperate situation even worse. The mental picture of Katherine's desperate tugs as she tried to pull free in those last minutes of her life is a bleak one. Thwarted by the immovable statue clinging to the murky bed of the pond. Like a ship's anchor hooked on coral, refusing to budge.'

Jennifer's cheeks went numb as the blood left her face. As a chill washed over her. Her grip on her Stress-Hog growing.

On-screen, Mabel shook her head as if picturing those last horrifying moments. 'Howard was questioned by detectives. He had a solid alibi, as he'd been spending the entire night with his mistress. And Ernest was charged with the murder of his daughter. It was never confirmed if the attack upon Ava by the speeding vehicle was linked to the incident – the dreadful murder of her mother. Nobody knows who was driving that car. Very, very mysterious.'

What was behind all this talk about a strange car? wondered Jennifer.

A family photo now filled the screen. It faded in, deliberately slowly, until it was clear enough to make out individual faces. Jennifer stood in the middle, dwarfed by her two big sisters. Their parents behind with wooden smiles slapped on their stiff faces. Stacey's expression was passive. Ava's lips downturned, eyes grave. Jennifer was the only one who appeared happy in the shot. A perky smile on a playful face, as if she'd been oblivious to the unease crackling from the family members around her. As the camera edged closer to Jennifer's young face, a yellow circle appeared around it as if added by an invisible pen.

There was a long pause before Mabel spoke again. 'Then we get to little Jennifer.'

Jennifer's fingers were digging into the hedgehog now. The chill numb in her cheeks replaced with a pulsating flash of prickly, unpleasant heat.

Mabel returned to the screen. 'Where does the youngest daughter slot into all this? We know from police reports that she'd been present at the property that entire day. Now it's said that her grandmother, after speaking with Ava, came back downstairs to find the girl fast asleep on the kitchen floor. Curled up in a ball, head resting on some tea towels. Jennifer told her gran she'd had a vivid dream about her mother during the night. Said she dreamed about her falling asleep and sinking under the water.'

Mabel pulled a face. 'I know, right? Spooky stuff. Is that the reason Sally went searching down by that pond? She never confirmed this. I'd say that seems likely. So what do we know about Jennifer's character?'

'You can't do this,' gasped Jennifer quietly. 'No. This isn't right.'

Mabel smiled. 'In a twist of fate, it turns out we can get some insight into the girl from someone who knew her rather well.'

Her cheeks on fire now. That squishy hedgehog at the point of spilling its insides. She urged herself to stop the film. One click and it was finished. She didn't move.

Cut to Mabel strolling across a bridge in a picture-perfect village. A backdrop of black and white Tudor-style houses and a bubbling stream. 'I've travelled to a beautiful part of the UK. The stunning Cotswolds in Gloucestershire. And I'm here to talk to one of my top fans. Exciting, right?'

Not exciting...

No.

20

As Jennifer watched the sassy Mabel approach a tubby guy in his late thirties, her heart rate increased to a worrying rate. Who the hell was this? How did he know her?

Mabel and the man shared a warm hello, a handshake and a big smile.

Mabel addressed the camera. 'This is Kenny. He is now a chef who lives nearby.' She motioned to Kenny. 'I'll let you explain how you are linked to the Moorby case.'

Kenny nodded, a pompous grin on his face as he used his index finger to push his round spectacles up his podgy nose. 'Firstly, Mabel, let me say how privileged I feel to meet you. I'm rather awestruck, to be honest. Such a huge fan of your crime channel. It always has me gripped.'

Mabel flashed a goofy smile in response to this. 'Aw, thanks.'

Kenny's face shifted to a shy, but slightly artful grin. *No*, it was a leer.

Jennifer hissed and snorted. *Jeez, wind your tongue in.*

Then it hit Jennifer like a slap across the face.

Kenny... Little gawky Kenny.

'Shall we take a stroll?' suggested Kenny.

Mabel nodded, and the pair trotted along the stream, following the cameraman.

Jennifer shook her head. This guy couldn't be Kenny. He didn't look anything like the shrimpy lad with the wonky eye.

'Before I moved here to start my job, I lived in Hackney with my parents,' explained Kenny.

'Wow, swapping London for this little gem must have been so wonderful.'

'Yes. I have always loved the countryside, Mabel. That's why my parents would book a cabin at the Moorbys' Barren's Lodge every summer. It became our special retreat. We all cherished that place. It felt like home. Well, until the last time we stayed – because that year, things seemed different. The atmosphere changed, becoming rather tense and strange.'

'You were at the cabin during that summer Katherine died?' asked Mabel, adding a note of drama to her voice, as if she didn't already know this information.

'Yes. We left the cabin two weeks before. Before *it* happened.'

'So, "tense and strange", you say. How do you mean? Talk us through that.'

Kenny pushed at his glasses again. 'I got the sense that all was not well. Normally, the Moorby family would be happy-go-lucky and helpful. The perfect hosts. Treated us like family. We were all especially fond of Ernest.'

'Not on that last visit?'

'Oh, no. Very different atmosphere entirely. It was like the whole family was ignoring each other. And us. Not Jennifer, though.' He raised his eyebrows high. 'Could never get rid of *that* one. She'd always be knocking about.'

Goosebumps rose on Jennifer's skin at the mention of her name. She didn't like this. Didn't like this at all.

Kenny cleared his throat and gave Mabel a coy smile and snorted breath through his nose. 'I'll be honest, I had the hots for her sister.'

'Ava?' asked Mabel.

'No, no. Not Ava. She was too old for me. I really, really liked Stacey.'

'Ah, OK. She would have been of a similar age, right?'

'A year older. So sweet and pretty. I'd get butterflies in the weeks leading up to my holiday at the thought of seeing her again. I was smitten. My first proper crush, you could say.'

'Did she feel the same?'

'She said she had a boyfriend. An older lad from the town. But I never met him. I think she was teasing me about that.'

'Right, playing hard to get, was she?'

Jennifer sighed. Was this a true crime series or a cringeworthy dating show?

Kenny nodded. 'I think so. But I never got the chance to be alone with her. Jennifer always made sure of that.'

'You sound annoyed. What did she do?'

'Jennifer Fincher was one strange child. She had the ability to pop up at the most inconvenient times. Like once, I'd almost convinced Stacey to join me and my parents on a trip into town for fish and chips and... *poof*, there she was.

Sometimes, it was like that annoying girl materialised out of thin air. It creeped me out. I was nice to her a few times, and she seemed to get it into her head that we were inseparable friends. And every year it got worse. She got more and more clingy and odder and odder. She'd always try to get me to go with her to this peculiar observatory place. And that last year. Christ! Where to begin?'

If Jennifer had been standing there now, she would have slapped that rude git and shoved him straight in the water. Horrible man.

The camera shuddered, and Mabel stopped in her tracks. 'This sounds intriguing, Kenny. Tell me more.'

The camera closed in on Kenny's chubby face. 'One night I couldn't sleep. It had been so hot and clammy. I decided to watch out the window for wildlife. Foxes and maybe a badger. Then I glimpse this shape standing there gawping right at me.'

'Jennifer?'

'Yep. She's just fixed on the spot... like a ghost. Like she'd been stuck in a trance. I moved from the window and made my way outside to find out what she wanted, but just like that, the girl had gone.'

'Odd.'

'I'd notice her pale face up in her window sometimes. At night, I mean. She'd be gazing out for ages. Fixed on... something.'

'Perhaps she had a crush on you, Kenny?'

'She probably did. I think she'd worked out I liked Stacey, and she'd purposely ruin our moments together. It's like... she always knew where to find us. And always knew everything that everyone was doing. She had to be sticking her beak into everyone's business.'

'Sounds like Jennifer was nothing more than an inquisitive young lady. I was much the same at her age,' stated Mabel, a hint of annoyance in her tone.

Too right. You tell that pudgy-faced jackass, Mabel.

'Then there's the dead girl.'

This got Mabel's attention. 'Say what?'

'She was fascinated with this girl who she believed had been hung from a tree. Penny. No, it was Polly. As Jennifer slept, the girl's spirit would visit her and beg for her help. I'd say she's the one who needed help, right? Jennifer kept asking me if I'd come with her to find Polly's remains. It became more than unsettling.'

Mabel raised her eyebrows and gestured that he should continue unloading.

'When I found out about the murder and her gran finding Jennifer asleep on the kitchen floor, I said, "That Jennifer *must* know something about her mother's death."'

'Are you suggesting that a nine-year-old child somehow murdered her own mother?' asked Mabel, a confused half-smile playing on her lips.

'No. I dunno about *that*. I'm saying that if anybody witnessed something that night, then you can bet your life that Jennifer did. Trust me, that girl never missed a thing.'

'But,' Mabel said, an edge of sharpness to her voice, 'why would she stay silent?'

Kenny shrugged and sighed through his nose. 'Like I said. A real oddball.'

Jennifer's grip on her hedgehog tightened even more. She raked her fingers into it, pretending it was Kenny's face. Then she made a huge mistake. She scanned the comments. Her brain couldn't cope. There were hundreds of them.

She read the most recent ones first.

Ernest is out now. Back at his home in North Sutton.
Residents are not happy about that.

Twenty-five years is not enough prison time... About
time that monster fessed up and admitted what he did.

Jennifer scrolled comment after comment. Conspiracy theories. Armchair detectives jumping in with their impertinent opinions. They got worse the further back she scrolled.

My money's on Ava. Not buying all that claptrap about
some car running her down.

Howard Fincher snuffed her out cos his wife was
screwing around. Framed his father-in-law. Watch this
space.

Stacey's guilty. She's proper fit though. I would. Ha ha.

Katherine killed herself. She could have untwisted that
chain. She chose not to. I reckon she wanted to die
down there.

Defo creepy Jennifer. I'm getting pure child-killer vibes.
Probably had help from her gypsy ghost friend of hers.

You can see the guilt in his eyes. Ernest did it. No
question.

Disagree. They've incarcerated an innocent man.

What is it with everyone and their ridiculous ideas? Stop

theorising and spouting nonsense. The jury voted.
Justice has been served, people. The end!

Jennifer closed the page. This hadn't been one of her better ideas. She put down her hedgehog, wiped the tears from her eyes and switched off her PC.

———————

21

The moon looked marvellous tonight. A magnificent bright yellow bulb glowing through a wisp of ethereal clouds. Reminiscent of a scene in a werewolf horror film, she decided. So low it almost seemed like you could climb a tree and poke it with an elongated finger. There was a scattering of stars, and Sirius dazzled incredibly brightly.

She wondered if Ernest was gazing up at the moon and enjoying its allure. Had he been able to view the moon from his cell? She'd often visualised a man with his face pressed up against a window, trying to get a glimpse of the life that was slowly passing him by. Fading away. Gone for ever. Wasted.

What had his cellmates been like? Did he make friends? Enemies? Did the prison officers treat him kindly? Had the food been edible or terrible? Did he ever contemplate ending it all?

She shook away these questions and remembered the apple she held in her hand. A perfect green apple washed and still wet. She took two big bites, swallowed, and gazed back to the moon as she ate.

But on her third bite, the texture of the apple changed, and the taste became bitter. She shone the phone torch onto the piece of fruit. Inside, she saw a brown, rotten area that she'd chewed around and taken a small nibble from. It was about the size of a ping-pong ball. She grimaced. The entire apple had appeared unblemished and normal to the eye.

Like me, she thought as she threw the apple away.

Normal on the outside.

Rotten to the very core on the inside.

22

J ennifer watched as Ernest tried to unlock the padlock on the outbuilding's door. He'd not seen her standing there, and she was tempted to call out a greeting to him. She didn't. Instead, she stood back and observed him. The padlock didn't seem to budge, and he tutted as he tugged at it. Then he stopped, let go of the lock and listened. It was as if he could sense someone was there. Anger and suspicion flashed in his eyes.

Jennifer let out a feeble cough. 'Hey, Grandad. Only me.'

The outrage on his face faded as he turned to her. 'You're back.'

She stepped out of the shadows. 'Be careful. Those wasps will get the hump and attack you.'

'I stuck a fumigator inside,' he said, then pretended to check the lock by shaking it.

'Right, good idea,' she said, not wanting to point out that she knew full well he'd been planning to go inside. 'Any more problems?'

He laughed without humour, swatted several wasps, then made for the main house. 'Come on.'

Jennifer followed, stealing a glance at the dilapidated building as she went. That place creeped her out.

When they reached the house, Jennifer stopped dead and let out an audible gasp. 'Holy crap!'

Outside the front door stood a tall white statue. A marble angel with outspread wings.

Jennifer put a hand over her mouth. 'Is it... God, is it... the same one?'

'Nah. Not tall enough, for a start. Close match.'

'You need to call the police again. This is getting out of hand.'

'Kids. Young tearaways. They'll soon get bored and leave me be.'

'We both know that's not true. You need to do something,' urged Jennifer. 'Did you see anything? Did they *leave* anything else?'

He gave her a questioning glare, raised one eyebrow and said, 'They did, as a matter of fact. A note.'

'Where is it?'

'Tore it to shreds.'

'But what did it say?'

He grunted and shrugged.

'Grandad, what did the note say?' she repeated more forcefully.

'It's a deadline to leave town. Ten p.m. next Friday. One week's time. Mighty generous of them.'

'And did the note mention what happens after that deadline elapses?'

'That next time they'll bring a length of chain,' he said quietly.

Jennifer took a few deep breaths and stepped closer to the statue. She ran a hand along the angel's smooth wing. 'I wonder if this is new. We might be able to find out where it came from.'

'What does it matter who bought the flippin' thing? The entire town wants me gone. I've seen that petition to make me sling my hook. Well, let me tell you this for free. I own this house. I own this land. Me! If those bastards want me gone, let them try to make me go. I don't intend to leave unless it's in a coffin!' With that, he stomped inside the house, mumbling something about making a brew.

As Jennifer studied the angel's austere expression and hairdo of ringlets, she wondered if she had something at home that could snap open that steel padlock on the door of the outbuilding. There was clearly something in there he didn't want her to see. But what?

23

D arkness greeted Jennifer as she opened her eyes. And caught a waft of something musty.

Thud. Thud. Thud.

Jennifer sat up and adjusted her eyes to the gloomy surroundings. She'd fallen asleep on her grandad's sofa, still wearing her boots. A tatty tartan blanket covered her legs, and she guessed he must've draped it over her while she slept. She struggled to recall even sitting down, let alone passing into a deep slumber. How long had she slept here like this?

She yawned, and her groggy head hurt.

The noise again.

Thud... Thud... Thud.

Closer now. Was somebody here? Out on the grounds? Inside the main house?

Throwing the blanket aside, she trotted across to the window and peered out into the darkness. Rain pattered against the glass. She couldn't see a thing. A sudden thought struck her. *My bike. My bloody bike is out there.*

Without even considering the dangers, she grabbed her helmet from the coffee table and charged outside. Once in the front courtyard, she stopped and listened. Nothing but rain at first... Then something else. A sound like wood snapping that made her jolt.

Jennifer made her way to the outbuildings where she'd left her bike. She breathed a sigh of relief when she found it was still there. But as she clambered over the barn gate and got closer, she noticed how wet the scooter was. At first, she assumed it to be rainwater. A closer inspection suggested it was something else entirely. She took out her phone, flicked on the torch and danced the beam over the scooter's body. Whatever covered it was red and slick. Paint? Blood? Some type of smeary oil?

A noise from within the woodland area opposite caused her to freeze. It sounded like a person shuffling through the undergrowth, followed by an echoey knocking.

'I have called the police! You hear me?' she shouted, sounding braver than she felt.

The shuffling stopped.

'You won't scare us. So sod off!'

A nerve-shredding silence. Even the rain had stopped.

Jennifer fixed her eyes on the trees ahead, and she wanted to shout out another warning or curse, but she couldn't speak now. Her instincts were screaming at her to turn and flee. However, fear had rendered her motionless and mute. She prayed for another thud or rustle just to shatter the grim quiet that had swallowed up the place.

'Jennifer?'

'Jesus!' she cried, her heart thumping as a harsh torch beam flittered across her midriff.

Ernest stood on the driveway, wearing a dressing gown

and a scruffy beanie almost covering his eyes. In one hand a cricket bat, the other a chunky silver torch. 'I didn't mean to startle you.'

Jennifer gestured to the woods. 'There was somebody over in the trees. I'm certain of it.'

He shone the light into the wooded area and trailed it across the spindly tree branches and the spiky shrubbery. He lingered over a mossy log. 'A couple of foxes would be my guess.' Then he danced the beam under the wavering willow tree. 'Can't see anything.'

'Grandad... Look. My bike.'

He stepped over and inspected the scooter with his torch. Red liquid glistened under the powerful beam. 'I'll open the gate. Wheel it up to the house, and we'll hose it down. Quick now! Don't leave it out here again.'

'I only intended to stay for twenty minutes.'

'You were dog-tired, lady. Didn't even finish your drink before you flaked out. Come on,' he said, fishing out a set of keys as he shuffled over to the gate to unlock it.

As soon as the gate swung open, Jennifer wheeled her messy scooter through the gap. She peered back into the shadows as she went, convinced that somebody was still crouching there watching them.

Something else worried her, too.

She realised that her grandad didn't seem the tiniest bit fazed by all this.

24

Sunday
(Five days before the deadline)

The party was in full swing when Jennifer arrived at Stacey's house; the garden jam-packed with people, young and old. She spotted David's parents, Jim and Marge, sipping glasses of fizz under a gazebo with Ava and several other grinning guests. As well as a table loaded with cakes, drinks, and snacks, there was another table loaded with presents of all shapes and sizes, and although a bunch of kids were charging around playing, she couldn't see Harriet among them.

Her plan had been to breeze in for a fleeting visit, wish her niece a happy birthday, then slip back out unnoticed. Upon seeing the size of some of those presents, she suddenly felt a tad embarrassed that her gift wouldn't quite compare.

Not that she'd been stingy. She'd put a lot of thought into her present.

Her dad was slouched in a bistro-style chair, swigging from a can of beer. His face carried a pensive expression as well as fuzzy stubble. His sullen presence was incongruous as he sat there alone, surrounded by chipper and chatty partygoers. Not one person was attempting to socialise with him. He'd not noticed her arrival, as he seemed to be occupied with throwing David's parents a snarky glare.

Jennifer knew her dad resented Jim and Marge Bamford. This derived from the fact that David's folks were everything he wasn't. Successful, generous, outgoing. His hatred of the pair had gradually manifested over time, and instead of trying to conceal his dislike, he chose to blank them. And so they reciprocated, making family gatherings a tad uncomfortable. But, whereas Howard was thorny and reclusive, the Bamfords were carefree, untroubled and talkative. Just not with her dad. Fortunately, these social occasions were infrequent.

A gaggle of kids raced past her, with her nephew, Evan, chasing them. She waved him down. 'Hey, you. Where's the birthday girl?'

'Summer house. Sulking,' he said in an apathetic voice before hurrying off with the other youngsters, who were now gleefully smacking each other over the head with long balloons.

Jennifer carried on past the main party, across the wide pristine lawn, and down to the summer house. The Dutch-style wooden cabin was quite a size. The sliding door lay open, and she found Harriet sitting on a giant orange beanbag behind a wooden bar made from reclaimed pallets. One of David's DIY projects.

'Hello, missy. Happy tenth birthday!'

Harriet peered up, eyes red-rimmed, and lips downturned.

'Bad day?'

Harriet shrugged.

'Here. Happy birthday.' Jennifer handed her the card and present she'd brought with her. 'It's just a little something. And I put some money inside the card so you can buy yourself something else. You can open it now if you like.'

Harriet wiped her tears and unwrapped the present. Studied the small unicorn with big round eyes. 'Aw, it's so cute.'

'It's no ordinary unicorn. You can squeeze him. When you're, you know, cross with someone or having a rubbish day.'

Harriet clamped her small hands about the unicorn and smiled through her tears. 'Thanks, Aunty Jennifer. I think I'm going to use her a lot.'

'I use mine daily. Mine's a hedgehog. His name is Stress-Hog. I have always been fond of the spiky little creatures.'

'I like hedgehogs as well. They have such sweet faces. I'll call mine... Miss Uni-Stress.'

Jennifer sat down on the beanbag. 'Good name... So why are you hiding down here on your big day? I mean, ten, that's a biggie.'

Harriet drew her knees up to her chin. 'It's meant to be my party, but my brother has invited all his friends, and they are spoiling everything. They are so... so noisy and annoying.'

A loud boisterous yell, followed by the cackle of rowdy children, filled the air, as if to illustrate her niece's point.

'Yeah, but I saw a couple of girls out there too,' said Jennifer.

'I don't really have that many friends. Not like Evan. He's Mr Popular.'

'Me neither. Friends are overrated.'

Harriet turned to her and gave her a quizzical pout. 'You don't like people very much, do you?'

Jennifer smiled. 'Did your mum tell you that?'

Harriet shook her head. A bit too quickly. 'No. I just get the feeling you don't.'

'I guess, if I'm being honest, I prefer my own company.'

'Oh. So you don't have a boyfriend?'

'Nope.'

'Don't you want one?'

Jennifer tried to recall the last time she'd been out with a man. Over two years ago, she guessed. One of the guys from the theatre group who'd eaten his Italian food like a frantic chipmunk. The huge dollops of ketchup he'd splattered all over his linguine had been off-putting enough, but the final straw had been his constant scanning of his phone. Every time she'd spoken to him, his eyes had flicked back onto that stupid device. He'd not asked her one single question about herself. And that wasn't even the worst date she'd endured over the last decade.

Jennifer nudged Harriet with her shoulder. 'Not really.'

'But don't you get lonely?'

Jennifer considered the question as her niece gazed at her with woeful eyes and an inquisitorial expression. 'I guess. Sometimes I do. Just a tiny bit.'

Harriett gave her unicorn a good pinch. 'Is that why you keep going to see the bad man?'

'Who is he?'

'Mum and Dad talk about him sometimes. They get a bit mad. They don't like you seeing the bad man. Neither does Grandpa Howie.'

'Um, well. It's hard to explain why I go there. Have you ever had an itchy scab that you really, really want to pick and rub? Even though you should leave it well alone, you just have to pick away at it.'

Harriet crinkled her nose and pulled a confused face. 'Yes. Cos if you pull it off, Mum says it will leave scars. But I don't understand.'

'Things happened at that house. When I was only a bit younger than you.'

'Nasty things?'

'I'd say more confusing things. Things that I *need* to remember, pumpkin.'

'And going to the bad man's house helps you to remember?'

'Yes. It's helping.'

'Harriet, are you in here?' called David.

'Down here,' said Jennifer.

David moved to the bar area, took off his shades and smiled. 'Girly natter?'

He had his hair slicked back in a ponytail and wore a loud Hawaiian shirt, crisp shorts and sporty flip-flops.

'Aunty Jennifer got me a stress unicorn,' said Harriet.

David smiled. 'Cool. Go and show your mum, would you, love? She's searching for you in the house. Quick now, you need to say bye to one of your friends. And don't forget to thank her for coming.'

Harriet nodded, kissed Jennifer on the cheek, then raced off.

David rubbed his hands together and offered Jennifer a

thin smile. 'Cold beer? Got some in the fridge. Or do you have your bike?'

Jennifer got up. 'Go on then. No bike. It's having some repairs done this weekend.'

David opened the fridge and grabbed the beers. 'Can I talk to you about something?' He popped the lids off the bottles and handed her one. 'It's quite important.'

Don't tell me – about the bad man.

Jennifer sipped the beer and nodded. 'Sure.'

'Come on then, why do you keep going up to *his* place? What's with that?'

'I have an itch that won't go away.'

David pulled a disgusted face. 'You're driving everyone bonkers with all this bullshit.'

'I get that, but it's important to me.'

'Ava is livid. Your dad is worried sick, and Stacey is freaking right out about you being hurt. Why would you want to upset your own family like this? You don't owe that bastard anything.'

'No. I don't.'

'So why? Help me understand, for fuck's sake,' he said, tilting his bottle of beer at her.

'I have my reasons.'

David took a noisy swig of beer and shook his head. He moved closer to her, and she caught a waft of a rather nice spicy fragrance. He also stank of booze.

'We've always got on well, right? So can I speak frankly?'

'Yep.'

'Are you plotting something? Are you involved in what's happening up at that house?'

Jennifer swigged her beer. Said nothing.

David moved even closer. 'Because if you're playing

games with that old loon, you are putting yourself in grave danger. And you're upsetting your sister. *My* wife. You know how flaky she is.' He spoke in a composed voice, but his tense body language contradicted his tone. 'Why not have a word with her, hey? Put her mind at rest. Promise her you'll stop visiting him. Would you do that, please? For me?'

'None of you need to worry about me.'

David placed a hand on her shoulder and got a bit too close for comfort. 'We *do* worry. All of us.'

Jennifer noticed how glazed his eyes were. He'd clearly necked a few this afternoon.

'If you ever need to talk. Properly talk. About anything. You can always confide in me. I mean that, Jennifer.'

She gave him a tight smile and stepped away from him. 'Cheers for the beer. I'll head down and find Stacey.'

David winked at her and closed the gap between them again. 'Make sure you get a slice of that cake I made. Call me a bighead, but it's pretty darn good.'

'Try to stop me.'

Jennifer peeled away from David and hurried away from the summer house.

Had her brother-in-law just tried to get a tad fruity with her?

25

S tacey poured the white wine into her glass until it reached the rim. 'A total bloody embarrassment. He has sat there with a face like a cow munching on an angry wasp and done sod all except swig beer after beer without talking to anybody. Why even bother to show up?'

Jennifer noticed a splash of wine on the kitchen counter, and her eyes hunted for some kitchen roll. *Force of habit.*

Stacey gulped back the wine. 'David's parents bought her an iPad for her birthday. What did *he* get Harriet? Oh, that's right, a cheap-arse toy set that he most likely got from the corner shop on the Eden for a fiver.'

'Thought that counts,' said Jennifer.

'There was little thought that went into that. He never does anything for us. David's dad built that swing set and climbing frame out the back for the kids. He always makes the effort.'

'Dad can't help being—'

'A skint loser,' interrupted Stacey, her tone surly.

'I was going to say a little strapped for cash.'

'Why do you always have to defend him? He hasn't had a proper job for over five years. Face it, he's an idle sponger. The scourge of the taxpayer.'

'Don't be mean.'

Stacey sipped her wine through pinched lips. 'Why do you always have to stick up for life's no-hopers? Stop seeing the good in everyone. It can get a little irritating. Sometimes a deadbeat is just a deadbeat.'

Jennifer pulled a face. Her sister was on one today. The drink, obviously. Only the drink would bring out this spiteful side of her.

'Materialistic,' she said faintly.

'Sorry?'

'Nothing. Thinking aloud. Something for my play.'

Stacey hit back the wine, put the glass on the counter, poured another. 'Harriet's not having a good day. Only three of her friends turned up. And one's already left because she has a second "party" to attend.' She used her two index fingers to air quote the word party. 'I don't know why that girl's so unpopular. It breaks my heart to think she's got no close friends.' She snatched up the wine and drained half in one hit.

'She's a bright girl.'

'Oh, yeah. You should read some of her English projects. She's going to be a literary genius, mark my words. Must take after you and... Mum... She loves a story, that girl.'

'Can I read some of her work?'

Stacey smiled, grabbed her phone and started searching. 'Let me read you this. Where is it?... Um, oh, here we go... "Everything". A poem by Harriet Bamford.

'Under a sombre, moonlit sky, a cold truth, a long, heavy sigh... *everything* ends.

'In shadows cast, where dark clouds gather, a silent pain lingers... *everything* ends.

'Fading light, parting loved ones, echoes of pain... *everything* ends.

'Stars will fall, their brilliant lights fading, mountains crumble, yet no one will see... *everything* ends.

'Yet, in the void, where darkness reigns, a new beginning grants a sprinkle of hope...

'Yet, still, hope fades, because... *everything*... ends.'

Jennifer gave her sister a sad smile. 'I love that. I really do.'

'It's quite bleak though, isn't it? Maybe a bit too bleak.'

'No, it's stirring. And... honest.'

THE SUN SLIPPED OUT from broken clouds to beam down onto the guests. Jennifer watched her dad crush a beer can, cast it aside, then head for the fruit punch that had been unpopular with the attending guests. She half expected him to pick up the entire glass bowl and guzzle it. Instead, he picked up the ladle, studied it and started filling a plastic beaker, concentrating as though it were the most complicated task in the world. He picked out some bits of fruit and tossed them back into the mix.

Stacey and Ava sat alone, chatting in conspiratorial voices.

Jennifer closed her eyes and enjoyed the sun on her face. For a moment she slipped away and pictured herself on some glorious Mediterranean beach instead of being stuck here with her family. Which was odd because she wasn't even fond of the heat or of beaches. Then she heard Ava mutter, 'Nobody tell him that's the kids' booze-free punch.'

'The kids hate it,' said Stacey flatly.

'What do you expect? You stuck a load of fruit in it,' Ava told her. 'Should have filled it with Skittles. They would have lapped it up then.'

Stacey grunted. 'Rum would have been safer with Evan and his pack of rampaging goblins. Where are they, anyway? It's too quiet out here.'

'Probably trashing your house,' said Ava.

Jennifer caught David's eye. He stood under one of the gazebos, talking to his parents and another couple. She averted her gaze and approached her sisters.

'Sit down. Have some wine,' suggested Stacey, nodding at the free garden chair at their table.

Jennifer's eyes flicked to Ava, who had her elbow rested on the table and her chin nestled on one hooked finger. Her expression was one of distracted contemplation. Jennifer offered her a warm smile.

In response, a flash of hostility showed in her sister's dark eyes. Or *ex*-sister, as may be the case. If she'd spoken the truth during their last get-together.

'I'm going to walk Dad home. He can barely stand,' said Jennifer.

'David's going to order him a taxi,' said Stacey.

'He won't take a taxi. He'll complain it's a waste of money and walk anyway. He always does,' said Ava.

'He can't go home on his own in that state. I'll walk him,' insisted Jennifer. 'Nice to see you all.'

'Oh, don't go,' whined Stacey. Her eyes were glossy and sparkling. 'Sit. Come on, you.'

As Jennifer sat, Stacey jumped up. 'I'll grab you a glass. We're having a drink, and I won't take no for an answer,' she stated as she trudged off.

Ava studied Jennifer with keen eyes. 'Well?'

'What?'

'Just ask already. Go on. I can tell you've been wanting to ask me something today. I can read you like a book,' said Ava, her tone monosyllabic.

'You won't get grumpy?'

'No.'

'Do you ever wonder about who tried to run you over that night?'

Ava's face didn't change. She let out a small sigh. 'I guess.'

'Why were you down that lane so late?'

Stacey returned with the extra glass. 'What lane?'

Ava picked up her wine. 'Jennifer's dredging up the past again.'

'Jeez, don't bring the vibe down even more,' said Stacey.

'I watched a YouTube film. A documentary of sorts. It got mentioned, that's all,' said Jennifer.

Ava and Stacey shared a pained look, then both gulped their wine.

Ava broke the brief silence. 'I'd been out that night,' she said in a resigned tone. 'Some friends dropped me off, and when I got to my room, I realised I'd lost my purse. I took a torch down the lane, assuming it had fallen out as I got out of their car.'

'And someone drove at you?' asked Jennifer.

Ava nodded. 'I spotted headlights snap on, and some dickhead tried to hit me with their car. I was forced to plummet into a ditch. I cut myself to shreds. I'm sure they did it on purpose. They were aiming right at me.'

'Likely a drunk driver,' said Stacey.

Ava pulled a face. 'Parked up on that dead-end lane? Yeah, sure. They were waiting for me. Or waiting for someone.'

Jennifer's mind flashed back to that VW van as it deliberately tried to back into her. For a moment, she considered sharing this experience with her sisters. Then, a moment later, decided not to. 'Who dropped you off?'

Ava shrugged. 'Some lads.'

'Who?' asked Jennifer.

'Just some lads from the Eden. Doesn't matter.' Ava took a deep breath and gazed into her wine. When she spoke again, she sounded weary. 'It has always bugged me. Some twat almost killed me, and all these years later, I still don't know why.'

Stacey cleared her throat. 'Best not to dwell on all that. And best not to fill your head with rubbish, Jennifer. Those films are morbid and wrong. Those unscrupulous people shouldn't be permitted to delve into such tragic affairs that have devastated other people's lives. It's sick.'

Jennifer persisted. 'That YouTuber interviewed Kenny. You remember him? He had a wonky eye.'

'Nope,' said Ava, a little too quickly.

'He came from London every year with his family. He had the hots for Stacey,' Jennifer said, trying to keep the annoyance out of her voice. She'd always believed Kenny had liked her, and hadn't been impressed by those things he'd said.

Stacey smiled and groaned. 'Oh, him. Yeah. A persistent bugger, that boy.'

'What the hell did he have to say?' asked Ava.

Jennifer sat up straight and took a small sip of wine. 'He had plenty to say. *Plenty!* You should see it. I'll send you both the link.'

'Don't bother. I won't watch it. I refuse to open that door again,' said Ava.

Jennifer turned to Stacey. 'Kenny said he asked you out. But you rejected him. You told him you already had a boyfriend.'

Ava laughed and shook her head.

'What's funny?' Jennifer asked.

'She won't want to talk about this,' said Ava.

Stacey's cheeks flushed.

Ava crossed her arms and shot Stacey a contemptuous look. 'We can't talk about Stacey's "secret boyfriend" because she'll have a massive meltdown.'

Stacey's nostrils flared, and despite her indignant expression, she kept her voice level as she said, 'Oh, give over, Ava, there was no boyfriend. I used that as an excuse to fob off that annoying Kenny.'

Ava leaned in closer. 'The folks had some epic barneys over it. I can remember. Ask Dad. Go on. I'm sure it'll all be fresh in his memory.'

Stacey shrugged. 'Mummy dearest was just being paranoid. And I expect Daddy was too busy planning his next hook-up with that slut Felicia Macclesfield.'

'Mum became obsessed about this mystery boyfriend. It drove her mental. You telling me that was all in her head? Because I recall her endlessly nagging you about him,' said Ava.

Stacey shrugged again. 'I was fourteen. I wasn't even into boys. And you were the one who snuck off to that party on

the Eden. Mum banned you from going. She knew there'd
be drugs and older guys there. You just went anyway and
pissed her right off.'

Ava chuckled darkly. 'Now you're talking bollocks, and
you know it. OK, you're right. Mum didn't want me to go, but
she wasn't that bothered. She was never that bothered about
my life. You and this older mystery boy were her primary
concern. Not me taking a few Es at some shitty house party.'

'Like I said, I was only fourteen. I didn't have a
boyfriend.'

Ava threw a wine cork at her. 'You liar.'

Stacey's face clouded with anger. 'You were off your head
that night. Which is why you dropped your purse. I reckon
all that happened was you stepped in front of that car
because you were so out of it.'

'Come on, who was this special fella? Why have you
never come clean about him?' said Ava, disregarding her
sister's comments.

Jennifer sank down in her seat. As her older sisters
continued their debate, they'd not noticed that David had
edged over to their table and was in earshot of their discussion. *How much did he overhear?*

'She even found a box of rubbers in the grotto. And they
sure as shit weren't mine. So stop lying, Stacey. It's boring,'
said Ava. She sounded drunk now, and a hint of belligerence
was creeping into her tone. 'Who were you shagging, hey?
Come on, why all the secrecy? It wasn't that little freak
Kenny, was it? Did he keep sneaking back?'

Stacey opened her mouth to speak, clocked David, and
her mouth fell shut. Her cheeks flushed even redder.

David beamed. 'Yeah, tell us, Stacey. Come on. Tell us all
who you were shagging.'

Stacey bit her lower lip and shook her head. 'David... I didn't—'

David cut her off. 'I mean, you could shout a little louder about all this. I'm not sure my parents and the other party guests quite heard the full story over there.'

Stacey drank her wine and clammed up.

David continued with a cordial smile on his face. 'I bet my mum would love to hear all about how my lovely wife was humping older boys at the tender age of fourteen. Such a wonderful story. Hey, I'll give Harriet a shout too. I bet she'd like to hear it. That really would make her birthday a memorable one.'

Despite his smile and relaxed voice, Jennifer only had to look at David's hard eyes to understand how infuriated he was.

David scanned the table. 'So, more drinks for anyone? No? All had plenty? Good.' With that, he snatched up two handfuls of empty glasses and strutted off.

'David, wait,' called Stacey lamely. 'I'll give you a hand.'

'Nope. You crack on, love,' said David, marching into the house.

Stacey spun to face Ava. 'What the hell?'

Ava pulled a silly grimace. 'Sorry! But he'll get over it. Men don't like to think that anyone else has poked their wife's honey pot before them. You've just hurt his macho ego.'

'Don't be so crude,' Stacey snapped, getting up from the table. 'He'll have the hump with me all day now. So thanks a bunch for that.' And she made a beeline for the house.

Ava raised her eyebrows and caught Jennifer's eye. 'Whoops. Trouble in paradise.'

'Who the hell is Felicia Macclesfield?' asked Jennifer.

'Dad's fuck buddy. Not now. Back then. That's who he was with… *that* night.'

Jennifer searched the garden for her dad. Located him sitting alone, drinking punch and scrolling on his phone. She remembered his affair being mentioned in Mabel's film, and she'd been keen to find out more. Now she had a name to work with, she was even keener to get him on his own.

'Felicia was his alibi?' asked Jennifer, now gazing back to the house, where she could see David and Stacey through the window. Her sister looked distraught, and David was jabbing an accusing finger at her.

'Yep,' confirmed Ava.

'Did Mum know about her?'

'Course she did. I once overheard them have an explosive argument about her. She's still here. In North Sutton. I heard on the grapevine she lives in one of those nice townhouses on Shaw Lane. Word is, she came into some money. Inherited a big plot of land, which she sold on and made a decent bit of cash from.'

'Have you ever spoken to her?'

Ava's eyes narrowed. 'I've met her a couple of times. Dad tried to reconnect with her five or six years back. Guess he found out about her windfall and thought he might worm his way back into her life so he could get his sticky mitts on her money. I'm guessing she told him to sling his hook.' Ava flashed Jennifer a lopsided smile. 'I shouldn't have said what I did at the restaurant. About us no longer being sisters and all that bollocks. I was having a bad day.'

'It's fine.'

'No, it's not. It's no secret that I'm pissed at you for going to see him. But I can't stop you. I was out of order.'

'I understand.'

Ava studied her closely. 'Do you?' She grinned and opened her mouth to speak, when a smashing noise snapped her attention away.

They both turned to see Howard on his back, the flattened punch table under him and an assortment of plastic cups scattered about the grass.

'For fuck's sake. Dad has well and truly killed the fruit punch now,' moaned Ava.

Evan and his mob of hyper friends were straight on the scene, hooting and jeering. Some of the guests looked outraged. Others were openly laughing. One kid, a mean-faced boy with a mop of messy red hair, picked up some fruit chunks and threw them in Howard's face, much to the amusement of Evan and the other horrors in his pack.

Jim raced over, attempted to pull Howard up, slipped and fell into the mess.

Harriet and another girl with splashes of freckles on her cheeks shared a quick look; then both broke out into a fit of silly giggles.

'Who needs to book a party clown when you've got Dad, hey?' quipped Ava, rolling her eyes.

Jennifer nodded in agreement as she watched her dad clamber to his feet. He wobbled away from the carnage without even acknowledging the damage or offering Jim a 'thank you' for trying to assist him. Jim, who was now on his back, trying to get up. He was a big lump of a man, and this wasn't going so well.

Ava finished her drink. 'I guess we should really lend a hand.' She picked up a wine bottle and tipped the dregs into her glass, making no attempt to go over.

They looked on, indifferent, as Marge and another man, who were now on the scene, each tugged at an arm.

'I'll follow Dad and make sure he gets home OK,' said Jennifer.

Ava shrugged and sipped her wine. 'Good luck with that.'

And both sisters watched as their shambolic father staggered away from the sorry remains of his granddaughter's tenth birthday party.

26

D aylight ebbed away as the pair set their eyes on the three concrete tower blocks that signified the start of the Eden estate. Even with the sun setting into a pleasant orange smudge beyond the structures, the place still held a daunting, hostile vibe. Jennifer had always been fearful of it.

Ask anyone in North Sutton who lived on the estate, and they'd tell you –

The Eden isn't all that bad. It has a bad rep, but the people who live here are salt-of-the-earth folk.

Ask anyone who didn't live there, and you'd get an altogether different evaluation –

Full of drug dealers and rowdy gangs of youths. You venture into the Eden after dark at your own risk.

The council had invested in better housing, fortified cameras and stricter policing, so the streets were safer now than they'd been a couple of decades back. Nevertheless, the area still oozed an air of menace, which seemed to manifest itself inside every shadowy corner, long alleyway and shrouded window.

The idea of her dad living in such a place was a depressing thought. She watched him now, hands shoved inside the pockets of his jeans, striding ahead. She'd tried to engage him in conversation during the forty-minute trek here, but she'd struggled to get much out of him save the odd slurred mumble. He'd kept strutting with purpose in pensive, drunken silence. Jennifer's plan to needle some information from him had backfired, and now she was cursing herself for being stuck in this grim part of town. There'd be little point asking him about Felicia now.

But she did hate seeing him like this, and she guessed it was at least in part Stacey's fault. He'd been no doubt made to feel inadequate and cheap alongside David's fabulous parents. The magnanimous Bamfords who could do no wrong. Howard Fincher liked to make out he was shameless and unemotional, but she knew this stance was pure subterfuge. Deep down, he was self-conscious of his impoverished status and way too proud to accept handouts (discounting free drinks) from his offspring.

The tower blocks loomed closer, causing Jennifer to suddenly need the toilet. The path they were now on would take them right through the middle of the blocks. There'd likely be scores of teens milling around on this balmy July evening. She didn't fancy that route.

'I can get back on my own, Jen,' he murmured.

'I don't mind.'

'I'm not a lost dog. I can find my own way home.' With that, he retreated into sullen silence as he trudged on.

Jennifer blew out a long sigh and contemplated turning back. There would be no way she'd venture through the estate on her own at dusk, and she wouldn't want to stay at her dad's. Which meant another long walk back to her place, or a taxi ride. Someone once told her that quite a few taxi companies charged triple to enter the Eden. Others outright refused to venture in during the hours of twilight.

He took a sharp right and started off down some steep concrete stairs.

'Where are you going now?'

'Shortcut.'

Jennifer trotted down the steps behind him. Urban area gave way to trees and bushes and scrubland. Jennifer's heart rate stepped up a notch when she understood that his supposed shortcut would send them into a dingy underpass set beneath the motorway.

'We should go the other way,' she suggested in a shrinking voice.

'It's fine. I always head through here.'

Two black bollards were fixed at the tunnel's entrance. A brown puddle of stagnant water greeted them as they entered. Along with the word JANK, written in a pink, bubble-style font that seemed to jump right out of the dirty-white wall that was lined with square lights. Pools of yellowish liquid that Jennifer attentively avoided as she walked. More loud graffiti on both sides.

She almost welcomed the intermittent *thrum, thrum, thrum* from the vehicles above as they went. Any noise was preferable over silence, echoed footsteps, or her father coughing in that solitary passage.

Jennifer stole a glance behind, seeing nothing but a black hole where they'd entered. The same awaited them on the other end, but just to add to the creepiness, the wall lights were flickering by their exit. All that was missing from this textbook scary scene was a maniac in a hockey mask appearing in front of them, brandishing a meat cleaver. Yet on her dad trotted, oblivious to her unease or the fact they would be easy pickings down here for a gang of muggers.

The underpass seemed to shudder and move as something heavy passed overhead. Jennifer decided motorway bridges were much safer. Who ever thought these grim passageways were a sensible idea?

The way out of the tunnel was mere footsteps away.

Then she caught the sound of laughter.

Jennifer froze, her heart racing. 'Dad?'

He stopped, pulled a face and staggered sideways. 'Kids.' He waved a dismissive hand. 'Come on.'

More laughter. People were on the outside of the tunnel. But she couldn't see a thing in the darkness. Her legs didn't want to move, and she was having to clench her pelvic-floor muscles because she was so in need of the loo.

More laughter.

Thrum, thrum, thrum.

Her dad's face. Drawn, pale and clueless, as he stood by the exit. Behind him was a backdrop of nothingness.

Pitch-black.

It's important to just breathe.

The unknown.

Breathe in deeply... exhale.

'What's the matter with you, Jen?'

She couldn't move. Why? What was stopping her?

'You wanna stay down here all night? You like this place or something?' he slurred.

'I only wanted to walk you home,' she whispered. 'I didn't want you to get run over.'

More laughter. This time rowdier and with it swearing and unruly chatting. Not kids. *Teenagers, at least.*

'Come on,' he ordered, ignorant of her growing dread.

Somehow, she forced herself out into the darkness. The laughter and voices eased as they passed by the group. Six or seven lads. She wasn't going to stop and count. Some were sitting on the steps, others slouching against the railings.

The group observed them with undisguised hostility. One tall lad, wearing a red Adidas baseball cap worn backwards and a black tracksuit, sniffed and spat. A stocky younger lad with a squashed nose and a tattoo on his neck said something Jennifer didn't catch.

A mixture of cigarette smoke and sweet vape smog encompassed the group. Some were drinking cans of cheap cider.

Jennifer caught their brazen stares and baleful sneers. They were a nasty-looking bunch. Their intent was obvious. They wanted to intimidate them, and they were enjoying making them feel apprehensive. She willed herself not to make eye contact with any of the lads as she took the steps.

Her dad misjudged the third step and slipped. This mishap earned him some spiteful laughter from the group. He stopped and turned to face the gang. He needed to hold onto the railing to stop himself from stumbling back down. 'Don't you laugh at me. You don't want to do that, boys.'

Jennifer's blood went cold. 'Dad! Leave it.'

The smouldering animosity radiating from the gang turned Jennifer's insides to liquid and her legs to stone.

But her dad laughed out loud. 'You're not scared of these daft wankers, are you, Jen?' He stepped closer to the lads. 'You really don't need to be. They won't hurt you. They won't fucking dare!' He spat those words so vehemently it made Jennifer shudder.

Even some of the teenagers appeared a tad wary now. As if their confidence had been broken by her dad's total lack of fear.

But one of the gang, undaunted, flicked a cigarette end at him.

Jennifer saw the orange butt whizz over his head. She flinched and held her left eye as though it had struck her in the face. This conjured a vivid memory of a teenage Ava screaming at her. Momentarily confused by why she'd just remembered this, she almost didn't notice the can of cider spinning through the air and heading her way. It bounced off the top of her head, and although it didn't hurt, the idea that they'd had the audacity to throw something at her stunned her.

Then the threats spilled from the group.

'I'll fucking lay you open!'

'You want your face carved up, slut?'

To Jennifer's surprise, the more intimidating and foul the threats, the more amused her dad became. He picked up one of their thrown cans of cider, necked it and smacked his lips in appreciation. 'Ah, nice. Any more you want to send my way, you pointless little wankers? Come on, don't be shy, you bunch of pussies. I've encountered more terrifying fuzzy-haired sheep than you lot.'

The harrying and goading continued, and her dad lapped it up. One of the youths swung himself over the railing and got right in his face, roaring and shouting appalling insults. Her dad exploded into a spitting rage and made a grab for the youth.

Jennifer had never witnessed her dad lose his cool. Not

really lose it. Nor had she seen him deal out violence. To say she was stunned by his action would be a massive understatement. She heard, more than witnessed, what he did to the lad. A dry cracking sound, followed by a hideous scream of agony, was confirmation enough that the boy's wrist had snapped. As her dad used all his power, and the metal railing, to force the limb downwards to its breaking point.

The lad fell back, howling in pain. The noise was chilling.

Jennifer now expected the entire gang to fly into action. To attack as one. She envisioned knives being pulled and the pair of them being dragged into the underpass, where they'd be mercilessly hacked and kicked to death.

Breathe in deeply... exhale.

Her dad smashed his fist against his chest and stepped closer to the group. 'I'll end you! All of you. Do you hear me?' he boomed as he eyed them with challenging stares. He spoke like some almighty, tyrannical deity addressing his pitiful minions. As if he could crush the lot of them in the blink of an eye if they dared to oppose him.

As the lad with the broken wrist lamented on the floor, the fight left his comrades, and they edged back. Sneers were now replaced with uneasy expressions. The nasty threats changed to worried muttering and urgent whispers laced with fear.

Her dad grabbed her arm, making her flinch. 'Come on. Move.'

Somehow, she did. Each step was a huge chore. 'What did you do?' she whispered.

A pitiful wail came from below. 'Don't touch it! No! Call someone!'

Jennifer wanted to put her hands over her ears to block out the sounds.

'Just a bunch of wide-boy pricks,' he growled. 'You live on the Eden, you learn to stick up for yourself, love.'

'But... but you broke his wrist!'

He kept walking. 'Nobody hurts my girls,' he muttered, almost to himself.

Jennifer wiped the cider that was running down the side of her face and caught a sickly chemical smell with only a hint of apple. She wondered if a prison cell would be safer than this awful estate.

27

J ennifer pushed open the door to her dad's dingy flat.
It smelled like fried food mixed with the occasional
waft of rotting rubbish. Like the smell you get when
you open a festering bin. She didn't want to go inside.

A grating cough grabbed Jennifer's attention. There was
a man on the street staring at them.

'You all right there, Howard?' asked the man, his deep
voice loaded with suspicion.

Jennifer smiled uncertainly at the man.

He offered her a frosty glower by way of response. The
man, who must have been close to sixty, had a long, mean
face, bushy eyebrows and a pointy chin, with a tuft of greyish
fluff sprouting from it.

Howard waved a dismissive hand and staggered into the
house. 'Yeah, yeah, Bruce.'

'Right then. OK. I'll speak to you later about that stuff we
need to collect,' said Bruce, his voice cold and slow.

'Yeah, OK,' said Howard, irritated.

'Well, I'll see you then.' Bruce threw her another glare

before crossing the road and going into a ground-floor flat opposite.

As she entered her dad's flat, she couldn't shake the suspicion that the creepy man was still spying on them from one of the darkened windows.

'Dad, open some windows; it's a bit whiffy in here,' she pointed out.

He ignored her and shuffled off into the gloomy kitchen. Moments later, there came the distinct sound of a can cracking open.

How could he be living like this?

A coarse shout from outside caused her to jump. She backheeled the door shut and stepped further into the hall-way, praying the youths hadn't followed them. She was still reeling from what she'd witnessed her dad do to that young-ster. That awful snapping noise his wrist made would haunt her to her dying days.

Jennifer walked into the kitchen. The stench in here became so overpowering, the urge to cover her mouth and nose was almost impossible to resist. The state of the place was evident, even in the low light. Grease-smeared worktops, a bowl loaded with manky fruit, and putrefying washing-up left on the side. Bottles, cans and wrappers strewn every-where. The floor under her Dr. Martens was sticky and foul.

Howard sat at a messy table filled with newspapers and bottles, sipping from a can of beer. 'I'd offer you something, but I'm guessing you wouldn't accept it.'

Jennifer wasn't sure if this was all an act, or if he was genuinely unbothered by the fact he was living like a complete slob.

Jennifer said nothing and phoned for a taxi. The relief when the operator said they'd send a car in ten minutes helped calm her down, and the shakes subsided. The sooner she left this estate, the better. Now the urge to use the toilet was getting close to unbearable, but there was no way she'd set foot in his bathroom. The idea of how bad it must be in there made her stomach lurch.

'Will those boys call the police?' she asked.

He responded with a shrill, sardonic laugh.

'They won't just leave it. Surely you can't go around hurting teenagers like that without any repercussions?'

'People around here don't tend to call the police.'

'What does that mean? They'll seek justice for themselves?'

'Most likely. They'll probably get me at the local boozer.'

'There's a pub on the estate?'

'Yep. A total dive. I love it.'

She sighed. 'In that case, I suggest you keep a low profile.'

'Stop trying to mother me, Jen. It's just weird.'

'OK. Right. But you shouldn't stay here. In fact, go pack a bag right now. You can crash on my sofa for a few days.'

As soon as these words left her lips, she cringed at the very idea of him sleeping on her lovely, clean sofa. She'd have to cover it in some old sheets first and remove all her new cushions. She couldn't have his greasy hair contaminating them. She felt bad for thinking like this, but she couldn't stop herself.

'They won't come here. I'm fine,' he slurred. 'I'm quite capable of looking after myself.'

'Clearly. But it's still not safe.'

Jennifer had never witnessed her dad so much as push another person. One reason the violent act had been so shocking was because she didn't realise he had it in him.

A sobering thought.

Another thought struck her. A very unpleasant one. She shook it away quickly and said, 'Felicia Macclesfield.'

His eyes widened with suspicion. 'Who told you about her?'

'Do you ever see her these days?'

'She wouldn't give me a squirt of her piss if I were on fire and begging for help. The self-righteous old crow that she is these days.'

'You were seeing her, though? Around the time... around *that* time, right?'

He snorted through his nose. Gulped his beer. 'We're not talking about this.'

'Why not?'

'I said we're not talking about that moody old boot! Or your mother... or any of it.' His eyes burned with rage. 'None of it! Understand?' His breathing became harsh and wheezy. 'Will you stop and give it a rest? Why are you always such a nosy bloody cow? Hey, why?' He angrily grabbed his nose and wiggled it. 'Always sticking this into places it's not wanted.' He gritted his teeth, went to say something else, then seemed to change his mind.

'I'll wait outside for my taxi.'

'How did you know she was in the water, Jen?'

'What?'

'When Sally found you on the kitchen floor, one of the first things you said was, "I'm sure she's still in the water." That's why Sally checked the pond. Did you see something? Hey? What's all that about? Come on, tell me. What did you see?'

'I... I need to go.'

'Go on then,' he snarled, 'off you trot. Why not go and see that murdering nutcase you seem so fond of these days?'

Jennifer walked down the hallway towards the door.

A chair scraped on the tiles, and he stomped after her. 'Why is it that you are so unafraid of that man? Mm, tell me that.'

Jennifer opened the door. The fresh air was gloriously satisfying. She breathed in a greedy intake.

'Why are you so sure he's innocent? Tell me! Do you believe him? Do you trust him?' he gabbled, growing increasingly delirious and irate.

She didn't answer and stepped outside.

He came after her, arms waving like he was fighting off an invisible foe. 'Or do you really believe that he deserves a second chance? After what he did. Is that what this is? Because I'll tell you right now, no one else in this town will forgive him. Never! I certainly won't. It should be his bones that get broken. If I ever see him, I'll break his arms, his legs and his bastard fucking neck.'

Jennifer stopped and stared at him. Waited for him to finish his slurring rant.

'You're a fool, Jen. Your head is in the clouds, you ditzy cow... You are... you're breaking my heart.'

'Please don't call me Jen. I don't like it. Go to bed. Goodnight, Dad.'

'Is there another reason for you helping him?' he asked, his voice wavering and softer all of a sudden. 'Tell me what you're playing at. All I—'

'Goodnight,' she repeated, cutting him off. 'My taxi will be here shortly.'

As she walked away from his flat and into the dark, empty close, he slammed the door behind her.

She gazed about the area, and her heart sank. It really was the pits here. Someone once told her that if you ended up living in the Eden, you'd hit rock bottom. All Jennifer knew was this: she couldn't wait to depart this abysmal area. The edgy neighbourhood was inauspicious enough to shatter anybody's psyche.

She walked fast to the end of the close and waited. It was silent. A little too silent.

She caught sight of those three foreboding tower blocks in the near distance, and a horrible thought came to her. What if the taxi failed to turn up? The idea of heading across this estate on her own made her feel sick with fear.

Distant sirens shattered the silence, and she pictured an ambulance crew racing down to collect the injured lad. Then she heard voices. A gaggle of youths was heading her way. She wondered if it might be the same group that they'd had that run-in with earlier. The prospect of facing those lads filled her with dread.

Jennifer considered slipping away and finding a spot to hide, but then she spotted headlights approach. She almost jumped for joy when she clocked it was a taxi. She waved at it like a mad person and got inside the vehicle before it had even come to a proper stop. 'Hello. Thank God you're here.'

'You look keen to leave,' said the driver, checking his mirrors and moving off with zero hesitation.

As they drove out of the Eden, it was hard not to feel upset – despite her relief. Her grandad was rattling around in that huge house out in the middle of nowhere, and her dad was stuck here. As she caught one last glance at those three tower blocks, something came to her. She'd driven down this side of the estate before. In her dad's car when she was young. He'd been frantic and going out of his mind with worry.

They'd been searching for someone. *Ava*. They had been searching the estate for Ava. Her dad and sister had ended up having an argument. She remembered it clearly now. Her sister's expression morphing from a baffled pout to outraged sneer. The very idea he'd had the gall to seek her out had vexed her. That he'd had the front to embarrass her in front of her friends, who'd viewed the confrontation from the roadside with sly grins on their faces.

'Mum wants you home. Get in the car, Ava,' he'd demanded.

'No! Tell her to stop suffocating me.'

'Get in.'

'Tell her you didn't find me.'

'Ava, come on, you know I can't.'

'For fuck's sake!'

'Ava, enough.'

'I hate that bitch. She can smoke drugs and drink a bottle of wine every night, while I can't even go out with my friends. She loves controlling us. And she controls you. And you let her. It's pathetic.'

'Just calm down and get in the car.'

Ava had yanked open the door and got into the back seat. 'This is such bollocks,' she'd hissed. 'And you can wipe that smug look off your face, miss goody-fucking-two-shoes.'

'Stop swearing at your sister.'

Jennifer was sure Ava had bickered with their dad the entire journey, though she couldn't remember the rest of their exchange. She'd likely zoned out and ignored them.

28

She slapped herself three times. It didn't help. She couldn't wake up. Or focus. Or contend with the day ahead.

It annoyed her when people said they were tired. *Oh, I didn't sleep a wink last night.* She wanted to grab them and scream in their face. Bellow at them and shout, 'You don't have a clue what you're talking about! You have zero idea what it's like to be so fucking exhausted you want to smash your face into a brick wall to knock yourself the hell out. When you want to make the pain stop so badly, you'll try anything. Anything! That's right, "the pain". It *is* pure pain. It is bloody torture. When you desperately want the suffering to end, it is nothing but agonising torture. Sleep deprivation and insomnia are no joke, you know? No joke at all. So don't spout your idiotic bullshit to me. Got it, you dumb fuck-head?'

Of course, she never did reply that way. She'd smile weakly and offer up some simpering guidance to the pathetic complainers. 'You should try cutting out caffeine. I hear magnesium supplements work a treat.'

She'd often been told that she was chatty and outspoken. She'd always secretly laugh at this. Not only was that nonsense, but if she opened up and told people what she really thought of them, they'd see her in a different light. They didn't know her. Nobody did.

And thinking about all this made her heart race and skin feel clammy. She splashed cold water over her face and gazed at herself in the mirror. She didn't like what she saw gawping back at her. The reflection sickened her. Repulsed her. She repulsed herself. Hated herself.

If she had an ounce of dignity, she would fill the sink and drown her miserable self. But that would take an epic amount of courage, which she didn't possess. She admired those poor souls who could pluck up the fortitude to cut open their wrists or step out in front of a speeding train. But this wasn't an option for her. Nope, she needed to face up to things. Her world would come crashing down around her. Life would never be the same again. But maybe... just maybe... she'd be able to view her reflection in the mirror without detesting what she saw peering back at her.

'I need to be brave. I need to be brave. I need to breathe,' she told herself in a bout of rapid whispers.

It's important to breathe. No one can hurt me here. I'm safe. This is my safe place, she said. *Hand on heart. Eyes glued shut. Breathe again. Empty my muddled mind. Relax. Let those crazy thoughts fizz away.*

Fizz and pop.

'I'm sorry, Mum. I'm sorry, I'm sorry, I'm sorry.'

And then she cried for so long she wasn't sure if the tears would ever stop flowing.

But they did.

And after the tears were all gone, she silently screamed at her vile reflection until her insides were on fire.

Then, once again, she wished she could transform into a small bird and fly far away from this godforsaken place.

29

Tuesday
(Three days before the deadline)

The woman opened the door and grinned. The type of grin you'd give an unwanted cold caller before giving them a polite brush-off, Jennifer decided. She tried to gauge her age. She looked like she could be in her early fifties, but she guessed her actual age was closer to late sixties. Her face appeared smooth and wrinkle-free save a faint cluster of crow's feet. Her silvery hair was up in a high bun, held in place with a red claw clip. She wore tight black leggings and a green and white Adidas sports jumper.

'Felicia Macclesfield?'

'Yes, that's right.'

'I'm Jennifer Fincher.'

Felicia's eyes widened, her grin faded, and she stood a little taller. 'Howard's youngest?'

'Yes. Sorry for this unannounced visit. I just... Can we talk?'

'In you pop. Come in.'

'This is a stunning house,' said Jennifer as she followed Felicia inside, admiring the interior of the pristine town-house as they walked. Everything looked clean and new. This home was owned by a meticulous individual, no doubt about it. Even the scatter cushions on the plum-coloured velvet sofa had been methodically positioned. She caught the scent of something homely and familiar. White musk fragrance oil, if she wasn't mistaken.

'I really like your home. It's so... immaculate.'

'A place for everything and everything in its place. I like to keep things in order. But you should see the neighbour's house. Theirs puts mine to shame,' said Felicia in a self-deprecating manner.

Jennifer doubted that. 'I like to keep things in order myself. I'm a bit OCD. Might be why I'm still single at my age.'

'Bah, men are messy. Trust me, you're not missing much. Tea? Coffee? Something stronger?'

'Water would be nice.'

'I have a jug in the fridge. Two ticks. Take a seat.' Felicia scurried off.

Jennifer perched on the edge of the sofa. She spied a framed photo of Felicia on an elegant glass table next to a bright pink begonia. In the shot, Felicia was standing on a white sandy beach with a marvellous turquoise sea behind her. She must've been in her late thirties, and she wore a skimpy white bikini that revealed a fabulous, bronzed body and shapely legs.

Felicia returned with a jug full of water, ice and lime. 'I

guess things are a tad tense in your family. With everything going on.'

'It's been difficult, yes.'

Felicia poured the water and smiled sadly. 'Poor thing. You were so young. It broke my heart. So horrendous.'

Jennifer nodded and accepted the proffered glass.

Felicia repositioned a coaster on a glass table, delicately placed the jug onto it, then sat in a square armchair opposite Jennifer. She took a tiny sip of her drink. 'So, are you here to give me a piece of your mind? Or do you have questions?'

'The latter.'

'Thought so. Howard always talked fondly of you, Jennifer.' She gave her a conspiratorial wink. 'I got the distinct impression that you were his favourite. Don't tell your sisters.'

'He talked about us?'

'All the time. I felt like I knew you all back then.'

'Oh,' said Jennifer, not sure how she felt about her dad discussing his daughters with the woman he was sleeping with on the sly. She tried to keep her face impassive. 'Was it an ongoing thing? You and him?'

'Four months before... before what happened. And almost a year afterwards.'

'Why did you break up?'

Felicia pulled a face. 'The drinking started. I mean the daily drinking. Look, Jennifer, I think there are some things I need to tell you. I have never had the chance to put my side of things across. Not to those who matter.'

Felicia closed her eyes as though in pain. 'I don't want to speak ill of the dead,' she continued. 'I don't want to start rubbishing your mother's memory. What I'm going to tell you *is* the truth. If it sounds like I'm bad-mouthing Katherine, then I apologise in advance.'

'I'm just looking for some answers,' Jennifer said softly. 'I'm trying to piece things together.'

'Yes. I understand your curiosity. And I'd be the same in your shoes. I'd need to know everything. So I'm going to tell you some things that might be a bit uncomfortable to hear.'

'It's fine.'

Felicia sat up straight, sipped her drink and jutted her chin. 'Your mother... Now how can I delicately put this? She didn't believe in monogamous relationships. Her desire was to have a more... let's say, open marriage.'

'Come again?'

'Katherine got in with a crowd that Howard described to me as outlandish and free spirited.'

'Like hippies?'

'Sort of. This group were all into poetry, self-portraits and, um, wild sex parties.'

Jennifer sipped her water, feeling her cheeks glow hot.

'Katherine tried to get Howard on board with her way of thinking. Tried to tell him to loosen up and that they should try new things.' Felicia cleared her throat. 'This was before I was on the scene, I might add. Anyway, he said Katherine gave him the ultimatum. Get groovy, or they were heading for the rocks. So, although he'd been reluctant, he agreed, and they both went along to some club out in the countryside somewhere.'

'My parents attended a... a swingers party?' Jennifer asked in a shocked whisper. She almost said *orgy*, but she'd never been a fan of that word, and saying it out loud felt incredibly inappropriate somehow.

'Apparently so. And it didn't go well. He said Katherine

was really into it. He suspected it wasn't the first time she'd attended. But he hated it so much he got very drunk and... how can I word this? He ended up more of a spectator than a partaker in the event. Whereas his wife had more than one dance partner. If you get my meaning.'

Jennifer coughed and spluttered. 'Right. OK. That is... oh, wow.'

'It broke him, Jennifer.'

Broke him? she almost replied, but stopped herself.

'When they drove home the next day, he told me he got so upset he had to pull the car over so she could take the wheel. And during that drive, she called him a total embarrassment. Then she said some words to him. Words he repeated to me, which I've *never* forgotten. She said, "Howard, you ruined what should have been a magical night. You spoiled it because you're too uptight and bloody narrow-minded. I'm trying to keep our marriage alive, and all you can do is get pissed and stand around like a timid prat with a flaccid cock, when you should've been having the time of your life." Howard told me the ordeal of seeing his beloved wife doing those unspeakable things not only destroyed his marriage but ruined his life. He couldn't shake the images. It drove him insane with anger, resentment and jealousy.'

Jennifer guessed the images in her own head would keep her awake for the next decade, because she'd more than jumped down the rabbit hole here. Plunged headfirst into a maze of thorny madness. A place she'd struggle to leave. She gawped at Felicia and blinked, unable to offer any response.

'The real arguments started then. Almost daily. And Katherine told Howard to man up. All but ordered him to go out and find another lady friend. Said he should "just get it all out of his system". That's right, she demanded that he find someone else to even the score. Perhaps in doing so, he'd stop obsessing over what she did. That "lady friend" turned out to be me. And we hit it off. Our relationship quickly grew.'

Jennifer nodded dumbly. Still speechless. She tasted metal in her mouth. This wasn't uncommon; it happened sometimes when she became anxious.

'But Katherine went ballistic. Sex... sex was fine. Howard seeing someone he had a connection with. Someone he liked and bonded with more than he did her. Nope. She wasn't allowing that. It broke the rules. *Her* rules, of course. In her world, you were allowed to have twenty sexual partners as long as the end result was something meaningless and unemotional. She delivered another ultimatum. He had to give me up, or they were over. He wanted to leave her. But she warned him that if he didn't stop seeing me, she'd make sure he never saw you girls again. She threatened to turn you all against him.'

'May I have some more water, please?' muttered Jennifer, somehow finding her tongue to speak.

'Let me,' said Felicia, getting up and giving her a top-up before sitting back down. 'There was plenty going on, by all accounts. Your father said he needed to be part of your world.'

'What do you mean?'

'Ava was being a pain. Running around with some bad apples from the Eden estate. Taking drugs, going to dodgy parties, getting up to mischief with unruly lads. He'd often be scouring that awful place in the night, searching for her.'

The memory of sitting in that car, viewing those tower

blocks and hearing Ava's angry words flashed through Jennifer's mind. 'Did he moan about me?'

'He told me you were quirky, inquisitive and funny. You enjoyed drawing and exploring – you were always keeping busy. I do recall him being worried about your strange sleeping habits. He said you had vivid dreams. And that sometimes you'd sleepwalk. Said your zany imagination would sometimes get you into trouble. But Stacey would usually be his top concern. I think she was a bit *too* popular with the boys for his liking.'

'Did he ever mention her boyfriend?'

Felicia drew in her lips. 'Yes, he did. And I remember Katherine became obsessed with finding out who this lad was. She gave your father a real hard time. Told him if he was a proper man, he'd find out who this mystery older chap was and give him a good thrashing. Tell him he had no right to be chasing around with a fourteen-year-old girl.'

'Did anyone see him?'

'Yes. Your mother saw him. Or so she told your father. Said he was at least nineteen or twenty. She chased him off the grounds of Barren's Lodge once or twice.'

An image of the faceless man in the boilersuit popped into Jennifer's head.

Why can't I recall his features?

Felicia lifted her chin, and Jennifer noticed the woman's eyes were wet with tears.

'What's wrong?' asked Jennifer.

'I need to get something off my chest. Something I did all those years ago and I'm not proud of.' She took in a long breath. 'I did it because I loved him. I trusted him. But the loyalty I once held for that man does not excuse the fact that I lied for him, and I shouldn't have. I'm ashamed. And I sincerely regret it. I thought I was doing the right thing. But I got it wrong.'

'Dad wasn't with you that night,' Jennifer said almost instinctively as the truth clicked into place. 'You gave him a false alibi.'

Felicia wiped the tears with the back of her hand. 'You know? He told you?'

'I guessed.'

'I told the police that he stayed with me in my flat the entire night. From eight o'clock onwards. But that wasn't true. He turned up at gone midnight, reeking of booze. Said he'd "done something foolish" and asked to stay over. Said if anyone asked, that he was here all night. He fell asleep on the sofa.

'When we heard the news about your mother, he pleaded with me. He swore on your life and that of your sisters that he'd never touched her. But he knew they'd pin him as the culprit. They'd find out about everything. The sex parties, their unsettled marriage, his affair with me. He was terrified he'd be made culpable. So I told a lie. I said he'd arrived earlier than he had.'

'Why are you telling me?'

Felicia sat in silence for a few moments, her head bowed. 'Life's cruel, isn't it?' She fell silent again.

Jennifer was about to agree, but also ask her to specify what she meant by that, when Felicia spoke again. 'I finally have everything I ever wanted. A wonderful home that looks like something straight out of a trendy magazine. Enough money to do whatever I please. Holidays whenever I want. Now it will all be taken away from me.'

'I don't follow.'

'I'm sick, Jennifer. Pancreatic cancer. I'm living on

borrowed time. I spend my time wallowing about in a depressed, self-pitying sadness. Instead of using my last bit of time wisely, I sit here, drink tea, watch mind-numbing trash on the TV, and curse myself for not making the most of my life.'

Jennifer didn't know how to respond. What could be said that wouldn't sound like a pathetic cliché?

'I clean the house like a mad person, and I walk on my treadmill like a hamster in a wheel until I'm so fatigued I almost collapse. It helps take my mind off things for a short time. Because when I stop pushing, I feel empty and sick.'

'I'm sorry.'

'So that's why I'm unburdening this secret. Before it dies with me.'

Jennifer nodded. 'Thank you for sharing it with me.'

'After your mother's passing, I saw a different side to your father. He changed so much I barely saw anything of the old Howard in him. I knew I wouldn't be able to stay with him. I wasn't strong enough. No, that's not true. I wasn't prepared to deal with him. I didn't want to be stuck with a drunk, sullen pessimist. I didn't want that in my life. I wanted happiness. Fun, warmth, and someone who wanted to show me kindness and love. Howard Fincher became a wretched manacle that I had to detach myself from. He took and refused to give back. That makes me sound heartless. I get that. But I tried to fix him. I did, Jennifer. He didn't want to be mended.'

Jennifer saw genuine pain on the other woman's face and believed every word she'd spoken. She'd suddenly noticed how wrinkly Felicia's neck appeared. As if it didn't belong to the younger face attached to it.

'So I have lived with what I did. And after seeing the person Howard transformed into, I have often questioned what exactly he meant by "done something foolish". Because if your grandfather has spent all those years locked away because of my lie, I'd never forgive myself.'

Jennifer finished the water. Her blood became as cold as the liquid in the glass.

'And I'm only talking now because of my situation. That makes me a callous bitch. I get that. I do.' Felicia's breathing was erratic, and her nostrils were flaring. 'I'm not proud of what I did.'

Jennifer bit her lower lip as she tried to think of something to say. Her mind went blank. No, not blank. She visualised her dad snapping that youth's wrist, and she almost threw up the water she'd just finished.

30

Wednesday
(Two days before the deadline)

The grotto had never been her place, Jennifer recalled. This spot was Ava's. It had always been overgrown and hidden away, but now the stone structure could hardly be seen under the weeds and clumps of wildflowers growing around it. She spotted the small white flower of the dead nettle plant and clusters of the purple bell-shaped flowers of the foxglove.

Jennifer took the stone bridge over the narrow, dried-up stream that circled the structure and walked inside the grotto. Made of cobblestones, it was a curved, oblong shape, though they all used to call it the circle grotto.

Her grandad once told her that one day he'd explored this part of the grounds and just stumbled upon this place.

Told them all it popped up as if by magic. She suspected that was a big fib and recalled her mum telling her that Ernest had built it, but nobody knew why, or how he'd even acquired the stones to make it. The grotto had no purpose. Or even a roof. But it made a great hideaway for Ava. A place to smoke cigarettes, drink cheap booze, and keep out of Jennifer's way.

It was damp inside and smelled of rot. A wooden ledge had been constructed across the top, which at one time you could sit on and use as a lookout spot, but that no longer looked safe and was now covered in a mass of multicoloured fungi.

As she ran her hand over the large stones, she decided the grotto was a bit like a small castle. But being in here evoked an uncomfortable emotion. More than that. A distressing sadness flooded through her suddenly – she'd never been welcome in the grotto. As a child, she'd often venture down here. Yes, she'd explore this area even after her sisters had given her strict orders to stay away. Jennifer could almost smell the pungent cigarette smoke now.

On one warm summer's afternoon, she'd caught her eldest sister smoking inside. Much of the memory seemed hazy. Apart from Ava's fierce eyes when they'd fixed on her. When she'd understood her little sister had caught her in the act of taking a big puff on that stolen Marlboro Light.

The fog cleared in her head. The picture becoming sharper. That white box with the gold pattern. She'd picked the box up from the floor and read the bottom of the packet. 'Smooth original flavour. How can cigarettes have any flavour? That's weird.'

'Go away.'

'I don't understand the point of smoking these.'

'I don't understand the point of *you*. So do one.'

'I want to play in here.'

Ava had jumped to her feet. 'Put them down. Now, frog face!' With that, she'd flicked the cigarette end straight into her face, catching her just under the left eye.

Jennifer flinched at the memory. Almost sensing the hot ash burning her skin all over again.

Then Ava had thundered towards her, screaming, and slapped her across the side of the head.

The noise of the strike had echoed around the smoky den. The packet had fallen from her fingers as she'd put her hands up to her stinging face.

Ava had ripped her hands away from her face and growled, 'I told you more than once. You do... *not*... come... and... play... here.' She'd stabbed a long finger against her forehead. 'Now I'm getting bored with repeating myself to you.'

'Sorry. I'm sorry, Ava. I won't say you stole Mum's cigarettes. I promise I won't.'

Ava had sniggered. 'Do you ever gawp at yourself in the mirror and question where you came from? I mean, check out that fucking forehead of yours. Bloody spam head. You look like a giant egg with a ratty mop of hair perched on top. Just piss off. Your unsightly face is quite offensive to my poor eyes.'

Jennifer had started to shuffle her way out.

'Have you got any friends in your class? I bet you don't. I bet you are the most unpopular kid in your entire school.' Ava had laughed. 'Do you know why?'

Jennifer had shrugged.

'Because you're an ugly freak. You look like a freak. And you act like one.'

Jennifer frowned at the memory of Ava's bitter put-down and stepped out of the grotto. She was drawn to the foxglove growing all around the structure. The purple, bell-shaped flowers were pretty, and she kneeled to examine one tall plant that had several bees drifting around it. She wanted to touch it, but she knew it wasn't wise to handle it without gloves. Her gran had told her several times that the plant was toxic. But now she wondered just *how* toxic... It got her thinking that she should do some research and learn more about it. For her play, of course.

When Jennifer rose, she found her grandad standing close by, eyeing her circumspectly. 'Grandad, I thought you were seeing your probation officer today?'

'Seen her.'

'All OK?'

'Yup. She also wants to come and chat with you one day soon.'

'Oh. That's OK with me. Is that protocol?'

He shrugged. 'I guess it must be. What are you doing messing about down here?'

'Just wanted to check out the grotto. It's smaller than I remember.'

'About the size of a prison cell.' He gave her a weak, humourless smile. 'But with more air.'

'I can't imagine what it was like. Were you scared?'

'The first night... oh, that was a toughie,' he said, settling on a low stone wall, as if ready to talk. 'I couldn't stop shaking. All night I lay there with my arms wrapped around myself, shivering. I didn't think I'd ever warm up. And I hadn't even been taken onto the main wing for my induction at that point. I was so afraid. I'll never forget that grim night. That overwhelming sensation of utter hopelessness and despair.'

'It must have been so awful. What were the other prisoners like?'

'At first, every single one of those men terrified me. However, I soon learned that if I was to survive, I'd need to integrate. It took a long time to find my feet.' He crossed his arms. 'I suppose once I got my head around the idea that these were real people, with real problems, fears and regrets, then I felt less isolated. I met some characters over the years, I can tell you.'

'I don't know how people cope inside, if I'm honest.'

'Well, some can't cope. In my time, some men found religion. Some turned to drugs. Some even found peace. Many even welcomed their sentence as atonement for their sins. They understood they needed to be punished. Others... well, others were beyond redemption. They were wicked creatures who relished in tormenting others. You soon learned which cons you needed to watch. You showed them weakness, and they'd make your life a living hell. Some screws too. But some of the officers became good friends. These bonds took time to form. Years, in some cases. Not that I wasn't duped, of course.'

He sighed and gazed up at the sky. 'People have turned their back on me. They let me down. Broke that trust I'd believed we shared. I detested the ones who deceive and betray more than the scumbags who show open animosity. They were worse than rats. And they needed dealing with accordingly.'

'I wouldn't last a week. Did anyone try to hurt you?' Her

stomach was in knots, and hearing him sharing the reality of all this made her cold and uneasy.

He uncrossed his arms and leaned against the grotto wall. 'I had to pour hot water over an inmate to defend myself once. This thug called One Punch came after my pad mate. Stuck a piece of broken pool cue into the lad's eye and blinded the poor kid. I stopped the lunatic from taking his other eye, and he turned on me. Tried to stick the cue into my neck. I managed to shove him off, and the kettle was to hand... so I pulled off the lid and threw it straight into his face. His scream was hideous. The entire block said they heard it.'

'Oh no.' She flinched. 'Nasty.'

'I got a few pats on the back for that, I can tell you. I was treated like a hero for months. Everyone loathed that bugger.'

'Do you all have kettles in prison?'

'Yes, how else would we make a brew?'

'Seems dangerous.'

'We're not animals! We don't go round scalding one another at random. Sometimes, you do what needs to be done. Simple as that.'

'You're talking like you're still a prisoner.'

'May as well be. This place might be huge, but it's a prison. Only in this lockup, I'm rattling around all on my own. I have to cook my own meals, and I have nobody to play cards with.' He smiled. 'Apart from you. I guess you're now my part-time pad mate'

'You miss your friends from inside?'

'Some I do. I really do. I trusted some of those guys with my life. Still do *trust* them.'

Jennifer didn't like the way he said "trust". Nor did she like the way his eyes widened, as if glowing with suspicion. Was she being paranoid, or was he implying he didn't fully trust her yet? It was a very similar look to the one he'd given those police officers who came here. Perhaps he wasn't buying her forgive and forget attitude. She assumed he wanted to, but prison had made him a sceptical man who'd been left wary of everyone. If he'd been duped by so-called friends inside, then he wouldn't repeat those mistakes on the outside.

'Shall I stick the kettle on?' suggested Jennifer.

'Good idea. But no throwing hot water over my face,' he said, sounding serious before breaking out into a wide smile. 'And enough prison talk. You don't need to hear all that grim stuff. Let's change the subject,' he added with a wry smirk.

They started making their way back to the house.

'I killed a ladybird the other day. It was in my room. I squashed it under a tissue, and all night I felt awful,' said Jennifer, not sure why she'd had the sudden urge to divulge this to him.

'Why?'

'Good question. I don't have any remorse when I kill a fly. So why did I care so much?'

'Maybe because flies are ugly and dirty.'

'So? Is that how we decide if something gets to live or die?'

He shrugged. 'Mm, I never kill spiders. But I wouldn't think twice about smoking out a thousand wasps. They're little bastards. You can't trust them.'

Yet he'd not cleared those wasps out, even though he'd been using the outbuilding for... something.

I must get myself a crowbar, she considered.

'Anyway, you probably killed that ladybird on instinct. After what happened when you were young,' he said.

'I don't follow.'

'You don't remember? That's surprising.'

'Remember what?'

'Your room would sometimes get infested with ladybirds. The pesky things were regular visitors, and they'd congregate in the folds of the curtains, where they'd sleep in clusters. Your gran used to tell you to leave the curtains be, so as not to disturb them. She was often hoovering the buggers up. One night you started screaming, so me and your gran rushed in, and you were tugging frantically at your hair, yelling that the bugs were eating your head.'

'And were they? Or was I dreaming?'

'Well, we thought you were in the throes of one of your night terrors, but a handful of those ladybirds had made their way into your hair and were crawling all over your head and neck. You had to have a shower to get them all out.'

'Eew. Gross.' Jennifer recoiled. 'How do I not remember that?'

'I'd guess that in your head you remembered it as a strange dream. You didn't talk about it much afterwards. Your gran always assumed ladybugs were harmless. Turns out the house-dwelling variety can bite. They have additional spots on their faces. They can cause reactions.'

Jennifer scratched the back of her head, certain that she could again detect things crawling in her hair.

'Jennifer,' her grandfather said, giving her a concerned look, 'have you done something?'

'What? No. Why are you asking me that?'

'Is something worrying you? You seem like you want to tell me something, but don't quite know how.'

'The deadline is two days away. That's what's worrying me. Aren't you a little concerned about what these people have planned?'

'Nope.'

'Well, I am. And I think we should contact the police again.'

'We don't need to worry. Trust me. I have everything in hand.'

31

M*adness is coming to claim me*, she told herself. Like a train thundering along a track at full speed with no destination. No driver. No means to stop. No way of avoiding that inevitable collision with those who venture onto the tracks.

It's getting faster and faster, and it might derail before it collides. Hurtle right off the tracks and come crashing down into a twisted pile of destruction. Who's on board? Just her? Her family?

No... not them. Because they are stuck on the tracks. They are awaiting the inescapable collision.

It's coming and will destroy everything. Everyone. Smash them to pieces.

And she's caused all of this.

All her fault.

How do you comprehend when you've gone mad? she wondered. *Do you ever?*

When they lock you up in a tiny cell, you knew. She pictured desperate fingers clawing at the dirty walls.

Bloodied cuticles as nails snapped and tore. No windows. Why were there never any windows in those rooms when she saw those cells?

And why did she always hear those rasping little voices when the darkness came?

Ghastly and cold.

Why did I think about them? They'll surely come now.

She caught those voices in the darkness. She'd let them in once again.

'Yep, she has a fragile mental state.'

'Not sound of mind, that one.'

'Her headspace is muddled.'

'Let me out,' she whimpered. 'I shouldn't be in here. I need help. Please, I'm having a panic attack. I can't breathe!'

'Oh, but it's important to *just* breathe,' one said in a jarring voice with an edge of mockery. 'You need to breathe in deeply.'

'Don't say that! You can't say that! Let me out of this fucking room!'

The voice didn't let up. 'Exhale... Hand on heart... Is it beating fast? Too fast, I bet! Way too fast. Is that normal? I'm not so sure it is. Have you glued those sleepy eyes shut? I bet they feel heavy now. What's wrong? Scared you'll never wake up ever again? Scared you'll never open those peepers again? Does it feel like you're drowning?'

'Be quiet!' she hissed as she rolled over, grabbed a pillow, hugged it tightly, and bit into the material to stop herself from letting out a shrill scream.

'You know what you need to do,' said the voice, softer now. 'You'll understand when it's time.'

The sensation of a single tear rolling slowly down her

cheek calmed her racing thoughts. Down it slid, like warm treacle making its way to her chin. Gliding gently.

She wasn't awake yet. Not quite asleep either. Somewhere in between. Limbo land. But not oblivion. She craved the nothingness that oblivion would bring. If only for a while. Long enough for her to shut off her brain and let her body rest. Repair. A break from the world. From herself. And those bloody voices in her head.

Madness isn't coming, she decided. It had arrived a long, long time ago.

So, now the question was... What came *after* the madness?

32

Friday 08.00
(Fourteen hours before the deadline)

'Dale, what a surprise!' lied Jennifer, sticking her crash helmet under her arm.

She'd spotted the theatre director when she'd been riding down the high street. If she was honest, she'd expected to come across him, as he often frequented the Buzz Coffee Lounge most mornings, because his own business was located opposite.

He was sipping a big frothy coffee and reading a paper at a round table with a blue ceramic top. 'Hello, Jennifer. Long time no chat. Care to join me for a drink?'

'Sure. I've been meaning to call you, actually. About—'

'Let me nip in and grab you something. What would you like? I'd also recommend the apple turnovers.'

'Coffee is fine. No sugar. Thanks.'

Dale folded his paper, placed it down and offered her his funny one-sided smile that looked more like a grimace or compulsive twitch.

Jennifer thought he was an odd little chap. With his bald, shiny head and big specs always perched on his forehead. Specs nobody ever saw him wear for reading. And, as always, wearing that vintage corduroy blazer. Even if the sun was blazing, or they were stuck in a jam-packed theatre with no air, he'd be wearing that camel-coloured blazer. He never seemed to sweat though, and this had gained him the nickname *Little Prince* among some of the group's more churlish members. Which, she assumed, was a reference to a certain royal's notorious misconduct. Jennifer didn't find this particularly funny. She condemned any form of bullying, no matter how trivial, no matter if it was done discreetly.

And she liked Dale Appleton. Yes, his indecisiveness was sometimes maddening. How he ran a successful interior design and soft furnishing store was a complete mystery to her. She always imagined him flapping about with a client. 'These curtains and cushions would look sublime. No, on reflection, madam, these floral ones. Mm, no, let's go with this gold-leaf fabric!'

Dale scurried off, and Jennifer took a seat at the table situated between two low planters filled with blue flowers. The retro eatery was positioned close to the road, and between people strolling right past the table and cars rattling by, she didn't consider this the most relaxing place to sit and enjoy a caffeine injection and five minutes' peace. There was no room to put her helmet on the table, so she placed it between her boots on the ground.

Dale came back out and plonked back down in his seat. 'She'll bring it out in two ticks.'

'Lovely.'

'Everything all right with you, Jennifer?'

'Yep. Brilliant.'

Dale nodded. 'Good. Good.'

'Yep, good.'

He emitted an awkward cough and cleared his throat. 'Good.'

Jennifer decided to get to the point and break the uneasy moment. 'Sooo, *The Jeopardy of Love*. When are you auditioning? I'd like to be there.'

'Ah, now, so here's the thing. I've been meaning to email you back. Now I feel awful for forgetting.'

'What did you forget?'

'The committee decided *not* to run with *The Jeopardy of Love* for its autumn production. Sorry. I shouldn't have left you hanging.'

'You didn't like the play?'

Dale smiled. Or at least, raised the right side of his lip and exposed his misshapen teeth. 'Can I be frank with you?'

'I'd expect nothing less.'

'I didn't love it. *We* didn't love it. It doesn't have the panache I've come to expect from your work. I struggled to connect with your protagonist. I found her a tad maudlin. Isla lacked the pluckiness and pep you normally inject into your female characters.'

'She was a downtrodden wife. She led a very sheltered life, but she was a fighter in the end. Once Everett showed her a different path, she came out of her shell and shone. That was the point.'

'Did she? I'm not sure. And Everett... well, he came across as quite hubristic. If I'm honest, he wasn't much of an improvement on her overbearing husband. I was beginning to question Isla's sanity towards the end. And certainly her taste in domineering men. Could you even call that a happy ending? Out of the proverbial frying pan and straight into the raging fire, if you ask me.' He let a snorting snigger slip, but had the decency to appear embarrassed upon noticing Jennifer had kept her expression deadpan.

Jennifer was about to offer a curt reply when her coffee arrived. She'd tensed up so much she didn't even thank whoever had placed it there. She decided to stay calm. She had another card to play.

'Don't be upset,' he said in an insipid, soft voice.

'I'm not upset. Not at all,' she blurted, a little too quickly.

'We understand things are tough right now. With... with all that stuff going on.'

Jennifer sipped the coffee and, desperate to divert the conversation away, said, 'What's the play you're going to be putting forward called?'

'*Forbidden Heart*. Very, very edgy. I urge you to read it. You'll want to be involved when you take a look. I'm sure you will.'

'Did you write it?' she asked, annoyed with herself for using such an accusatorial tone.

'No, Mary did.'

'Mary? As in Mary, who's involved in scenic construction?'

'The very same. Turns out she's a writer too.'

'Mm. You realise she's seen *Cats* four times? She's fanatical about that play.'

'So? It's an innovative spectacle. Why is that relevant?'

'She'll likely have a singing hamster or dancing moose in her story. Is that what you're going for?'

'It's sounds like you are being a tiny bit sour about this,

Jennifer. Come on, don't be surly. Her piece is gripping. Her characters are rich and relatable. And I can confirm there are no singing animals.'

'So, what *is* the story?'

'A woman who falls madly in love with her beguiling brother-in-law. And her overpossessive sister who will go to any lengths to keep her man. It has all the elements we were searching for. But it also embraces some comical moments that balance the story rather well.'

Jennifer's mind flashed back to her recent encounter with David as he'd squeezed her shoulder. *We do worry. All of us.* She baulked at the memory. It made her rather uncomfortable. Like she had been the one who'd done something wrong. Should she have blasted him for doing that? Or would that have been an overreaction? Did he mean anything by it? She'd told herself he hadn't, but his wanton eyes had suggested he'd been transmitting more than just friendship vibes. But why? What could he possibly see in her, especially when he had Stacey?

Dale said something that she didn't catch due to a noisy van rattling past. It reminded her of the van that had run off the road, and this made her feel even more uneasy.

'Sorry, what did you say?' she asked.

'Are you all right?' Dale asked. 'You seem miles away. You're not too vexed about us picking Mary's play, are you? I'd be gutted if you are.'

'No. You're right. *The Jeopardy of Love* is awful. I wrote several drafts and hated all of them. It isn't the piece I had my heart set on. In fact, that banal rubbish was just a distraction.'

'I'm not following.'

'I chickened out.'

'Of what?'

'That's not really what I wanted to send you.'

'You're saying there's another play?'

'Oh, yes. And if I realised I had actual competition, then I wouldn't have wussed out and sent you that lousy rubbish.'

Dale rubbed his hands together and leaned in closer to her. 'OK, I'm intrigued. Why did you wuss out?'

Jennifer took a deep breath. 'Because it might be pretty controversial. It might be...'

'Yes?'

'I dunno, Dale. You know, it's not a good idea to talk about all this,' she whispered in a slow, intentionally secretive voice.

'Jennifer! Don't leave me hanging. What's the play about?'

'Murder... Mystery... Betrayal... But ultimately, it's a story about revenge.'

'Is there a name for this piece?'

'Yes. It's called *The Day She Died.*'

Dale's features were set in a strange, grave grimace.

Jennifer saw the curiosity burning in his pale blue eyes. She guessed he wanted to question her about this. How close to unravelling the truth this would take them. The town had been changed by her mum's murder. But there were lingering uncertainties. So many questions floating around. So many theories.

Jennifer also remembered that Dale was obsessed with productions based on real-life events, and he had a passion for true crime. Seeing *London Road*, a production based on an actual event and using real interviews, had been a pivotal moment for him. The musical about the impact on a community of the murders of women in Ipswich during the ensuing trial of the killer had inspired Dale. The idea of a play about ordinary people dealing with such a shocking experience seemed to really captivate him.

Amateur dramatics or not, Dale wanted big things for their group. He'd love to bring the Flair Play Drama Group into the limelight. What better way than to use a historic murder that happened right here in little old North Sutton? A murder that was still surrounded by so many questions.

Was she using this to her advantage? Yes, most definitely.

'I'd be so bold as to say it's a rousing and challenging piece. You could even say radical,' she said.

'OK. I'll read it. We'll need to be quick, because the group are currently set on *Forbidden Heart*,' he said.

Jennifer could see she had him now. 'The final act has yet to be written.'

'Hold up, so it's not even finished?' He sucked in his lips. 'How can we commit if we don't know how it ends?'

'The problem is, I'm not *sure* how it ends yet. That's still to be decided. And it depends on a few things.'

Dale gave her a confused, contorted smile. 'This is the most interesting conversation you and I have ever had, Jennifer Fincher. And we've had a few.'

She cracked a charming grin. 'Yes.'

'Send what you have. Today, mind you. Then we'll see what's what.'

'As good as done.'

'We will need to tread carefully. This must be depicted in a tactful, edifying and prudent way.'

'The Finchers have spent twenty-five years under a dark cloud that's never faded away. We've endured that darkness. Lived with the grief. You could say we've faded into the shadows, kept low profiles, lived anonymous lives. But why?'

'Because some people are cruel. Simple as that.'

'Do you recall what you asked me when we first met?'

Dale nodded. 'I'm sure I said, "So tell me, what's it really like to be part of the infamous Fincher family?"'

'Exactly that. And I said?'

'"Please never ask me that question again." So I haven't.'

'Well, today I'll answer you... Lonely and scary.'

'You did nothing wrong. Remember that.'

Jennifer smiled. 'It doesn't matter.'

Dale glanced at his watch. 'Oh, gosh. I really must dash. I need to get the shop open. I'll be looking out for your email. Today.'

'On it.'

Dale gave her the thumbs up, slurped the dregs of his coffee and headed off.

Jennifer took a deep breath and sipped her own drink. It was lukewarm now. She considered if what she'd just agreed to was a fabulous idea, or the most reckless decision she'd ever made. Perhaps a mixture of both.

As she traced her finger over the crazy pattern on the table, a lithe jogger wearing a loud orange headband came past, flashing her a grin as he went.

Jennifer beamed and felt her cheeks burn. The guy was quite a looker and a few years younger than her. She guessed he was probably just high on the pleasure of his run.

She gazed around the High Street, which was getting busier now as the town started to wake up.

Then she saw it. A grey Volkswagen Crafter, heading onto the narrow part of the street. She instantly grasped that it was the same vehicle she'd encountered before.

Then she realised something else.

The van's speed was increasing as it approached.

33

I t took Jennifer a few frightful seconds to pull herself up from the chair.

Now the van had mounted the path and was coming steaming straight for her. It smashed into a standing shop sign outside the nearby charity shop and sent it flying into the road. Something else went thud, and someone shouted frenziedly.

She leaped from the vehicle's path without a second to spare as the van slammed into the seating area. Jennifer fell sideways and hit the road. A metal chair spun a few feet into the air and came thudding down near her leg. The ceramic table smashed through the café's window, and the planter was pulverised under the heavy vehicle as it crushed everything in its way.

Jennifer gasped as the van continued its destructive course along the path... As it cut down the jogger in its deadly wake.

The cheerful man disappeared from her view.

The van veered off the path and slammed onto the road,

revealing the jogger once more. Now he looked broken and twisted, with one leg bent at a hideous angle.

The café owner came racing out, hands on her head, mouth gaping.

This time, the van didn't stop and raced off around the bend, almost fishtailing as it sped off. A car coming the other way was forced to skid to a stop, and the driver gave a long blast of their horn.

The café owner edged over to the jogger, one hand now hovering over her mouth.

Jennifer's mind swam. She touched her head. It felt wet, and when she peered down at her hand, it was glistening with dark blood. She stood and moved towards the downed man.

The café owner stood over him, shooing Jennifer away with a furious wave of her hand. 'Don't come over here, love. There's nothing you can do. Stay back.'

Jennifer's stomach lurched. She didn't need to step any closer to see that the poor man's head had been crushed. The path was slick with blood. She stood on a flattened shop sign outside the café that was covered in glass. It said *Come in for an egg-cellent breakfast and free, super-fast Wi-Fi*. She kept staring at the sign, too afraid to focus on anything else.

A commotion broke out all around her. A woman cried out. Someone stood near her said something in a distraught voice, but it was hard for her to breathe, let alone find her voice to say anything back to them.

After tearing her eyes from the sign, Jennifer discovered the street had filled with onlookers. Some people stood near the man, others watched from shop doorways, and at least two people had phones held up, no doubt filming the grim scene.

'Jennifer? Hey, are you OK?'

It took a while for her to comprehend Dale had returned.

'Let's get you inside. Come on,' he said, putting a comforting arm around her shoulders.

As they moved away from the destruction left by the van, she couldn't fight off the urge to gaze back at the man one last time. Someone had placed a blanket over the disfigured body.

That should've been me, was all Jennifer could think in that horrific moment.

34

Jennifer had been in a trance as the paramedic checked her wounds and Dale fussed over her, insisting she drink strong sugary tea, and keeping a blanket wrapped over her shoulders.

He also wouldn't let her move from the chunky green and gold sofa positioned in the store's front. 'She's in shock. She should be taken to the hospital,' he'd repeated to the paramedic four times.

Jennifer had kept protesting, telling them she would be fine. The cut on her head had produced a worrying amount of blood, but wouldn't require stitches and didn't hurt too much. It was her shoulder that ached horribly, although she didn't think anything had been broken when she'd plunged onto the road. Some strong painkillers would numb that pain.

But nothing would numb the shock of what she'd witnessed out there. That poor man. Had he died instantly? She couldn't help visualising the van's tyres rolling over his head and crushing it like an exploding melon. Even though she'd not seen it happen, the images wouldn't leave her head. The thought made her dizzy with anguish.

There were blue lights flashing outside. The street had been cordoned off, and she could see the café owner and another young lady sweeping up the glass scattered along the shopfronts.

Now a uniformed police officer was in the store. She had a petite and youthful stature, with dark hair styled in a bun and plump cheeks. 'Are you OK to talk?' she asked with a sympathetic smile.

Jennifer nodded, her fingers rubbing the dressing the paramedic had put on her head. 'My name is Jennifer Fincher, and the driver of that van was aiming for me.'

The police officer pulled a shocked expression and looked at Dale, who appeared just as stunned.

'Is that man dead? The jogger. He is, right?' asked Jennifer.

What a stupid question.

The officer nodded, her face set in a grim expression. 'He was pronounced dead at the scene. His injuries were catastrophic, and the paramedics are certain he died instantly.'

'Don't blame yourself, Jennifer,' said Dale.

The officer scribbled in her notepad. 'Jennifer, why do you think the van was aiming for you?'

'The same van tried to run me off the road. A few weeks back on Bicknor Lane.'

'Did you report this?' asked the officer.

Jennifer nodded her head, feeling her cheeks glow red. 'I was tired and riding my scooter. I put it down to road rage. At first, I assumed the driver took offence because I drifted into the middle of the road. I can disregard that idea now.'

The officer scribbled on her pad again. 'OK. What happened?'

'I was forced off the road. I fell off. The van tried to reverse into me, but a road sign got in the way.'

The officer frowned. 'And you say you *did* report this incident?'

Jennifer nodded again. 'Yes, to the officers who came to my grandad's house. About the rubbish some men dumped there. I told them it might be connected.'

'Did you see the driver of the van that day?' asked the officer.

Jennifer grimaced. 'No. Nor did I catch the number plate.'

'She's had a lot on her mind,' said Dale supportively. 'Can't you ask her these questions later? She's in a right state.'

'You have no idea who the driver might be?' asked the officer, ignoring Dale.

Jennifer shook her head. 'No. Didn't anybody see anything? Did they catch the registration?'

'There must be cameras all over this street,' chipped in Dale.

The officer's face dropped. 'Yes, we've got plenty of footage, but the van's plates are false, and the windows blacked out, so we are unable to identify the driver. Are you sure you don't have any idea who might've done this, Jennifer?'

'No.'

'OK. I need to take all your details. The team dealing with this case will no doubt wish to speak with you further,' said the officer. 'Sorry, Jennifer, what did you say your surname was again?'

'Fincher.'

The officer scribbled on her pad once again. Then she stiffened as her eyes flicked back up to Jennifer.

The name must have suddenly registered.

'Yes, it is,' said Jennifer, answering the question she knew would be coming next.

35

S he'd been sitting in quiet misery for a long time when her sisters arrived at her place, demanding to know everything. They both listened as Jennifer relayed the morning's disturbing events, then told them about the incident that had happened on Bicknor Lane, too.

Stacey, ashen-faced and disturbed, sat next to her and gave her a hug. Ava, her face set in a grave scowl, stood, shaking her head as if in disbelief.

'It will be on the news soon. They are going to appeal for witnesses,' said Jennifer.

'Are you sure it was the same van?' asked Ava, her tone suggesting she had little faith in her account of things.

'No doubt about it,' confirmed Jennifer. 'There's something else I need to tell you both. I went to see Felicia Macclesfield.'

Ava and Stacey shared a quick look.

'Dad wasn't with her all night. She lied for him,' said Jennifer.

Stacey's eyes narrowed. 'What? She said that?'

'She's regretted lying for him ever since,' said Jennifer.

'And what if she's *still* lying now?' said Ava.

'She's not. I can assure you she's genuine. And she told me plenty of other stuff. Painted a very different picture of Mum and Dad. And their relationship,' said Jennifer.

'What are you trying to do here?' asked Ava, eyes hardening.

'Dad broke some lad's wrist on Sunday. After Harriet's party,' said Jennifer.

Stacey looked stunned. 'Seriously? Our dad?'

'Yes.'

'You saw this happen?' asked Ava.

'I was right there,' said Jennifer.

Ava and Stacey shared another glance.

'I was there. I didn't imagine this! It happened right in front of me,' said Jennifer, dumbfounded. This pair didn't seem entirely convinced.

Ava pulled a face. Jennifer knew that expression. All too well. Her little disbelieving sneer.

Jennifer stood up and slapped her hands to her sides. 'God, why do you both hate me so much?'

Ava rolled her eyes and let out a weary, exasperated sigh. 'We don't.'

'You're lying! You've always hated me! Both of you.'

'Calm down,' cooed Stacey, standing up and trying to take her hand.

Jennifer yanked her hand away. 'No! I want you both to leave. Now, please.'

'You're in shock. You're not thinking clearly. What happened today has messed with your head,' said Stacey in a placating tone.

Jennifer glanced at her wristwatch. 'Just under six hours to go.'

'Until what?' asked Stacey.

'Until Grandad's deadline is up. Ten p.m. tonight.'

Ava frowned and in a weary voice said, 'What are you talking about now?'

Jennifer glowered at Ava. 'That's when they come for him. They are going to make him leave.'

'You stay away from that house. You hear me, Jennifer? You stay the fuck away from his place tonight,' Ava yelled.

Jennifer glared at her eldest sister. 'Are you going to stop me?'

Ava shrugged, suddenly entirely unruffled. 'If I have to, then yes.'

'Try it. See what happens,' snarled Jennifer.

Ava rubbed her forehead and groaned as if in pain. 'I'll put the kettle on, shall I? Try to chill out a bit.'

Jennifer stood tall. 'You will not. I have asked you to leave. So... leave.'

'Jennifer, please don't be like this. What on earth has got into you?' said Stacey, looking close to tears.

'Leave her, she's in a silly, querulous mood,' said Ava.

'Ava, she saw a man die, for Christ's sake. Have a bit of compassion,' cried Stacey.

'Look, I can't deal with her when she's like this.' Ava threw up her arms. 'She's like a bloody huffy child with a bee in her bonnet. Why did she have to start dragging all this shit up? I don't want to relive this nightmare again. Don't you understand that? This bastard cloud has followed us our entire lives. And I'm done with it now. All of it. In fact, by the year's end, I'm outta this bloody town. And I'm done with this cursed family!'

'Ava! What the hell?' gasped Stacey.

'I hope the mob do go after Ernest bloody Moorby. I hope they do run the murdering pig out of town for good,' shouted Ava, incensed. She glared at Jennifer. 'And stop trying to find conspiracies. Our dad did not kill our mum! Understand?'

'Why did he get Felicia to lie for him?' asked Jennifer, refusing to be cowed.

Ava groaned again. 'Oh, why do you think, you idiot? They were separated, and he was screwing another woman. It was obvious he'd be suspect number one. At the time, he didn't know about the evidence they'd found implicating Ernest. So he panicked. Now, for God's sake, can you stop being ridiculous.'

An image of a teenage Ava flashed through Jennifer's mind. It was such a crystal-clear picture. It was quite surreal. She was smiling for once. Offering her a warm, sisterly smile as she handed her a big mug of hot chocolate. 'Mum has made you your usual bedtime choccy and marshmallows, Jennifer. Drink up now. She said she'll come and tuck you in soon.'

'Thanks, Ava. But I don't want to sleep. I'm too scared.'

'Don't be ridiculous; there is nothing to be afraid of. It's all in your head. Drink it all up. This helps you snooze like a princess,' Ava had said with a big, kind-hearted grin.

'I will,' she'd replied, blowing on the drink before taking a sip. 'Mmm, really yummy and creamy.'

'Go on. Drink up now.'

Jennifer snapped out of the memory and eyed Ava warily. The flashback made her tense up. 'I'm rather tired, and I need to lie down for a while.'

'I don't think it's a good idea for you to be alone,' said Stacey.

'Well, that's what I want. So if you don't mind,' said Jennifer, pointing at the door.

Ava shook her head. 'You stay away from that place tonight. I mean it, Jennifer.'

Stacey gave Ava's arm a gentle tug. 'Come on. Let her have five minutes' peace.'

36

J ennifer stuck the crowbar she'd borrowed from her
landlady into her rucksack. She grumbled to herself
when she was unable to zip the bag shut. She'd have
to ride to her grandad's place with the damn thing
poking out of the top.

The news was on now. Once she'd listened to the report,
she'd have something to eat and make tracks. The idea of
food wasn't appealing, but she had the shakes and needed to
get her head straight before she attempted to ride her
scooter.

'Police were called to the collision on the High Street,
North Sutton, this morning at just after nine a.m. Aiden
Barker, a local solicitor and father of three, sadly died at the
scene after a grey Volkswagen van mounted the pavement
and hit Mr Barker while he was out for his morning run.
Officers have confirmed that the driver of the van failed to
stop following the collision.'

Jennifer's heart palpitated as footage of the cordoned-off

High Street came onto the screen. As the morning's events came flooding back with sickening clarity.

'Speaking at the scene, senior investigating officer Detective Sergeant Claire Wallace of the Serious Collisions Unit spoke to our reporter.'

A dark-haired detective in a hi-vis jacket addressed the camera. 'Our thoughts go out to Mr Barker's family and friends at this terrible time. And we are now appealing to witnesses to come forward.'

A still image of the grey van came onto the screen.

'If you were in the area this morning, we urge you to check your dash-cams in case you have captured footage of the vehicle, which may assist our investigation and help us locate the driver of this van. The van has blacked-out windows and damage on its wheel arch. It's quite a distinctive vehicle, and we ask that you contact us if you know anything about this van, or if you have recently seen it.'

Jennifer turned off the TV, walked into the kitchen and opened her cupboards. She hunted for something sugary to ease the shakes. She'd been contacted by a detective working on the case and advised they would be coming to interview her soon. But the deadline was fast approaching, so she couldn't hold off any longer. They would have to wait.

As Jennifer grabbed her rucksack and made to leave, her phone buzzed in her pocket. She took out the device and studied the screen. Harriet was calling.

She considered ignoring the call, then decided she should accept it. 'Hey.'

'Aunty Jennifer, I wanted to check you are OK. After what happened.'

'I'm fine, thanks for checking, pumpkin. That's sweet. How are you? Is that brother of yours still being a pain?'

'Please don't go up to that house today. I'm really worried something bad will happen to you.'

'Harriett, did your mum put you up to this?'

'No... I...' She hesitated, then said, 'I overheard her talking. She's afraid.'

'Is she home now? Is she there with you?'

Another hesitation. 'Um, um, no, she's gone to lie down in her room. She has a bad migraine. She gets them now and again. They make her upset, and she likes to be alone in the dark. Sometimes she stays in her room for ages. I thought it was because Dad snores at night, but I think she likes to be on her own.'

'Your mum sleeps in the spare room?'

'It's not really a spare room. It's *her* room.'

'Oh, OK.'

'Do you ever talk to yourself?'

The question threw Jennifer. 'Well... I do a bit. Why do you ask?'

'I wondered if that was normal.'

'I think so. Is everything OK? You sound a little lost.'

'I'm all right.' The little girl paused for a few seconds. 'Sometimes I hear Mum crying at night. I always ask her if she's OK, but she pretends she's not upset and puts on a brave face.'

Trouble in paradise indeed.

Jennifer was about to ask if Harriet ever heard her mum and dad arguing, but decided that was none of her business, and it wouldn't be right to prise such delicate information from her niece, who suddenly seemed vulnerable and uncertain.

'Mum said you nearly died today. Is that true?'

The image of the dead man flashed in Jennifer's mind again. 'Wrong place, wrong time. I'm fine. Look, Harriet, I need to go. Thank you for calling; it's sweet of you. You take care.'

'Be careful. Please.'

'I will. You too, missy. You too.'

37

Jennifer cut the scooter's engine as soon as she came out from under the willow tree. The sun had been blazing all day, but now it had dipped down, and immense, steely clouds were forming.

She rolled the scooter the rest of the way, parked it out of view and walked past the main gate to the front of the outbuilding where the wasps lived. Here were two large wooden doors secured with a bulky chain that she knew she'd never break open. She tried to find a gap to peek through, but there was nothing.

She made her way back to the gate and clambered over it. The coast was clear. She moved to the side door and gave the padlock a tug. Now she wasn't quite so confident the crowbar she'd borrowed would do the job, but she told herself she'd have to give it a try. She glanced over her shoulder, dropped her rucksack and pulled out the crowbar. The wasps were stirring and buzzing in her face as she jammed the end between the door and frame. Her first tug didn't seem to do much, so she got a better grip and put all her weight against it.

'You'll never open it with that!' boomed her grandad's harsh voice.

Jennifer dropped the crowbar. It clattered down, and the wasps got angrier. 'Grandad,' she said, without turning to him. She couldn't stand to face him.

'If you're so desperate to snoop in there, you should've asked,' he said, his voice scornful. He shoved her out of the way. In one hand, he had a set of keys and in the other, a bottle of whisky. He reeked of the foul booze. He was wearing blue trousers, a beanie hat and a green raincoat.

'I was just... I... I was going to...' she gabbled.

He slammed a key into the padlock. 'You think I'm hiding something? What, hey? What do you reckon I have stashed up in here?' He tugged the lock free, tossed it aside, and shouldered the wooden door into that old building open, sending the wasps into a frenzy. 'After you, young lady.'

Jennifer eyed the dense, frightful darkness.

Her grandad took a deep sip from his bottle. 'What are you waiting for? You wanted to go snooping. So go.'

Jennifer stepped inside. It stank of rot and oil. The intense noise of the frenzied wasps was daunting in the dark. She kept rubbing her arms, convinced they were landing on her.

A light clicked on. The cavernous building was practically empty. Save for a few rickety units loaded with junk, some old tyres and a long wooden table. A table on which a shotgun lay, next to rows upon rows of red cartridges in neat lines.

'Grandad... you shouldn't have this! Why have you got a gun?'

'I'm supposed to sit back and take it? Is that what I should do?' he yelled belligerently.

'They'll send you back. They'll send you back to prison for good.'

He snatched up the shotgun. 'If they do, they do. It doesn't matter to me. What do I have out here?'

'Me,' she said weakly.

'Do I?'

'Yes!'

'I'll not sit idly by any longer. If they want a war with me, I'll give the bastards one!'

'I thought you said it was only some kids who would get bored.'

'This won't end well.' He grabbed handfuls of shells and stuffed them into his jacket pockets. 'You should go.'

The wasps were everywhere now, and one stung Jennifer on the neck. 'You need to get rid of that gun. We'll speak to the police again. Make them listen. They'll have to do something.'

'Fuck the police!' he spat and marched out of the outbuilding.

Jennifer followed him, glad to be leaving the swarm of agitated wasps. 'Grandad, please.'

'The police didn't listen twenty-five years ago. And they won't listen now.'

'Give me that gun. I'll get rid of it.'

He laughed. 'Will you? Or maybe you'll turn it on me.'

'Grandad!'

'What did you expect to find in there?'

'I don't know.'

'Don't lie to me, lady. You're just like your mother. I can see the signs. I can see when you're lying to me.'

'You're drunk. And you're scaring me.'

'Then leave. Go on, get outta here. Judas!'

'No. I won't leave you like this. You'll do something you'll regret.'

'Ahh, whatever,' he hissed before ambling off in the direction of the house, gun resting on his shoulder and swigging the booze as he shuffled.

Jennifer thought about the day her mum had died.

The drunken argument Mr and Mrs Ragbourne had seen from the holiday cabin.

And the aggression oozing from the old man now he had booze driving him.

Not just booze. *Whisky.* The stuff he'd been drinking that very day.

Jennifer checked her watch.

Just under twenty minutes to go.

38

After bringing her bike up to the house and locking the main gate, Jennifer found her grandad perched on a stool in the gloomy kitchen. Rain pattered against the window. Two candles flickered on the table where the whisky bottle and shotgun sat.

He didn't acknowledge her entrance. He stared forward in a dreamlike state.

'Shall I make you a strong coffee?' she suggested.

'No.'

Jennifer saw the clock on the wall. Watched the second hand ticking by. 'I know deep down you don't want to go back inside.'

'You don't know anything about me,' he said.

Jennifer's eyes dropped to the shotgun. 'They probably won't even come.'

'Oh, they'd better.'

'So, what, you're going to just shoot them?'

'Nope. I'll warn them first. They'll have one chance to leave and never return.'

'And if they refuse?'

'Then I'll shoot them.'

'Where did you even get that thing?'

He flashed her a wolfish grin. 'A friend. An ex-con who owed me. He'd be here with me now if I'd asked him. I told him the gun would be enough to see off the cowardly shits who have been targeting me.'

Jennifer pointed at the bottle. 'Is this wise? Guns and booze are not a great combo.'

'I disagree.'

Jennifer grabbed the bottle, removed the lid and sniffed the liquid. 'How do you drink that nasty stuff?'

'I don't drink it for the delicious flavour.'

'I'm surprised you can stomach whisky at all.'

Her grandad's eyes narrowed. 'Why? Because it's a stark reminder of what happened? You're right, it is. And that makes me mad.'

'You want that?'

'Tonight, I do.'

Jennifer placed the bottle back on the table. 'Can I hold the gun?'

He raised his bushy eyebrows and smiled. 'Why?'

She shrugged. 'Never held a gun before.'

'Go for it.'

Jennifer gingerly picked up the shotgun. The weapon felt cold, heavy and well-worn. It felt wrong.

Her grandad grabbed the whisky. 'You'll need to click the safety off if you want to use it. I have already chambered one round, so don't blow your own toes off. There are two more in the chamber.'

'I don't want to use it.'

'You certain of that? Why are you really here, Jennifer? Huh? You here to put an old man out of his misery?'

'Don't say that. I'm here to help you.'

'You won't get a better chance. You could blow my head right off my shoulders at that range. I won't stop you. One pull of your finger and I'm done for.'

'Don't be ridiculous.'

'You want revenge for your mother, don't you?'

'You said you're innocent, so why would I need to take revenge?'

'Yeah, but you don't believe me.'

'I do.'

'Liar!' he thundered.

Jennifer flinched and almost dropped the gun. 'I want to believe you. I need to. If you did do it... then... I'm a terrible judge of character.' She shook her head, desperately trying to stop the tears that were now pricking at her eyes from falling. 'And I don't think I am.'

But perhaps he was right. Had she let the doubt gradually creep in? She didn't want to tell him that. Not while he was in this state.

He rubbed a hand over his balding head, with its faint shadow of hair. 'If you're not going to use the thing, put it down.'

Jennifer considered making a dash with the gun. He'd not be able to use it if she took it away and hid it somewhere.

As if sensing what she might be planning, her grandad stood and ripped the weapon from her grip. Then he took a big swig from the bottle and left through the back door.

Jennifer gazed at the clock again.

Five minutes left before the deadline.

39

Jennifer jogged after her grandad and found him marching towards the gate. The sound of a diesel engine rumbled nearby, and her heart thudded wildly. She wanted to call the police, but if they came out here and found her grandad waving a shotgun about like some madman, he'd be done for.

Headlights streamed through the gate, and she saw a van edging through the willow tree branches. The lights were on full beam and blinding. Rain slashed down like a million needles in the dazzling light.

The driver dimmed the lights and killed the grumbling engine.

'Grandad! We should go. Now.'

'No,' he said, standing in the shadows and keeping out of view from the van's occupants.

Jennifer could make out three shapes inside. 'There's at least three people,' she whispered.

The van's doors creaked open. One figure emerged from the driver's side. Two dropped out from the passenger side.

The sight of the dark figures was terrifying. As they moved closer to the gate, she noticed they were armed. The driver, the tallest of the three, carried a shovel. The other two were wielding a cricket bat and pickaxe. Jennifer tried to work out if the van was the VW Crafter, but she couldn't quite tell in the gloominess.

The three figures were closing in. All three were wearing black clothes, dark baseball caps pulled right down, and surgical masks.

The driver reached the gate and shook it. 'Ernest Moorby! Show yourself, you old prick!'

The coarse male voice sent a shudder of fear through Jennifer. These men weren't messing about.

'Get out here. Come on, you fucking coward! Out here now, Moorby.'

Jennifer's heart was in her throat as her grandad raised the gun, stepped out of the shadows and strutted to the gate. 'Evening. Right, take one more step and I'll unload this into that big mouth of yours.'

'Shit, shit, shit, he's gotta bloody shotty,' shouted the driver, stepping back from the gate.

The shorter figures followed suit.

Ernest took aim with the gun. 'Make one more move and I will fire. You understand?'

'Ease up, old man. Don't do anything stupid,' said the driver, now talking in a slow, deep voice that sounded familiar to Jennifer. 'Calm down. We all know you won't fire that thing. Is it even loaded?'

Ernest sneered. 'I tell you what. I'm a terrible shot... But I have three chances. And we're at close range. I reckon I'll hit at least one of you. You fancy taking that chance, you lanky streak of piss?'

The driver held the shovel tightly and sneered. 'You're talking shit, you old muppet. Put it down, there's a good chap.'

Ernest tilted the gun up and fired a shot. The booming sound echoed around the countryside, and the three figures cowered.

He waved the gun and growled, 'Right, you gobshite. Mask and hat off. Do it, or I'll put a hole the size of a football in your guts. And throw that shovel to the side. Far as you can. Go on. Now. Don't mess me about.' He spoke with a firm, stern finality that confirmed none of his requests were up for debate.

The driver tossed his shovel aside, and it clanged as it hit concrete. Then he tugged off his hat and mask.

Jennifer recognised him straight away. Her dad's neighbour from the Eden. *Bruce.*

Another wave of the shotgun. 'Come on, you two parrots copy this ugly donkey. Hurry up.'

'Please don't shoot,' pleaded Bruce. 'That's my nephew.'

The shorter figure unmasked, revealing a young, petrified face. The lad couldn't have been older than seventeen. He had an unruly mop of shaggy hair that almost popped out of the cap when he removed it. 'Don't. Please, mate. Please be careful with that thing.' He dropped the pickaxe.

The figure in the middle didn't move, but his chest was rising and falling.

'Well, you gonna make me pull this trigger? Or you gonna play ball, hard man?'

The figure still didn't move.

Jennifer knew who this was now.

40

E rnest took aim. 'I'm going to count to ten. One... two...'

'Stop!' Jennifer raced over to the gate. 'What the hell are you playing at?'

The man tugged off his face covering. 'You need to get in that van and leave with us now, Jennifer!'

'Howard Fincher,' hissed Ernest. 'You... you total arsehole.'

Howard gave him a repulsed glare. 'I won't let you take my daughter from me! I won't.'

'Why? You took mine from me,' growled Ernest, teeth bared.

'Can we all please calm down and talk about this? Grandad, please put that gun away,' said Jennifer.

'Talk. They didn't come here to talk,' said Ernest. He jabbed the gun at the driver. 'Go take a long walk on a short cliff path.' He straightened his coat, turned and stomped away. She noticed him loading another cartridge into the shotgun as he walked.

'Dad, please. Put that bat down and come inside. This is insane.'

'Bruce, you and Carl had better get going,' said Howard.

'You want us to leave you here? Is that wise? That prick is wasted and waving a shotty about,' said Bruce.

Howard nodded. 'I can handle him.'

'You sure? That mad old-timer might stick a slug in your guts,' said Bruce.

'Go on. It's fine. We need to talk. It's time we had it out.'

Bruce and his nephew trudged back to the van, warily gazing back at them as they climbed inside the vehicle.

'Dad,' said Jennifer, 'the bat?'

He threw the weapon aside. 'Happy? Now he has a gun, and I have nothing.'

The van started up, and Jennifer observed as it turned around in the courtyard.

It wasn't the VW van with the damaged wheel arch.

JENNIFER and her dad walked into the kitchen to find Ernest rooting around in the cupboards, shotgun clasped in his left hand. He produced an unlabelled bottle and two glasses. 'Finish the whisky off if you'd prefer, Howard.'

'No, Dad. Leave the whisky. It doesn't agree with you. I don't like it when you drink that stuff.' She gave him a fierce glare to assert her demand and let him grasp this was a command not a request.

'I guess I'll have whatever that is, then,' said Howard.

'Spiced rum,' said Ernest.

'Grandad, could I get one of those too?' asked Jennifer, pulling up a chair and placing her phone on the table.

Ernest grabbed another glass and put them down with a smack. He poured three huge measures, pushed one over to Jennifer and slid another towards Howard. 'Drink up.'

Howard eyed the drink like it was poison, then snatched it up and took a sip. 'Don't expect me to say sorry.'

'Was all of it you? What did you throw over my bike?' she asked her dad.

'Fake blood. Carl, Bruce's nephew, got it online. And yeah, it was me. All of it. I enjoyed every minute,' said Howard, sounding pleased with himself. 'Bruce's mate runs a waste collection service, and he was happy to provide us with plenty of junk. We raided skips, pallet yards, stole charity offerings, and even emptied a few dog shit bins.'

'Dad!'

'Don't you start, Jen. Don't you dare. You caused this. Was I supposed to sit by and do sod all while you fraternised with the enemy? While you came here cosying up with the beast who killed my wife? Your mother?' He gulped down the rum, pulled a sour face and threw the glass onto the table. 'Now, I'm not sure what your game is, but we're done. I want you to go now. And I want you to never come back here. No more pissing around. Are we clear? You will stay away, or things will escalate all over again.'

'Did you start that petition as well?' she asked.

Howard let out a short, bitter laugh. 'No. What good would a petition do? What are a few signatures going to achieve? Get fucking real. Now, I said leave.'

Jennifer shook her head. 'I'm not leaving you two alone.'

Ernest snorted. 'And what were you hoping to accomplish by tossing crud at my windows like an immature delinquent, Howard? Did you believe that a few eerie messages and a couple of bags of trash would make me leave? You are a bloody mindless twat.'

'Oh, don't you worry, Ernest, I will send you packing. One way or another, you'll leave North Sutton. And you will stay away from my daughter. That is a solemn promise. You think a shotgun will protect you? Think again. I'll keep coming for you until you beg me to pack your bags and drive you out of this shithole myself.'

'Big words. Not such a pushover these days. Found a bit of backbone at long last,' said Ernest.

'Why did you do it, Ernest? What drives someone to murder their own daughter in such a way?' asked Howard quietly.

Ernest gritted his teeth. 'You'd better stop talking.'

Howard stabbed a finger at Ernest. 'Stop denying it. I want to hear you say it. You got drunk out of your skull, you argued with her – and you lost your temper. Just admit to what you did. Put us all out of our misery.'

'Please, can you both calm down?' said Jennifer. She felt like a referee. No, a mediator, stuck between two men who had spent the last two and a half decades detesting each other. Both men had no doubt contemplated for many hours how much they'd like to destroy the other. And how much they'd like to see the other suffer.

Ernest put the shotgun down on the table. 'I was shouting at her because of how she'd been treating *you*. I tried to make her see sense. Tried to stop her from destroying her marriage. I got angry. I lost my head.' He refilled his glass to the top. 'You might think I was oblivious to the things she was into. But you'd be wrong. I was shocked to realise that my own daughter had been behaving in such a way. That wasn't how a mother should act. She was a disappointment to me. The way she treated you, Howard, filled me with disgust. I was utterly ashamed of her.'

'That's why you did it? You killed her because she was...' Howard's voice trailed off, and he frowned.

Jennifer caught her dad's eye, and he swallowed as he gave his neck a nervous rub. Jennifer wasn't willing to admit that she was aware of the infidelity. Aware of the parties and her dad's disgust at having to endure her mum's debauched behaviour.

Ernest let out a long sigh. 'If you want the truth, I'm certain she regretted having children. She craved a different life. And, as much as she loved her girls, she started to resent them. She pretty much told me she'd made a mistake having children so young. She wanted to be free and go off on her own. To find herself and embrace all that stupid, free-spirited nonsense.'

'What, you reckon I didn't have a clue about all that? I saw the change in her. It broke my heart. Ruined what we had. Wrecked our marriage.'

'I didn't kill her, Howard. I didn't kill my Katherine. I was so drunk, I wasn't even capable of making it to the toilet let alone down there to that water.'

'What you mean is you were so pissed you can't even remember what happened, can you? You've denied it all this time, but a tiny part of you wonders if you did kill her. In court, you confessed to experiencing a blackout, Ernest. There are gaps in your memory, and that scares you. It scares the fuck out of you!'

Ernest's face dropped, and in that moment, he appeared so ancient, haggard and forlorn. So fragile.

'I-I...' stammered Ernest.

'And if you can't remember everything, then you can't be one hundred per cent sure, can you?' said Howard.

Ernest shook his head frantically. 'No, no, no. Never. I would never have hurt her.'

'Admit it. Admit that a tiny part of you is worried that the jury got it right. You might not want to accept it. But be honest with yourself. Be honest with us. There's a chance you are guilty, and you can't bring yourself to accept that reality. Because if you are, then life wouldn't be worth living, would it? I refuse to accept that during all those years, you didn't lie in your dark cell mulling over the facts and considering, what if they are right and I am wrong?'

Ernest's red-rimmed eyes dropped to the gun. 'If you were speaking the truth, I'd have already ended my life. But I know it's not true. You hear me? I know it! And talking of the truth, it's about time you admitted that bitch Felicia Macclesfield lied for you. I don't believe you were with her all night like she claimed you were.'

'I was,' said Howard, crossing his arms.

'No.' Ernest thumped his fist down onto the table. 'Bullshit. You made her lie for you. Why?'

'Don't attempt to deflect this onto me, you slippery sod,' growled Howard.

Ernest placed his hand on the barrel of the gun. 'I thought about you a lot in prison, Howard. About your feeble, downtrodden husband act. You played that well back then, didn't you? But we both know that deep down you have a dark side. A cruel streak.'

Jennifer reflected on the moment she'd seen the man in the work overalls treading through the wheat. She imagined the man with her dad's face. Then her mind shaped the face into her grandad's features. And then it became a faceless blur again.

She shook the images away and focused back on the men in the darkened kitchen.

'I have learned to stand up for myself,' said Howard. 'Back then, though, I was a doormat. I should've put my foot down and put a stop to things. I was weak. I regret being weak.'

'Why are you so keen to get me out of town? Hey?' asked Ernest. 'I'm sure this goes deeper than a half-arsed attempt to keep me away from Jennifer. You want me out of the way in case your secret is finally exposed.'

'I'm telling you now, Felicia didn't lie for me! I was with her all night.'

'Felicia *did* lie for you, Dad. She told me herself,' said Jennifer quietly, shocked that she'd let the words come out.

41

Jennifer had the impression her dad was going to thump her. She'd never been the recipient of his anger, and now the hatred burning in his eyes frightened her.

His face twitched, his lips drew into a tight line, and he clenched both of his fists so tight they turned bone white. 'You sneaky little cow! What the hell are you playing at? You're on a witch hunt against me now? Your own father? I'm so disappointed in you. So, so disappointed.'

'And now the truth finally comes out. I knew it. I always knew it,' said Ernest with a nasty glint in his eye. He picked up the gun and struggled to stand. For a moment, it appeared as though he'd topple.

'She's talking rubbish. Felicia isn't exactly my biggest fan these days. She's stirring the pot, that's all. And you fell for her nonsense, Jen. Are you stupid, or what?'

'She's dying, Dad. She doesn't have much time left. And she wanted that lie off her chest.'

These words had an instant impact on her dad. His face dropped, and his anger fizzed away. 'What do you mean?'

'Cancer,' said Jennifer. 'It's terminal.'

Howard poured himself a hefty rum and knocked it back in one hit. His face took on a greyish hue in the candlelight. He looked grizzled and bony. *Old.*

Ernest levelled the shotgun at him. 'Time to spill the beans, Howard Fincher. Time to tell us why you made that mistress of yours lie for you.'

Howard rubbed a hand over his stubbly chin and closed his eyes. 'Stop waving the gun about, you old fool. Put it away before you blow a hole in one of us; then I'll tell you.'

'Please, Grandad. You've had a lot to drink, and you might accidentally fire it. Please put it down now,' she urged.

Ernest lowered the gun slightly, hesitated, then pointed the barrel at the floor.

Howard poured another drink. 'Katherine had all but moved in here, and I was struggling to connect with her. That's when she became obsessed with finding out who Stacey's mystery fella was. She wouldn't stop going on about it. The day before she died, she came back to our house. We got into a huge barney. She told me if I was any sort of father, I'd find out who this guy was and give him a good pasting. That a real man would put a stop to their liaisons. A real man would have seen off their daughter's boyfriend.'

He took a long gulp of rum. 'I told her we'd only make things worse. We'd just drive Stacey closer to the guy and put more of a strain on our relationship with her. I said the best plan would be to let things run their course. Stacey would soon get bored with this lad. But she wasn't prepared to try this approach. She couldn't stand the idea that this older guy was taking advantage of one of her daughters. The idea that he was sneaking around right under her nose and making a fool of her. She said it was technically rape.'

'She was right. And you should've dealt with the situation. That girl was only fourteen,' pointed out Ernest, his eyes narrowed.

'The next day, Katherine found out this guy was coming up to see Stacey around ten o'clock that night. She overheard Stacey on the phone, or so she told me... I'd started to question her. I wondered if Katherine had got it all wrong. That there was no boyfriend, and she was just being a neurotic mother. I mean, nobody else had seen this guy, and Stacey outright denied everything. She still denies it to this day.'

He rubbed at the deep creases in his forehead. 'Like a good boy, I did as she told me. I came over to Barren's Lodge after dark. I parked my car in a dark spot under the trees, and I waited. I was so nervous about the whole thing. The idea of collaring some lad I didn't even know and beating him up and threatening him. This made me feel sick to my stomach. I'd already been to the pub and necked five pints. I remember my heart was racing so fast, and I was sweating like mad. I actually thought I might have a heart attack.

'I'd only been waiting fifteen minutes when I saw someone walking quickly away from the property. I was so annoyed with myself. Because I assumed I'd arrived too late and missed the dirty bastard going in. So much stuff was going around in my head. And now the very idea that this piece of shit had just been with my daughter... I saw red. I started the car, and before I'd even thought about what I was doing, I drove down the lane and aimed straight at them.'

'Jesus, you almost killed Ava!' said Jennifer.

'It was a miracle she got out of the way. But at that point, I had no idea it was her, did I? I came to a stop and waited. My head was spinning. I considered getting out and telling them next time they wouldn't be so lucky. But there was no movement from the trees. I panicked, thinking perhaps I hadn't missed after all. Or the lad had hit his head when he'd dived out of the way. God, the idea of me driving away and leaving my Ava in the ditch like that... it sickens me.'

'So you assumed you'd run over Stacey's boyfriend, which is why you originally asked Felicia to give you an alibi,' stated Jennifer.

'Yes. When I discovered it was Ava, I felt so ashamed. But I could hardly tell the truth. It was too late. I'd laid the foundations for that lie and had to stick with it, or risk burying myself. I knew I'd likely be in the frame for your mum's death already. And if I'd have said I'd been there... said I'd been pissed and almost run over my own daughter, I really would've been suspect number one.'

'You're a bloody fool, Howard,' said Ernest. 'A damn fool.'

'If I had been ten minutes earlier, I would've seen Ava's friends drop her off, and I might have twigged it was her coming back down the lane... But it didn't look like my Ava. The darkness and—'

'The fact you were drink driving,' said Jennifer.

'Ava was wearing a baseball cap. I'd never seen her wearing one of those. How was I supposed to know she'd borrowed her friend's hat?' moaned Howard.

'Dad, you should've told the truth. You wasted police time. You confused their investigation. How much time did they spend trying to tie that incident to Mum's murder?'

'I'm aware of that. I've had to live with my mistake. At the time, it just seemed easier to stick to what I said. I kept the lie up and said I was nowhere near Barren's Lodge, and Felicia backed me... But when all is said and done, it changes nothing.' He glared at Ernest. 'What happened down that lane doesn't change what happened in the house. And down by that water.'

'I need some air. I need... some fresh air,' said Ernest, his face ashen and his whole demeanour drawn and unhealthy. He stumbled to the door, opened it and traipsed outside.

Jennifer made to follow.

Her dad grabbed her arm. 'Jen, the jury *didn't* make a mistake. You know that, don't you? Deep down, I think you do. That old man needs to keep telling himself he's innocent. He has to. There is no other option other than to keep contesting the truth. If he stops doing that... if he admits defeat. Admits they were right, then what's he got? There's nothing left to cling to.'

Jennifer peered outside. The rain had stopped. Her mind was in overdrive.

Her grandad might have gaps in his memory, but he wasn't the only one who couldn't remember everything.

Her memories were also missing, jumbled and confused.

That man in the field wearing the overalls.

That glass.

The aroma of that potent whisky.

Her mum's blood dotted on the floor.

But there were pieces missing. Important pieces. She just knew it.

What the hell is it I can't recall? What's missing? Why won't my mind let me see it?

She urged herself to remember. The frustration of it was

making her angry. She turned and hurried back into the main lounge. Flicked on a dim light. Stepped inside. Span the dusty globe. Gazed around.

She closed her eyes and could smell the pungent whisky once again.

What was I doing in here that night?

42

She pictured her parents on their wedding day. She struggled to recollect much else about the event. Just that dance. That dance was etched in her mind. The coy smile on her mum's pretty face, strands of ringleted hair falling down over her cheeks as she slow danced with her new husband. *Her daddy.*

She'd been a bridesmaid, as had her two sisters. Her parents were still very young. They were going to settle down into a little love nest. A new build on the edge of North Sutton's Parsonage Park. The deposit paid by Mum's rich parents.

Many years later, she'd found out that her mum had been rather reluctant to marry her dad despite them having three children together. It had been her mum's parents who'd pressured her into getting married. She'd also discovered that they hadn't been entirely happy with their daughter for having three children out of wedlock.

She could recall her dad smiling like the cat that who'd just got the cream and then some. Perhaps he'd been punching above his weight. She'd not thought much about that back then because she'd been so young, but she now guessed, looking back, it was plain for anybody to see. Howard Fincher had been lucky and fallen on his feet with Katherine Moorby.

The guests all stayed silent and watched with warm smiles as the pair slowly moved to 'Nights in White Satin' by the Moody Blues. She loved the song. It was so beautiful, yet so sad and haunting. At the time she'd been confused by the lyrics and assumed they'd been singing about knights, and for years when she caught that song on the radio, she'd envisaged gallant knights with satin cloaks draped over their suits of shining armour as they elegantly rode their mounts. She'd felt a bit daft when she later read the song's lyrics and discovered that Justin Hayward's words were nothing to do with knights and she'd totally misunderstood the meaning behind the song. Now she found it impossible to listen to it without breaking down into a sobbing mess.

She closed her eyes. She couldn't stop thinking about that jogger. That poor, poor man. It was so tragic. So needless.

They'd showed a photo of him on the news earlier. It had been all over the internet too. The image of his handsome, joyful face wouldn't shift from her thoughts. He had kids. A wife. A life.

His agonising death was all her fault.

Now she struggled to breathe. Her windpipe seemed to be obstructed. Like she'd swallowed some thick glue that was gradually hardening.

She heard her mum's sweet, caring voice echo inside her head. *Glue those heavy eyes shut. It's time to sleep now, sweet pea. It's finally time to sleep, my special little girl.*

43

Jennifer kept spinning the globe, watching it turn as the dust particles danced around it. She'd been so lost in her thoughts as she'd searched her memories of this room that she'd almost forgotten about everything else.

The silence in the house became rather harrowing. She raced back into the kitchen. The candle's flame flickered in the breeze from the open door. The room was empty. She stepped outside. 'Dad? Dad?' A rising sense of panic almost drowned her. She couldn't leave those two men alone. It would end in disaster. She raced into the grounds.

When she reached the pond, her chest heaved and her ribs ached from the effort of the run.

She found her grandad at the pond's edge, gazing into the murky water, the shotgun held to his chest as though hugging it. Her dad stood on the other side in silent contemplation, also peering into the water.

The scene appeared jarringly odd. Surreal, even.

Both men were extremely drunk. They looked terrible.

Crestfallen and defeated. They'd had the showdown that they'd both wanted. They'd said the things they had held onto for twenty-five years. The outcome probably wasn't what they'd expected. She got the sense that these two men perhaps didn't loathe each other as much as they'd convinced themselves they did over those long years. Years full of hatred, regret and devious plotting.

Jennifer believed her dad was telling the truth. He had no reason to lie about almost killing his own daughter with his car.

But did she believe her grandad? He'd admitted he had blacked out. Admitted he had some gaps in his memory. He'd been drunk. So drunk that he was certain he would never have made it down here in such a sorry state.

Yet here he was, blitzed out of his skull, at the edge of the water, standing at the same spot where her mum had died. He'd not even used his walking stick to get here tonight. She still suspected he didn't need it. He'd kept himself in tiptop condition and was no ordinary old man. He was strong, sharp, fearless.

If he'd made the trek here today, in his eighties, she decided it would have been a walk in the park when he'd been in his fifties.

He kept telling himself he wasn't guilty. And he believed that to be true. However, that didn't make it so. She understood that now, no matter how hard that was to process.

So how does the final act end? she mused.

A sudden image popped into her head of her mum as she closed her eyes and slid down into a bath overflowing with warm, bubbly water. She'd had a nightmare. A terrible nightmare about her mum drowning in a bathtub.

A sequence of images flickered through her head.

The statue. The chain dragging.

Then she imagined being in that dark water.

A tightening sensation around her neck.

The extreme pressure on her chest.

Lungs filling with water. The panic. The raw terror. The overwhelming hopelessness.

The coiling chain strangling her. Choking her as the water snuffed out her existence.

The chain hooked on the angel's wing, refusing to budge.

Clawing at the metal. Nails splitting. Fingers useless.

'I need to leave this place,' mumbled Ernest. He tossed the gun into the water. 'I need to leave.'

As the gun sank into the darkness, Jennifer wondered if he meant leave Barren's Lodge or the place where his only daughter had died.

As her grandad's shape faded out of view, her dad dropped to his knees and cried. Cried like she'd never seen a man cry before.

It made her want to cry, too. Made her heart ache so much she needed to press her hand against it. She'd never been good at dealing with people when they got like this. Did she go over and offer some kind words? Tell him it would all be OK? Hug him? Place a comforting hand on his shoulder and let him know she'd be there for him?

Jennifer did none of those things. Instead, she took one final look at the water.

She didn't intend to return to this spot ever again. All that could be found here was more pain and sorrow, which only served to make everything feel so much worse.

She left her father to his solitary agony.

44

She'd told herself not to come here ever again. Told herself that if she did, it would make everything worse. It might be what finally plunged her over the edge of that hole she'd been edging ever closer to. The chasm. The dark pit where total insanity awaited her. Where there'd be no turning back once she fell in.

It isn't nice to think of yourself as mentally ill, raving mad or unsound of mind, she decided. But she'd known for some time now that if she didn't get proper help, she'd flip, do something really stupid and end up being sectioned. End up in a centre where deranged people went. Where she'd spend her days half-baked on mind-bending medication, gazing endlessly at the same spot for hours on end as her mind and memories slowly diminished and her brain turned into lumpy mashed potato. She decided that might be better than what she'd been dealing with. She'd managed to suppress things over the years. Somehow, kept things in order. But since her grandad's release, keeping it together seemed altogether impossible.

That song, 'Nights in White Satin', kept playing in her head. It seemed to be stuck on an endless loop. Like it would never switch off. The wedding reception had been here, in the grounds of Barren's Lodge, she now recalled. She pictured her parents dancing and smiling again. Her grandparents had joined the dancing as soon as the next song kicked in, though she couldn't remember what the DJ had played after the Moody Blues. Something more upbeat and livelier, because soon more guests were drifting onto the dance floor, and she'd been doing funky dance moves with her sisters as they all found their confidence, lost their inhibitions and boogied the night away.

The memory made her heart ache. Everything had been so wonderful then.

Now she longed for this torment to stop.

There was only one way to set herself free of this.

Her world was about to be crushed.

But there was no other option now. She would confess. No matter how much damage it would cause.

Today she would unburden. Today she would tell the truth.

45

J ennifer noticed the distant light glowing faintly inside the observatory. She also caught a faint whiff of rancid smoke, so she made a beeline for the building.

When she arrived, she climbed the ladder and proceeded onto the deck. She gazed out across the field and could see a fire far off in the distance in Cobble Wood. It didn't appear to be a controlled blaze, and she hoped that firefighters would be on the scene soon and put the blaze out before any of the surrounding woodland was burned. A stolen car, she guessed. She considered calling the emergency services, then realised she'd left her phone on the kitchen table.

As Jennifer started to head back down, something else caught her attention. For a second, she convinced herself she'd spotted a shape moving around in the crop below. She fixed her eyes on the spot for a good twenty seconds. Nothing now. A flash of the figure in overalls came to her and, with this vision, a sense of dread that made her blood run cold. Like it had done when she'd seen the figure as a child. She guessed she was imagining things. It had been a long day.

Jennifer headed back down and entered the observatory. She noticed straight away that her grandad didn't look right. His face was drawn and chalky under the orange glow of the overhead light. He doubled over, held his stomach and let out a low, croaky groan.

Jennifer put her hand on his shoulder. 'We should go back to the house.'

'I love it down here, Jennifer. When I was inside, I... I would often think of this place. Think about you happily drawing and playing. You were such a sweet girl. Such a...' He groaned again.

'It's best you rest, Grandad. Come on.'

He shook his head and fixed her with a dejected expression. 'I don't feel so... well. I don't...' He spoke as though he was out of breath.

'You should take things easy. Come now.'

He pressed a hand against his side and applied pressure. 'I should never... have... gone back... there... never,' he said quietly.

Jennifer wondered if returning to the pond had triggered something in his muddled mind. Had he seen something? Had that place nudged a memory? Perhaps a memory he'd tried for so long to suppress?

'I told myself I would never go there.' He fell against a cupboard, knocking some paintbrushes, easels and pots over. He steadied himself. 'My heart feels strange. I don't like it. It's like I have a ghost inside my chest.'

'Grandad, it's important to just breathe. Take in some air. Can you do that?'

'Don't leave me, Jennifer. I'm... I'm scared. Please don't leave me,' he pleaded. 'Not alone.'

'I'm right here. You just drank too much. That's all. It's been a stressful night.'

He blinked. His eyes were wild and glassy. 'No. Everything is blurry. What is that? What is that at the window?' he cried.

'Nothing. There's nothing at...' Her voice faded as she turned around.

Because there *was* something at the window. A face. A masked face that caught her by surprise, made her jolt back, knocking over the doll's house.

46

She peered up the stairs, and her entire body trembled. She could almost hear those harrowing screams now. The first time she'd been so scared, she thought her sister was dying. She'd kept asking herself how a fear of sleeping was able to cause someone to get so worked up? Where did that girl venture off to in her sleep that was so frightening it would cause her to make such a silly fuss?

She'd listened at her sister's door. Listened to those things her mum said. Things she'd always say to *her* when she'd been afraid. Not of sleeping, just scared in general. She'd used similar words when she'd been worried about a sports event, was being picked on, or if she didn't want to go to school because she'd not finished her homework and was having a minor meltdown.

It had annoyed her when she'd first heard her mum say these things to her little sister. They were special words for *her*. Not for stupid, annoying Jennifer. She remembered thinking that the world revolved around Jennifer. She got all their parents' attention. All their love and support. Once she'd hit puberty, all that flew out of the window for her. What did she get? Blamed for everything that went wrong. Branded a slut by her mum for wanting a boyfriend. Every time her mum uttered a word to her, it would be some type of accusation or derisive comment. It became so frustrating.

On that night she recalled so vividly, she'd pushed herself against the wall outside her sister's room, keen to learn what was causing her distress. Listened to her mum's soothing words.

'Come on, you, breathe in deeply... and exhale. Hand on heart. Hey, keep those eyes glued shut now. That's it, Jennifer.'

'I want some more hot chocolate. And I need a wee,' Jennifer had lamented.

'Any more to drink and you'll be peeing all night. And you already went five minutes ago. This is why you can't sleep, pickle, too much fussing at night. It's all in your head. You don't need to go. Mum knows best. Listen to me. Glue those heavy eyes shut. It's time to sleep now, sweet pea. It's finally time to sleep, my special little girl.'

'But I'm not even sleepy. Not even a little.'

'Mm, those big dark shopping bags under your eyes say differently, missy. I'll stay right here until you drop off. I'm not going anywhere.'

'But I want my own bed. I don't like staying here.'

'What? You love this place. Why do you keep saying that?'

'I do. But I don't like sleeping *here*. I can't sleep like I can at home. Where I don't have funny dreams and wake up all hot and sweaty. And I prefer it when Dad tucks me in, too. Where is he?'

'Just think about one of your lovely, special drawings. That amazing hot air balloon. Picture that floating in the sky. And breathe. Empty your muddled mind. Relax. And let those crazy thoughts fizz away. Fizz and pop. Fizz and pop. That's right. Fizz and—'

'But the balloon might explode and crash! The people on board might fall out and die. I might dream that. Now it's in my head, I might dream it! I might see them all bent. Limbs broken and bones sticking out.'

'Or they might float off to a magical island where everyone is happy and they all sleep like tiny, untroubled babies.'

She shook away the memory and walked into the lounge. Now, of course, she understood. Now, she saw things from a totally different perspective. She'd been an immature, green-eyed and bitter teenager. Why didn't she see all this back then? Why had she been so selfish and cruel?

As she took in the sights and smells of the lounge, she stiffened. Her grandad's leather recliner was no longer in the room. She gaped at the spot where the chair once stood, and the urge to run out of the room hit her. She backed away, hands at her sides, breathing hard as if the air itself was sharp and heavy. It seemed difficult to draw it into her lungs.

The globe was still here. Her eyes moved to the floor, as if she'd still find the broken glass and the thick droplets of blood. Her mum had been so angry with her grandad that day. The way she'd torn into him had been awful. It was no wonder the family staying at one of the cabins had over-heard the exchange and reported the incident to the police. Grandad had merely been trying to make her mum see sense, but she'd gone ballistic.

She'd drifted downstairs and tried to wrap some kitchen

roll around her mum's cut, and she'd snapped her bloody hand away and ordered her to go upstairs. Yelled at her to stay away from her. She didn't want to catch her back downstairs again. But she'd only been trying to help stop the bleeding.

She could do nothing right that summer. It was like her mum detested her; she couldn't even look at her without an expression of total disdain or pure disappointment. Had she pushed her away one too many times? Even if she had, it was still hardly a valid reason to do what she did. Her mum's petulant behaviour towards her didn't excuse her actions, and she knew that. Even back then she'd known it, though she'd tried to convince herself she'd had sufficient reason.

Suddenly she became aware that somebody else had come into the room. They were standing behind her.

47

'Grandad, where the hell did they go?' whispered Jennifer, fumbling with the key to lock them inside.

'I can't breathe,' gasped Ernest, his hand clasped against his neck. He sank down on a wooden bench and started coughing.

The door handle moved downward as the intruder attempted to open it. There were several whacks and thuds, followed by heavy footsteps.

Jennifer caught a flash of movement outside and instinctively moved to her jeans to grab her mobile, remembering once again that she'd left it in the kitchen. 'I've rung the police,' lied Jennifer, calling out the words with a confidence she didn't feel.

The handle turned again, confirming they'd come back to the door.

'You'd better go away now,' she shouted.

They jiggled the handle, and another powerful thud against the door made the entire doorway shudder.

Jennifer stayed silent and tried to listen. She was certain they had moved away from the door once again. Had the intruder gone to find something to bash it open?

No noise now. Apart from her grandad's harsh breathing.

She'd glimpsed the intruder's face when they'd glared in through the window. They were wearing a black beanie and had a bandana or scarf covering their lower face. Red with a white paisley pattern. She was sure the intruder was a man, though she couldn't be certain.

'Who is that? What do they want?' gasped Ernest breathlessly.

Jennifer went to the art chest and yanked open drawers. Threw stuff aside in a desperate attempt to locate something she could use to defend them. Aside from pliers and long paintbrush that had a sharp tip, there wasn't much to hand. Then she spotted a glass jar full of bits and bobs. She grabbed it, tipped out the contents and stole a glance outside. Saw no sign of the figure out there.

Just the spiky bushes and shadowy trees dancing outside the windows.

'Are these windows glass or plastic?' Something told her it was real glass.

Confirmation of this came as one of the panes shattered with an ear-piercing crash and showered the observatory in shards of glass.

48

'What are you doing here, Ava?' asked Stacey, trying to keep the shock from her voice.

Ava gave her a quizzical glance. 'I have been trying to get hold of you all shittin' day! What are you playing at?' There was a hint of scorn in her tone, and her eyes were dark and full of mistrust. 'Harriet is going out of her mind with worry. She's convinced you and David are on the verge of separation. She's been calling me in tears. Thinking all sorts. Said you two had a big fight over... *him*. I bloody guessed I'd find you out here.'

Stacey turned away from her sister. 'Yes. I came to find him. To find Grandad.'

'Why?'

Stacey felt so drained it was difficult to stand straight let alone face her sister's wrath. Her shoulders felt like she had two sandbags weighing her down. 'Do you ever look back at those things we did to Jennifer and loathe yourself?'

Ava gave a nonchalant shrug. 'We were kids. We were

mean, yes, but kids do mean shit. Time to get over it, wouldn't you say?'

'Are you for real? We weren't just mean. We were wicked to her. It's probably why she is the way she is. Why she's so different... so detached from the real world. She never used to be like that. We did that. We sucked the joy from that girl and made her the lost, solitary person she is now. Don't you feel any guilt?'

'Oh, give over, Stacey. Jennifer should have been diagnosed properly as a kid. We all said she had special needs, but Mum insisted that we were wrong. *She* should've got her help. But that's not on us. It's not like she's the only person out there living with undiagnosed problems and coping just fine.'

'We tormented her. We drugged our own little sister.'

'All right, I admit that was messed up. But you're the one who continued with that stupid experiment. Even after I said we'd taken things too far. You're the one who needed her out of the way.'

Stacey recalled Ava searching for those blue sedatives in her mum's room while she kept watch in the hallway. She'd found them on the bedside table, wrapped in a white drawstring bag next to her sleep mask. She'd stolen an entire strip. There'd been loads, so they had guessed the theft would go unnoticed.

Ava had left the room with a big feral grin slapped on her face. 'We'll do it tonight. I'll offer to make the hot chocolate, and you can crush one up into powder and mix it in.'

Stacey had nodded with an eager smile. 'One? Maybe two? To make sure.'

'Wow, you really want her to sleep tonight, don't you, hey?' Ava had said with a knowing smile.

'It's for the best.'

'Yeah, best for you. Got plans with your mystery lad?'

'No! I just want rid of her, same as you do. Besides, it will help. A young girl needs proper sleep, right?'

And so they'd secretly used their mum's sedatives to drug Jennifer.

And why? Because they couldn't breathe without Jennifer being in their business. She didn't miss a bloody thing. She seemed to know everything. She drove them both mad with her constantly nosy behaviour.

Questions, questions, questions. The annoying demands, habitual quizzing, persistent griping at them and digging into their private affairs became so galling they'd ended up hating her. They'd just wanted a break. But they didn't even get that during the night because she'd never stay asleep for longer than two hours. If she wasn't wailing about her intense dreams, or complaining that she couldn't switch off her mind, she'd be wandering about Barren's Lodge. Drifting about like a ghost in the night, seeking them out, inside and outside.

Jennifer suffocated them, and they were both too uncaring and self-centred to give her the love and support she needed, despite their mum needling them. 'You're her big sisters. She loves you both, and you treat her like dirt. Stop thinking about yourselves all the time and be the big sisters she needs for once in your lives.' But in saying these things, their mum still kept placing Jennifer's welfare on their fragile teenage shoulders despite the fact they evidently despised the girl.

During that last summer, things got worse. As their parents' divorce loomed and their mum became withdrawn and distant, she'd sometimes lock herself away in her room, take those pills and be dead to the world, leaving the children's grandparents to deal with everything.

But more often than not, it got left to Ava and her to pick up the pieces. Left to handle their disturbed sister's strange habits and emotional issues. In response to this unjust turn of events, they'd take it out on Jennifer by doing horrible things to punish her.

They'd once buried her favourite stuffed toy, Reggie-Hedgy, deep in the grounds of Barren's Lodge, where they knew she'd never find it. They'd stomped her cherished hedgehog sanctuary to pieces and blamed the badgers. Sabotaged her favourite drawings.

They acted like vile human beings. But Stacey was much worse than Ava. So much worse.

'I told you to stop giving her those pills,' said Ava plainly, breaking Stacey from her grim reverie. 'I warned you things would get worse.'

They'd later learned from their mum that those sedatives were not even prescription drugs. She'd obtained a big batch from one of her hippy friends. Some creep she'd no doubt been screwing on those days when she'd go missing until the early hours. God only knew what was in them, but they made Jennifer flip. Her dreams had been bad before, but as the tiny blue pills took hold of her, they did weird things to her mind. She'd struggled to differentiate what was real from what she'd dreamed.

'She needs my help,' Jennifer had said to them after one of her intense dreams. 'A girl. She came and spoke to me.'

Did they comfort Jennifer? No. Instead, they'd fed her a horrid tale about the dead girl's soul being trapped inside a puppet their sister liked to play with. They'd both found this hysterical. Then Ava had taken things a step further and kept hiding the puppet in various spots in Jennifer's room. She'd also named the creepy thing Polly Puppet, burned its eerie face with a cigarette and snapped off its strings. She'd even gone so far as to tell their distressed sister that Polly Puppet was disfiguring herself because Jennifer hadn't made any attempt to find her real body.

These cruel tricks resulted in Jennifer having more disturbing dreams about the ghost of the girl in the woods. The girl she'd come to believe was called Polly.

It had been around this time when her severe night terrors really kicked in. Only now she didn't always wake from those nightmares. No, thanks to those strong pills they fed her, Jennifer got stuck inside her own messed-up mind and often couldn't come to consciousness and escape the twisted terrors she was being subjected to.

Stacey shook her head and bit her lip at the memory of it all.

'I know what you're thinking about. Don't go there. OK, just don't,' stated Ava.

'Did we really mean it? Did *I* really mean it?'

'I believed so at the time. I only went along with it because you were so set on following through with the plan.'

Stacey put a hand over her mouth and almost choked on a gasp. 'And you didn't try to stop me?'

Ava huffed as if she'd really come to the end of her tether now. 'Oh, give it a rest. Nothing happened, did it? Get a hold of yourself, Stacey.'

'How can you say that? We led her out there. We led her out there with sick intentions! She looked up to us. Expected us to protect her. We were her big sisters, and we—'

'Stop dredging up all this stuff. You're as bad as her. We were young, thoughtless; we were mean cows, but it's all history now.'

'We made Jennifer drink your Mad Dog 20/20. Remember? The red grape one you liked so much. Mum smelled the drink on us straight away. Do you reckon a tiny part of Mum understood? What we'd been trying to achieve?'

'No.'

Stacey's own words echoed around her head. Her vile teenage voice. 'We'll take Jennifer to find this Polly. Take her out to that island of trees where the girl keeps asking her to search.'

'It's nice the girl has a real name now,' Ava had said with a sneaky grin. 'She doesn't like playing with that toy anymore. Huh, funny that.'

'Mm, now I can't think why.' Stacey had laughed out loud. 'Classic. Jennifer totally believes there's a tortured soul stuck inside that ugly puppet.'

'Hey, we both know it *really* is trapped in there,' Ava had said, suddenly serious. 'This is no joking matter.'

'Geez, girl, you have such a warped mind. I reckon you watch too many horror films.'

Ava had let out a nasty laugh. 'Oi, you also played your part in convincing the dopey cow.'

Stacey had sniggered and shrugged. 'Well, maybe I played a tiny part.'

'That sister of ours is so clueless. She'd believe the moon was a giant Ice Gem if we told her it was.'

'Would it really be our fault if our little sis roamed off while we were out there? If she happened to step into the path of a giant combine harvester? I'm sure it would do the entire family a favour if she just... went away. Don't you reckon, Ava?'

'Why not just bash her with a hefty lump of wood, leave her in the field and be done with it?' Ava had said, only half sounding like she was joking.

'Would we get away with doing that?'

'If one of those machines ran her over, there wouldn't be much of her left.'

Stacey recalled that grim sound of a thousand furious birds quarrelling when they'd reached the copse... and then they'd suddenly stopped, engulfing the three girls in a queer, unnerving silence. With just the far-off rumble of the gigantic combine harvester.

Stacey, recoiling at the horrid memory, sobbed.

'Right, I'm speaking to David. You need professional help. You can't be a mother to Harriet and Evan in this sorry state.'

Upon hearing the names of her children, Stacey broke down even more.

'You can't keep beating yourself up over this! Christ, you were a kid, Stacey. You're not that person anymore. Do you hear me? Just let all this stuff go. Please. You're doing my head in now. Jennifer was too young to remember most of that stuff.'

'She needs to know. She must be told. All of it.'

'Come on. We're out of here.'

'I tried to forget. I have tried so hard, Ava. But I can't. I'll never be able to forget. Not ever.'

'This horrible place is fucking with your head. You can't handle it.'

'I need to see Grandad. I need to speak with him alone,' cried Stacey.

'No. You do not speak to that man. I won't allow it. Understand? You have nothing to say to him. Nothing!'

'Grandad,' Stacey sobbed, her words blurred and incoherent. 'Grandad.'

'What's this stuff with Jennifer got to do with Grandad?'

'Nothing!' she cried. 'Everything!'

49

A second observatory window smashed.

Ernest jumped to his feet, yelling curses, threatening to kill the unseen attacker lurking in the blackness outside.

Jennifer stood in front of her grandad and raised the glass jar. 'Stay back! You're not coming in here. I won't let you!' She heard a mighty crash behind her and spun to witness her grandad topple sideways and fall against the doll's house, putting his hand straight through its roof.

Jennifer turned back in time to catch half a garden slab smash against another window, pulverising the pane and sending jagged shards inwards.

'Stay down, Grandad,' she cried.

Two large, pointy, triangular pieces of glass were left in the top and bottom of the window frame. Then the top piece wobbled, slid free and dropped like a guillotine, smashing to bits as it hit the floor.

'Stop! Just stop!' yelled Jennifer as she crouched down to her grandad. 'Are you hurt? Grandad?'

'I'm OK,' growled Ernest. 'I'm going out to face them.'

But that wouldn't be necessary. Because when Jennifer gazed back up, she saw the intruder had already climbed in through one of the broken windows.

50

'Talk to me. Stacey? What's going on here?'

Stacey wiped away her tears with the back of her hand, but more filled the void.

'Why are you in such a state?' asked Ava.

'You were there. That day when those arseholes beat me up. I glimpsed your face in the crowd before they started thumping the crap out of me.'

'So? I wasn't with them. I was with my friends, who happened to be there when that lot started on you.'

'Yet you appeared happy to stand by and watch me get kicked and punched. You were happy to do nothing while they stole my house keys and ripped off my necklace.'

'What was I supposed to do?'

'You didn't even try to stop them throwing my stuff down the drain.'

'It wasn't my fault you couldn't stand up for yourself. You let those idiots treat you like that. Nobody ever dared any shit like that with me. Do you think it would have helped if I came running to your rescue every five minutes? Get real. If I'd stepped in, it would've made things worse.'

'You sure there's not more to it?'

'Meaning?'

'You wanted to punish me for what I did. You always knew, didn't you? Maybe not knew... but suspected, right?'

Ava's face darkened. 'I don't understand what you're saying here. What did I suspect?'

'That I was to blame! For Mum.'

Ava shook her head and screwed up her face. 'OK, yeah, I blamed you for messing around and driving her nuts. Before you'd even hit fifteen, you went about acting like you were a grown woman. Can you imagine what that must've been like for Mum? What if Harriet did the same thing to you? You were a little bitch during that summer. Perhaps a part of me did secretly enjoy seeing you get your face punched in. There, is that what you wanted to hear? Happy now?'

'Then you didn't have a clue. Not really.'

'Ah, you're hurting my head. Yes, you caused her heartache, but what happened to her wasn't on you. You didn't kill her, so you can stop with all this now.'

You didn't kill her.

Those words hit her like a speeding truck, and Stacey held her chest, bent over and sobbed so hard she could barely breathe.

'What the actual fuck? You're freaking me out. Stacey?'

And Stacey looked up at her sister, fought back the tears and felt her face burn red hot with shame.

The look she gave her must've conveyed all there was to say. Because Ava's face dropped; she took two steps back and kept shaking her head. 'No. No... No, no, no. What is this? What the hell is this?'

'I'm sorry. I'm sorry... I'm so, so sorry,' whispered Stacey.

Ava's lips drew back into a snarl. 'What did you do?'

'It all happened so fast. I had to pick a side.'

'Tell me what you did.'

'I... I... I should've stopped him.'

51

Silence filled the air as the three of them observed each other.

'You should have opened the door. I just wanted to talk,' growled the man.

Pure anger oozed from him, contradicting his words.

Jennifer gazed at the figure standing in front of them. As soon as he spoke, she realised who it was.

It made no sense. Why would he come here to hurt them?

She pictured the VW van hurtling towards her on that lane. The near miss in the High Street as it almost mowed her down. As it killed that innocent man out for his morning run. The figure in the wheat field, gazing at her intently. Now she pictured the mysterious figure's features as she recalled that day she'd first seen him out there. Really focused her mind on his face. His eyes. The shape of his mouth and nose. And the blank face in her mind shifted into a face she knew all too well. Or a younger version of that familiar face.

'You might as well take off the mask now,' suggested Jennifer. 'I know who you are.'

David didn't move. His chest rose and fell as his grip tightened around the hefty wrench clasped in his left hand. He wore a grey tracksuit over a black T-shirt and trainers that were slick with mud. He stank like foul smoke.

'I thought we were friends. I don't understand. Why would you do this, David?' said Jennifer.

'She's going to come clean. She's going to tell them every-thing. She's lost her marbles – and it's all your fault, Jennifer! All because you wouldn't leave things alone,' said David, his voice shrill and panicky. 'I tried to warn you. I tried to make you see sense. Why didn't you listen? I said you were upset-ting Stacey by coming here, but you didn't care. And now you've ruined everything! You have completely messed up her mind and smashed our world to bits,' he growled through clenched teeth.

'David, you are clearly very drunk. Please calm down. Can you please step back?' urged Jennifer.

'Yes, you drop that wrench and get off my property. Right now. Go on,' demanded Ernest, puffing out his chest, even though he looked about set to keel over. 'I'm warning you.'

David's wild eyes switched to Ernest and narrowed. 'Why did you have to come back here? You stupid old wanker. Why couldn't you just piss off and skulk away into the shadows like you were supposed to do? I hope you are both pleased with yourselves. You've driven my wife mad!'

52

'Sometimes I felt like we were stuck on an island living out here. Miles from anywhere. He kept promising to buy a car so he didn't have to walk here to find me. He'd come after work. It would take him over an hour, even using his shortcut through Cobble Wood and along the back fields. He was an apprentice at the gasworks on the Kings Road industrial area. It's quite a long way to walk, isn't it?' Stacey glanced up at her sister and wiped her wet eyes. 'Ava?'

Ava threw her a reproachful glare, but confusion was fixed on her face, too. Her mouth kept moving a touch, like she wanted to speak, but couldn't quite form the right combination of words. That didn't happen very often.

'I told Mum I wanted to go back home. I'm sure she liked having us all stuck out here, away from our friends. Away from the temptation of boys and booze and parties. She was so horrible to me that year. I could do nothing right.' Stacey spun the globe and closed her eyes. Why had it been so hard back in those days? All she had wanted was to be with David.

It had been all she ever thought about. He had been on her mind twenty-four seven. She'd pined for him. Stuck out here with her demanding grandparents, neurotic mother and annoying little sister. 'You were the only one who ever understood what it was like, Ava. What *she* was like.'

'She was struggling with life, but you know damn well she wasn't a bad mother, so don't try to paint this bleak picture. Don't make out you were some poor abused teenager living an abysmal life. She was trying to protect you. Surely you get that now. You're not a ditzy teenage girl anymore, Stacey. Surely you can see she cared.'

Stacey's entire body shuddered. Ava would never see things from her point of view. She was wasting her time even trying. She wasn't sure if it was even worth explaining to her. But she'd not come here to have this exchange with Ava. She'd come to speak with her grandad. And to stop her husband from trying to kill Jennifer again. She'd not mentally prepared herself for this encounter.

'He spent all those years in prison because of me. It was all my fault. I need to tell him to his face. I need to beg him for forgiveness.' Stacey didn't make eye contact with Ava as she spoke. She couldn't stand to view the expression on her face.

Instead, she remembered the intense exhilaration she'd felt when David arrived that night. Her heart had swelled in delight when he'd snuck onto the grounds and sought her out. She'd phoned him up and warned him it wasn't sensible. Told him that her mum was onto them and that they might get caught out. But secretly, she knew he'd still come. They'd both enjoyed the thrill of being so rebellious.

David had been working a late shift and came dressed in his overalls. He'd tied the top half around his waist and had been wearing a tight, white T-shirt that exposed his muscly arms. He'd been so buff and strong in those days. They'd hugged and kissed by the pond. He'd got frisky and said if he didn't have her that night, he'd go insane. Then he'd almost tripped over that taut chain stretched out behind them. 'What's all this about, Stacey?'

'I bet Ava a fiver she wouldn't be able to push this weird statue into the pond,' she'd said before kissing him on the lips again. 'Turns out that, for a beanpole, she's quite strong.'

'Yeah, but what's with the chain?'

'Oh, yeah, so Grandad was trying to drag it back out. He couldn't do it. Maybe you should try. I bet you'd be strong enough. You'd do it with one of those massive arms of yours.'

'Stacey Fincher, if you think I've walked all the way through that field and got wheat stuck in my boxers again, just to pull some rusty chain out of a stinky old pond, then think again.' He'd pulled her closer to him. 'I've come to pull off all your clothes and make you wet.'

She'd giggled. 'Oi, you. Stop it. We can't do that!'

'Yeah, we can.' He'd started kissing her neck and groping her bottom. 'Find a place. What about that stone circle where we had fun before?'

'Ava uses that to smoke. And she found that box of condoms you left in there.'

'About time we used those.'

'We will. Soon. When I'm ready.'

'Is Ava here?'

'Well, no. She's at a party on the Eden. But she might come back because she didn't feel too great earlier. Had one of her weird headaches.'

'She won't.'

'David! She might.'

'Come on, Stacey. What are you worried about? Is it your weird, nosy little sister?' He'd glanced around. 'Tell her to do one and stop spying on you. She clocked me in the field the other day. Did she tell on me?'

'She won't bother us. Not tonight.'

'Oh, right, did you give the little creep what for, did you?

'Mmm. Something like that, yes.'

They'd started kissing again. His hands were all over her.

'Get your dirty fucking hands off my daughter, you filthy scumbag!'

What happened in those next moments was always unclear in Stacey's mind. There was lots of shouting and name-calling. David had been taken aback by the barrage of abuse and said nothing. He'd taken it all with a silent grimace on his face.

Her irate mum had called him some awful things. So awful. She'd punched him in the chest. Shoved him. Told him she'd make sure he went to prison where he belonged. That he'd end up in a rank cell with the rest of the perverts.

She remembered trying to calm her mum down. Begged her to take a moment to listen. She'd not even done anything. They'd not even had proper sex yet. They were in love and wanted to be together for ever. But she just wouldn't listen to her. Wouldn't even give her a chance to get a word in as she ranted, threatened and slapped David. And he took it all, hands stuck at his sides. He looked completely mortified.

She had to put a stop to it. Her mum was ruining everything. David would never want to see her again after this embarrassing episode. If she remembered it correctly, she'd been the one who snatched at her mum's hair first. That was when her mum spun and smacked her hard across the side of the head. The scuffle was a very hazy memory. Her mum had grabbed her around the neck, and Stacey fell over, landed funny and struggled to catch her breath.

She'd only been winded from the fall, but David had lost his cool and taken action, believing she'd been hurt badly. She didn't know why he'd used that chain. He saw red, she guessed. She remembered peering up from the ground and seeing a scene that had haunted her ever since.

David had wrapped the end of the chain around her mum's neck and nastily hissed, 'Hey, how do you like that, you vicious cow?' The fear in her mum's eyes in that moment had stayed with her. As she'd clawed at the chain about her neck with desperate fingers. How he'd pulled harder and wrapped even more around her in response to her attempt to fight back.

'Oh, God! Stop now. Let go of her!' Stacey had shouted as she saw her mum's eyes bulge.

'You touch her again, and I'll come back and finish the job. Understand? Nobody gets to hurt her. Nobody!' he'd roared. With that, he'd let go, and her mum had stumbled sideways.

Still fighting to free the chain, she'd tripped, and with the chain still tangled about her neck, she'd pitched straight into the water.

They'd both gone to the pond's edge, mouths open wide in shock, as they gaped at the scene in horror.

Her mum had disappeared.

Stacey had gasped and almost jumped in after her. Or, at least, she was fairly sure she considered doing this.

When her mum's hands had broken through the surface, like two frantic fish trying to leap from the water, they'd both jumped back in shock. It had been too dark to make out how close her mum's face had come to the surface. She later read somewhere that if there'd been another two inches of chain, she'd have been able to push her face above the surface of the water.

Sometimes she played a different scene in her head where her mum's face did emerge. In that memory, Stacey spoke to her mum and admonished her for the ridiculous way she'd acted. She'd stood next to that pond, arms crossed, and in a calm voice said, 'Now, if you don't want to be dragged down there with that statue, I suggest you calm yourself down, lady, and let me have my say. I'll only save you if you listen and promise to take everything on board. Deal?'

Her mum, straining to keep her head out of the murky water, would splutter and plead for help. 'OK, I'm sorry, Stacey. I'll try to be more understanding. I swear I will. I should never have hit you. I was upset, sweet girl. Please help free Mummy now.'

'OK. We'll get you out. Don't panic. It's important to just breathe, Mum.'

'It's dragging me under. It's deep. Please save me, Stacey. I can't breathe anymore. It's so tight. Help me get it loose. I can't do it on my own. It's all twisted around my neck. It's pulling me down.'

'I'll get you out. I'm coming in to get you out.'

If only... If only... If only.

Stacey had a fuzzy memory of David putting his hand against her chest and stopping her from chasing straight over, although she could never be sure if this actually happened, or if she just liked to believe that it had. She'd never once asked him about that.

What she knew for certain was they'd both observed in totally stunned silence and did absolutely nothing. Stood like they were statues themselves, peering down in morbid fascination as the splashing hands became less frantic. As the movement of those skinny fingers died down to a slow drumming. And then her hands dropped back into the water and vanished.

Stacey often wondered why her mum spent those last moments splashing madly instead of attempting to free herself from that chain. But she knew the answer to that. Her mum understood she couldn't untangle herself, and this had been her last desperate attempt at getting her daughter's attention. Stacey always remembered noticing that her mum's right hand was bandaged. The shoddily applied dressing hanging off, limp and useless. That must've triggered the idea that led to what she did next.

Now Stacey opened her eyes and, trembling, locked eyes with Ava. 'I made the wrong choice, didn't I? I picked David. I picked a monster over my own mother.'

53

The jar in Jennifer's hand shook as she held it out in front of her. How could such a small thing seem so heavy? It was like she was wielding a bowling ball. Fear, she assumed. Fear was rendering her limbs useless. Her legs were weak too, and she was sure that if she moved one step, they would collapse under her weight.

She wanted to keep David talking, but her grandad had other ideas and lunged for the man, grabbed his wrist and tried to prise the wrench from his grasp.

The pair went crashing around the small space, and they must've hit the light switch because everything turned dark, and Jennifer somehow ended up knocked down on the floor. The jar rolled from her grasp, and her specs flew from her face. As Jennifer tried to push herself back up, a sharp pain in her hand made her cry out. She realised she'd fallen among the broken window shards, and she'd gone and put her hands straight into the sharp pieces as she'd tried to get up.

She glanced up to see a figure go crashing backwards

and fall against the art apparatus, causing paint tubes and brushes to clatter down around them. Her eyes adjusted to the gloom just in time for her to comprehend that this had been her grandad. He let out a long, hollow groan and held his side. She caught a flash of David's fierce grimace, his face mask now pulled down, as he crouched and searched the floor. She guessed he'd dropped the wrench in the tussle.

She touched her right hand and found a shard of glass sticking out of her skin under her left thumb. Pain seared up her arm, and for a couple of seconds she felt certain she would throw up, pass out, or both. She tried to compose herself. Out of the broken window, she noticed the blueish moon breaking through the clouds. And she heard her dad calling out her name.

'He's going to kill us!' shouted Jennifer.

Then David found the wrench and swung it at her.

54

'I told David to wait by the pond, and I ran back to the house. I don't remember having a plan at that point. Though, I guess I must have. I must've had a reason to go back to the house,' said Stacey.

Ava's face was impossible to read now. She'd stepped back away, so she was almost standing in the hallway, cloaked in darkness. This made it easier to keep talking. Unburdening everything seemed less scary when she couldn't see the threatening expression she knew would be stuck on her sister's stony face.

But then Ava spoke. 'You took his watch.' Her voice was quiet and empty of emotion.

'Yes. I took it,' Stacey said, recalling her grandad shifting in his seat and letting out a moan as she'd approached. The smell of strong booze had been heavy in the air as she'd tiptoed around that glass and edged closer to the intoxicated man. 'I could hear you walking about upstairs. You were running a bath. This was just after that car almost hit you down on the lane.'

'You took his watch,' repeated Ava, her voice harder now.

Stacey had struggled to free her grandad's gold wristwatch. She'd used some thick kitchen roll, careful not to get her prints on it, further evidence that she'd been in control and had planned things properly in her head. She'd struggled to get it free, which had caused her grandad to moan and mumble something inaudible in his slumber.

'Stacey? Stacey, is... that... you?'

Stacey remembered her stomach lurching when she'd heard Jennifer's voice. She'd sounded funny. Distracted and sluggish. Stacey had stepped away from her grandad and pretended to be scrutinising the globe, spinning it with an intent look, while doing her best to ignore her sister, who was standing in the doorway, wearing her light blue summer nightie. She'd looked like a chilling apparition staring straight at her, heavy-eyed and listless.

'I think Mum's in... the... bath... now,' Jennifer had mumbled drowsily. 'She's asleep in... the... water. With the bubbles... I can picture the frothy bubbles foaming over the sides... Someone should... wake her. They really should... wake her now.'

She'd been drugged out of her head and was in a languid, sleepwalking state. Stacey had stayed put and said nothing.

After getting no response, Jennifer had mumbled, 'Why is there so much glass? It's all over... the... floor.' Then she'd drifted away from the doorway, wandering off into the kitchen, where she'd fallen asleep for the night.

Stacey had rushed back to find David. He'd been pacing with his hands on his head, doing his best not to look at the water. She'd broken her grandad's watch strap and dropped it into the water, then told her boyfriend everything would be OK. She'd fix everything.

'Yes, I took his watch,' repeated Stacey, snapping out of the bleak memory. 'When you were running your bath and clunking about, you disturbed Jennifer, and she thought Mum was having a bath for some reason. She came downstairs, and she saw me take it.'

'So, you're worried she'll remember,' stated Ava.

Stacey nodded. 'All those scrambled memories are slowly coming back to her. I can't work out if she'd been awake or sleepwalking that night. Maybe she already knows. If not, it's only a matter of time.'

Ava stepped out of the shadows, her face pale and unreadable.

'Help me put things right, Ava. Tell me how I can fix this. Tell me what I need to do, because I'm going nuts here.'

'You can't fix this. Nothing you do will ever fix this,' whispered Ava.

Stacey shook her head, tears streaming down her cheeks. 'I made a bad choice. One bad choice. But I need to fix this.'

'You... you... you conniving cunt!' boomed Ava as she stepped forward and delivered a slap that almost knocked Stacey off her feet.

55

Never in her life had Jennifer been so pleased to see her dad. It clearly took a few moments for Howard to get the gist of things after he'd climbed through the broken window and took in the scene with a confused scowl. He'd spied Ernest down among the paints, groaning in pain, and found her cowering away from David, blood-covered hands up in defence. Jennifer knew another couple of inches and that wrench would've hit her in the face and knocked her senseless. It had been a minor miracle David's ferocious swing hadn't connected.

Now David had ceased his mindless attack to identify the new threat.

It was difficult to say which of the men sprang into action first, but they collided with a mighty crash and began grappling and throwing wild punches the moment they connected. Glass crunched underfoot, and the doll's house ended up pulverised in the brawl. Her dad somehow managed to get behind David, grabbed him around the neck, and held him in a powerful headlock as the other man bucked in a frenzy, thrusting the wrench backwards in a blind attempt to land a hit.

Jennifer caught a dull thud, guessing one had struck, but it was difficult to see clearly in the gloom with both men twisting and turning and scrambling.

David crouched and flung Howard over his shoulders, sending him crashing down into bits of broken doll's house, but he rolled sideways, got back up and flew at David the moment he found his feet.

David started swinging frantic shots with the wrench, and the pair were soon stuck in a fierce grapple.

What followed were vile curses, wild punches and even hair yanking. The savage fight was getting out of hand now.

Jennifer spotted her specs and made a grab for them before they got flattened in the chaos; then she scurried over to her prone grandad. 'What are we going to do? They're going to kill each other!'

56

S tacey's face burned from the hefty slap. She braced for more blows, but they didn't come.

Ava had left the room. She heard her say, 'Yes, police, please.'

Stacey rubbed two fingers against her throbbing cheek; it was wet from tears and hot from the slap. She had to find her grandad before it was too late. Because she had to look him in the eye, beg for his forgiveness, then accept her punishment. She took a last gaze around the room. She'd never be returning here. She knew that much.

Stacey raced after her sister and found her finishing up her call outside, near the back door.

Ava flashed her a harsh, disapproving glare as she approached. 'We're done. I need you to understand that this is the last conversation you and I will ever have, Stacey.'

'Ava, I—'

'Shut up. Just shut up.'

'I'm not sure what's going to happen to me.'

'All those lies you've fed us. All your fake grief about

Mum. Lies about how you and David met. When you introduced him to our family for the first time, claiming you'd hooked up at some music event. All of that was a pile of bollocks.' She shook her head. 'You've been scheming for years. Were you seeing him all the time? For all those years?'

'We stayed apart for a while. For months, we barely had any contact. In the years after, we kept our relationship a complete secret. We agreed we wouldn't announce we were an item until I was nineteen. We pretended that's when we first met. Everyone thinks we are the same age, but he's almost six years older.'

'How? How can a flaky little cow like you hide something like this? I... I don't know you at all, do I?'

'You do. You *do* know me. I'm me... I'm still me... I made a mistake. I made a silly mistake. I was young and stupid. My grief wasn't fake. I swear it wasn't.'

Ava laughed without humour. 'Wow. "A silly mistake." Is that what you'd call killing your own mother, framing your grandad, letting him rot in a cell for all those years, while we all went around detesting him? While the entire town loathed him. And then you two skulk off to play happy families.'

'I didn't kill her. We didn't kill her. Things got out of hand... I made a mistake.'

'If you say that one more time, I swear, with God as my witness, I will strangle you with my own hands. Is that clear?'

'It's true,' sobbed Stacey.

Ava was about to respond when a distant shout travelled up from somewhere within the grounds.

57

The wrench clanked down on the floor as the men tussled and threw more wild punches. Then, somehow, David found a way out of the commotion and jumped through the broken window, causing the remaining glass to break and clatter down.

Jennifer tried to grab her dad's arm and stop him from pursuing, but he leaped through the window and threw a flurry of punches that bounced off the back of the other man's head. Yet David kept walking, and it was evident that his persistence was infuriating her dad.

Jennifer's hand was soaked with blood, and thick droplets fell from her fingertips.

Howard was trying to stop David from running away by pulling at his tracksuit top, but he lost his grip and pitched forward. David spun, thrust up a knee and smacked him square in the face.

Jennifer carefully climbed through the window and raced over to pair. The blow had knocked the fight right out of her dad, but he wouldn't let up. He was still trying to climb back up to continue the brawl. David stumbled away.

'Stop! Please stop now!' shouted Jennifer, grabbing at her dad's wrist, trying to stop him from chasing after David. He was bloodied and disoriented, and she knew if he carried on for much longer, it wouldn't end well.

David stopped, grabbed a piece of broken slab from the ground and turned. 'I'll kill you, Howard Fincher! You take one more step towards me and I'll smash your ugly head in.'

'Let him leave, Dad. That's enough,' Jennifer urged, still holding him back. He had blood all over his neck and face. His right eye had become puffy, hindering his ability to open it. His appearance mirrored that of someone who had left a boxing ring after going twelve rounds with a heavyweight.

The light from the observatory came on. Her grandad unlocked the door and came outside. His appearance was equally terrible, and he was struggling to walk. His bottom lip was ripped and dangling down horribly.

Then Jennifer spotted her sisters approaching.

Stacey, distraught and snivelling.

Ava, face fixed in a furious scowl, her anger targeted at David.

'What the hell are you doing here, you stupid man? Haven't you done enough damage already?' Stacey cried as she gawped at her husband. 'You're making things worse!'

David said nothing. He simply glowered at his wife as if she were an annoying child pestering him.

Jennifer noticed blood seeping through his tracksuit top. His right arm seemed to be saturated in claret.

'You crossed the line. That man died. It's over. We can't hide from this anymore.' Stacey gazed at the ground with a crestfallen expression fixed on her face. 'You went too far,' she continued in a pitiful mutter.

David wiped away a thick stream of blood flowing from his nose. 'You... you and your fucked-up family. Why did I ever stay with you all this time?'

'For Christ's sake, would someone tell me what the hell is happening here?' yelled Howard.

Stacey's red-rimmed eyes moved to Ernest, and she held his gaze for a few seconds, then flicked them back to the ground. 'I'm so sorry, Grandad. Please believe me... I... I picked the wrong side... In a moment of madness... I picked the wrong side. I'm sorry!'

'You'll end up with all the other lunatics where you belong,' snarled David.

'Don't say that,' begged Stacey.

David shrugged. 'You want to play this game? OK. Sure, that's fine. I'll tell the police what you did. I'll explain how you throttled your own mother, stitched up Grandpa here, then made me complicit in your twisted crime.'

'That's a lie,' cried Stacey, stepping closer to David. 'That's a lie. You dare. You bloody dare!'

Jennifer's gaze darted between her family members.

Her grey-faced grandad looked frail and shocked.

Her dad's face wore an expression set somewhere between enraged and dumbfounded.

Ava's face was white as snow, her thin lips tight, her eyes ablaze with fury.

Stacey's cheeks were almost purple and wet with tears. Strands of her hair were sticking to her face and forehead. She looked terrible. Bedraggled and defeated.

David appeared exhausted, though his expression was resolute, and his eyes sparkled with hatred. 'Try me, Stacey.

I'll fight you all the way with this. Our kids need *me*... Not you. Not some fruitcake who spends most of her time locked in the spare room listening to the voices in her head. I'll prove you're a mental case. I'll get the best lawyers money can buy. I'll make sure you never see *my* kids again. You attempt to pin this all on me and you'll be sorry.' He turned to Ava. 'You're not buying any of this bullshit she's trying to spin here, are you?'

'Go fuck yourself,' said Ava.

David shrugged again. 'I kept her wicked secret. I'm guilty of that. But I'm not going to let her pin this on me. Simple as that.'

'So why come after me? Why did you feel the need to keep me away from this place? What would you have done if I'd have met you alone, David?' asked Jennifer. She kept her voice steady as she held his harsh gaze.

David dropped the piece of slab and dusted off his hands. 'I was angry with Stacey and took it out on you. Now I have calmed down. Now I have a clearer perspective on everything. I shouldn't have come here. That was stupid. I had too much to drink, and I let my anger get the better of me.'

'No, no, no. David, please. We need to put this right now. We do,' Stacey bleated, her voice shredded with desperation.

Sirens shrieked in the distance, and Jennifer wondered if it was the police or the fire service heading to the blaze in Cobble Wood.

'He's worried you'll remember what you saw that night, Jennifer,' said Ava, glaring at David. 'That you'll recall seeing Stacey take Grandad's watch.'

'What?' gasped Howard.

David ignored Ava's comments and spoke to Stacey. 'If

you want to confess, go ahead. But I'll be sticking to my version of events. I'm going home now. My mum is holding the fort.' He placed a finger on his bleeding nose and winced. Then he turned and walked away.

'David!' Stacey went to follow and hesitated, staring at Ernest. For an instant, she gave the impression that she was about to say something. Her big eyes were wide, glazed and bloodshot. Her shoulders sagged, and her face dropped. Then she followed her husband.

'Stacey, come back,' yelled Howard. He made to go after her, but Ava pulled him back. 'We can't just let them go, Ava! Stacey. No. Come back. You need to tell me what the hell is going on!'

Ava rubbed his shoulder. 'Leave them, Dad. By the state of you, I'd say you need to sit down before you collapse. Come on, I'll make some coffee. Then I'll tell you everything. And I called the police; they're on their way.'

'I don't understand what's happening here,' said Howard, sounding beside himself now.

Jennifer could hear more distant sirens. Her hand was throbbing like hell; she reckoned she'd need stitches when the glass came out. But all she could focus on in that moment was her poor grandad's downcast expression. He had his hand pressed against his chest, and she could see tears slipping down his cheeks. Then he clasped a hand over his mouth, fell to his knees and let out a string of choking sobs that altogether broke her heart.

Jennifer and Ava gently pulled the broken old man back to his feet and led him back to the house.

58

As Stacey ran through the high wheat, her acute misery started switching to profound hatred. Not only for her husband, but also for herself. Though right now, she despised that man so intensely she wanted to scream until her lungs collapsed.

In the early days, she'd struggled to cope with the crushing guilt, and David had been level-headed and sensitive; he understood how fragile she was. How hard it was for her to bury her guilt and anguish. She'd been a complete mess. Yet he was sympathetic to her needs. She'd never have survived those early years without him.

Once Stacey had become a mother, things slowly got better for her. It never disappeared. Not completely, but with other things to focus on, she was able to cope better. Able to hide the grim shadow and push back the sombre memories that were always lurking in her mind. Night-time had always been the worst. Twenty-five years of an intense mix of nightmares, insomnia and vivid flashbacks had taken their toll.

Over the years, David's compassion had faded. It reached

the point where he'd get furious with her. Tell her to stop living in the past. Once, he'd told her to take an overdose and do them all a favour so he could move forward with his life and find someone less disturbed and unstable. So he could find Harriet and Evan a suitable mother who would be capable of caring for them and wasn't mentally unbalanced and dangerous.

That had been around the time the voices started, and she'd moved into the spare room, where she spent those long nights alone, often coming close to losing her mind. The most recent breakdown had coincided with her grandad's upcoming release. When they'd learned that he'd be staying in town. This news had brought all her problems back to the surface once again. Only this time, she'd been unable to keep a lid on her intense emotions.

However, unbelievably, things had become even worse.

When her youngest sister had announced she'd been going back to Barren's Lodge.

Behind closed doors, David had also slowly been losing his mind. He'd been panicking and kept flying into irate rants, insisting that Stacey needed to assume control of the situation. If she didn't, he was prepared to take drastic action. When he announced that he was going to keep an eye on Jennifer and they might need to 'do something about her', she'd been furious with him and ordered him to leave her sister alone.

But then Jennifer started remembering things. After their family meal, David had stepped things up a gear, and when Stacey found out he'd run her off the road, they'd had a blazing row.

This had ended in real, terrifying violence when he'd smashed her up against the fridge, strangled her, then shouted right in her face, 'If she remembers what she saw you do, we're screwed! We have to keep her away from Ernest's house. Get that into your stupid head, woman!'

'You can't hurt her, David. You can't hurt my sister. Please don't.'

'In that case, you make sure the bitch keeps her distance. Or make that old prick leave. I'm going mental here dealing with this. You know what she's like. Once she gets a bee in her bonnet, she never lets up. She'll keep sticking her beak in and digging it all back up again. That little freak will chip away until she's uncovered the truth. Do you want us to lose everything? Do you? If the senior associates catch a whiff of my involvement in something like this, my days at that place are numbered. That's us ruined. Big house. Nice cars. Pension. Our life... All gone. All of it!'

'I've been trying to keep her away. I even made out Mum was drugging her, and I tried to manipulate her memories. Have you any idea how that made me feel?'

'All you did was make things worse. You probably just helped her remember.'

'I tried my best.'

'If I lose my position at work, I'll never forgive you. Have you any idea how hard I have worked to get where I am? No! Of course you fucking haven't, you bloody airhead.'

'It won't come to that. They can't prove anything.'

'Yes, they can, you dense cow. That—'

He'd become silent then, and Stacey knew he hadn't wanted to disclose his thoughts. Because she guessed he'd not wanted to give her the added ammunition regarding the other fingerprints found on that length of chain that the police had never tied to anybody else.

Instead, he'd said, 'You reckon your stupid secret petition will help? You think the town will really rise up and force him out? Think again. He's not going anywhere, and eventually no one will care. Yesterday's news. We need to force him to leave. We need to keep *her* away from that place.' He'd jabbed her in the temple with his finger. 'Start using this. Or I'll be forced to do something much worse. Next time I won't just scare her, I'll crush that nosy bitch under that van. Do you get what I'm saying?'

'I can't cope, David. I can't take this anymore. I can't, I can't, I can't.'

He'd punched her hard in the stomach and in a thunderous voice yelled, 'You ever even think about speaking the truth, I'll kill you. And your fucking dipshit sister. I'll kill your entire family if it means protecting our kids from this secret and keeping everything I've worked for. Do you understand, you dense, back-stabbing slag?'

Stacey saw a dark shape ahead of her in the field and broke out of her awful swirl of thoughts. She needed to try to concentrate on the here and now. On the possible ways she could resolve this. She needed to get her husband to stop and listen to her.

Around them, blue lights were flashing. Some were moving fast and were clearly heading for Barren's Lodge. There were more vivid blue lights in the distance, where coils of smoke rose into the gloomy sky. They weren't moving, and she guessed they were fire engines attending to the blaze in the nearby woods.

She knew what was ablaze there. David had promised to eliminate all evidence, and she imagined the fire brigade dousing the VW van, now a charred wreckage. That crappy van he'd had some crook steal for him. Some dodgy guy from the Eden he used to purchase drugs from back in the day.

When David found out about the man he'd killed on the High Street, he'd become close to flipping out and throttling her in the kitchen. If the kids hadn't been watching TV in the lounge, she might not have been able to get out of the house and run away from him. But his last warning to her had been a stark and terrifying one. He'd said if she came to Barren's Lodge tonight, he'd come searching for her and kill her.

Stacey thought she was now close to the place where the field met the copse that Jennifer once called the Forbidden Island. Close to where she and Ava had led their younger sister. Did destiny lead her to this place today? Was it karma that her world was crumbling around her and it was here she'd now lose all the things she loved the most? Was this punishment for those horrible things her younger self had done?

Who was that girl?

'David... David, just stop. We need to talk.'

He didn't respond. He coughed, then bent over and spat out some foul, stringy saliva.

'An innocent man lost his life because of you. You took things too far. There's no way out now.'

Still no reply. He kept going. Head bowed.

'You've made everything so much worse.'

David whacked the crop from his path with the back of his hand.

'What did you think you'd achieve? Hey? David, stop ignoring me.'

The wheat made way for overgrown weeds, dry branches and creeping vegetation as they approached the line of trees where the copse began. He gazed around, as if trying to get his bearings. In his haste to get away, she reckoned he'd gone off track and lost the path he was familiar with. The route he'd used in the old days.

'You want the truth, David? You want to hear something insane? I have spent all these years convincing myself I made the right choice. That I picked you because I adored you. That I picked you over my family because I believed we were destined to be together. That I chose you over my mum because I loved you so much, and it was impossible to comprehend a world without us being together... I'd even tell myself that if we didn't do what we did, then Harriet and Evan wouldn't be here... But the truth is, I knew a long time ago I'd made the wrong choice.'

David stumbled into the undergrowth. It was as though he needed to get away from her. That he couldn't face her and would wade through whatever stood in his path if it meant not looking at her. They passed a collapsed fence with bits of curled barbed wire sticking up from the posts.

'I would have left you years ago. God, I so wanted to. I'd dream of doing it sometimes. Pictured myself telling you to go fuck yourself and that we were over. But I couldn't do that, could I? Because all the time I was playing happy families with you, I was somehow able to justify what we did. How messed up is that? I was stuck with you. Stuck with a daily reminder of our hideous crime. Leaving you would mean I'd have to admit the truth to myself. Admit that I made the biggest mistake of my life when I stood by you that day.'

It was darker now they'd left the field, and she thought about Jennifer's dreams. When her mind had come here during those drugged-up slumbers. When she'd dreamed about Polly swinging from a tree.

If she had some rope, she'd have used it on herself right there and then. Would David try to save her if she did? No. He'd grab her ankles and pull with all his might. He'd apply all his weight until her neck cracked and her body went limp in his arms.

'Nothing to say now, David? Or has the beating you took from my dad finally shut you up?'

David emitted a derisive snort as he finally swung round to face her, but in doing so, he tripped and fell into a mass of bracken.

As he lay there, sprawled in front of her, she was unable to resist the urge to let out a scornful laugh. She truly despised him, and now she'd told him some home truths she felt so much better about herself. She'd spent so long being belittled by him, and in that moment, she saw him for what he was. A weak, pathetic, domineering bully.

'Don't you dare laugh at me.'

Stacey laughed harder. 'Why? What are you going to do?'

'I'm warning you.'

'Are you going to have one of your little temper tantrums? Is that what you're going to do?'

'Shut your mouth.'

'Are you going to throttle me and tell me I'm a useless, tragic wretch? That I'm not fit to be the mother of your perfect children? You're nothing but a little man with a big temper. A jumped-up little prick.'

Stacey struggled to make out David's features in the gloom as he shuffled about in the undergrowth, but she sensed the overwhelming wrath emanating from him. 'Everyone will find out what you did. Your parents will be mortified, won't they? When they learn what their special boy is capable of.'

Stacey heard his ragged breathing and knew the time was close. She was close to getting the reaction she needed. She willed it to happen. Because she was ready. The whispering voices in the dark had told her this moment would come. Told her that when it came, she'd be in a significant place. A place full of sorrow and regret.

'Oh, dear. Had the fight knocked out of you?' she said sarcastically. 'Come on, David, now's not the time to pussy out on me.'

'All you had to do was keep your head. We should have worked together and put things right.' His voice sounded distant and strange as he used a tree stump to pull himself up.

'By killing my sister? You expected me to accept that? I planned to kill her myself once. And you know how much that still haunts me.'

David said nothing and simply stood in the darkness ahead of her.

Stacey wanted him to come at her. She desperately wanted him to lose his cool and give her the justification she needed to hit him with the big lump of rock her trainer was planted on. She'd pushed it loose. Felt it move under her foot. She'd need to be quick. As soon as he came at her, she'd go for it. She even pictured herself cracking the rock against the side of his temple, and once he went down, she'd keep hitting him until he stopped moving.

But David didn't go for her. He walked on a few steps; then he keeled over.

59

Stacey used her phone's torch to examine her motionless husband. She considered this might be a trick, and he would suddenly leap up from the undergrowth, grab her and beat her senseless. Until she saw how wet his black T-shirt looked under the glow of the light.

She moved his tracksuit top aside, peeled back the sticky garment, saw the huge, gory gash along his side. She touched it with her finger. The wound gaped open and pumped out thick, dark blood. She examined him further, and when she rolled up his soaked tracksuit sleeve, she found another long laceration running from his wrist right up to his elbow. 'Ouch. Oh no, David. You've gone and got yourself in a right old messy state now, haven't you?'

She guessed he'd lost a huge amount of blood, and that clarified why he'd slowed up, bumbled into the bushes and hadn't throttled her when she'd said all those things. Her tough hubby had flaked out.

And so here he was. Lying at her feet and unable to defend himself.

She shone the light on his face. Right in his eyes. She poked his cheek and took his neck pulse. Faint, but there.

Distant sirens howled, but she saw no blue lights flashing nearby. Just pitch blackness.

She thought about David using that chain. How in that split second, he'd made the decision to unhook it from the rock and wrap it around her mum's neck like that. He could've pushed her. Used his body to block her path. Grabbed Mum and dragged her away from the scuffle. Even punched her. Anything would have been less cruel than what he'd done to her. He'd always said he acted spontaneously. He'd seen red. Wanted to protect her. She'd believed all those lies back then.

Now... now she understood what type of person he was. Spiteful. Ruthless and mean. Violent.

'Well, David. A dilemma. Do I leave you here and hope for the best? Or shall we make sure the job is done properly?' Stacey went over to collect the rock from the ground, and something else caught her eye.

She removed the item from the bushes and studied it under the light. She gasped and let out a jittery laugh. 'My God. No way!' It was a bottle of Mad Dog 20/20. The bottle was old, the label faded, but it was, without a doubt, red grape flavour. The same flavour they'd been drinking out here that day. Stacey was absolutely certain this was the bottle Ava had brought along that memorable afternoon. The bottle her older sister had thrown away all those years ago.

Stacey smiled and touched the weather-washed label. This was a sign. A clear sign. She smashed the bottle with the rock and selected a nice big piece from the fragments.

Stacey stepped back over to David. 'Did you think you

were some sort of action hero crashing about in all that glass? Mm? David? Hey, David?' She grabbed his left hand in hers and flipped it, exposing the wrist.

Her loathsome husband had threatened to lay the blame on her more than once. Told her in no uncertain terms that if she ever let the truth out, he'd turn it all around on her. That it would be his word against hers, and he'd make sure she took the fall. He'd not been joking. He'd proved that today.

She wouldn't let him do that again. No way would she stand by and let him blame her for everything. She knew she could never beat him once the police and lawyers got involved. He'd talk his way out of it, and she'd be demonised and left accountable for everything. Even if they did work out that those were David's fingerprints left at the scene, he'd still get himself off the hook. At least this way, she'd get to have her say, put the record straight, and he wouldn't be around to counter the truth with his bullshit. This way, she'd get a fighting chance.

Under a sombre, moonlit sky, a cold truth, a long, heavy sigh... everything ends...

Stacey grimaced and cried when she used that piece of glass bottle to slice open her husband's wrist. She felt warm blood spurting over her fingers. She hated him. Right now, she genuinely detested him.

But it hadn't always been that way, had it? There'd been some uplifting and pleasant moments in the time they'd shared together, hadn't there? There'd been times when she'd convinced herself they were happy. Brainwashed herself into thinking they were a normal couple who, despite all their issues, still loved each other. Plus, they had their lovely children.

But deep down, she knew she'd been a witless teenager infatuated with an older boy who'd showed her a bit of attention. A heedless idiot who picked this man over her own mother and then got stuck with him. There'd never been any genuine love shared between them.

The last twenty-five years had been a sham.

In shadows cast, where dark clouds gather, a silent pain lingers... everything ends.

The second wrist was harder to do, with the glass slippery in her fingers. As she hacked away at skin and vital arteries, her crying turned into chest-burning bawling.

And David didn't stir once during the entire gruesome procedure.

60

Three Months Later

'Hey, Grandad. Are you OK?' asked Jennifer, taking a seat on the bench next to him.

He seemed to have aged dramatically over the last few months. It worried her to find him looking so drawn and sapped. Had leaving prison and coming back into the real world taken it out of him so much? Sped up the ageing process?

She guessed it was more to do with what had happened after his release and the dreadful things he'd found out. The idea that his own granddaughter had caused his incarceration. He'd spent all those years desperate to clear his name, but when he had, learning the truth had been soul destroying.

'Dad still working? We should get going soon.'

'He's been fixing up the electrics in the second cabin, but

I'm sure he's getting ready now. You should see what he's done with the place. It'll be ready for guests in a week or so. Hard to believe we'll be having visitors coming here again.'

'I'm so glad he's staying here with you and he's out of that estate. And it's so good you've got company now.'

'Well, it seemed silly for him to be stuck in that poky flat when I have plenty of space here. But it was his idea to get the rentals reopened. This is his venture, not mine.' He chuckled. 'All I do is make the tea. Oh, he's done away with those bloody wasps and fixed up the roofs.'

Jennifer rested her head on his shoulder. 'Thanks. He needs something to focus on. This will do him good.'

'Yes. It's doing me good, too.'

'Are you sure you don't want to come today?'

'I read they've sold every seat, and that your play is causing quite the stir.'

'Yes. I'm so nervous. I don't normally get nervous about my plays.'

'I bet it's going to be amazing. But... all those people. I'd rather not. I'm not a huge fan of crowds. It would be too much for me, I'm afraid.'

'I understand. I'm not a fan of crowds myself. But I guess I should pop my head in and see what all the buzz is about. Oh, and I also need to contact Mabel Grice-Hutchinson and thank her for all the publicity. I'm sure it's helped generate more interest.'

'Mabel who?'

'She's a YouTuber. She did a documentary about what happened. And she's put together a new film updating her viewers on the case. It was extremely popular. Lots of people are intrigued by what happened here, Grandad, and not just people in the town.'

'Right.' He shifted, frowning.

'I understand you want to forget about all this and move on. Nonetheless, it's best if the truth is told. Better for everyone.'

'And this theatre play of yours... also *does* that? Tells the truth?'

'Oh, no, not entirely. Well, it does, in a way, I suppose. I had to make adjustments. It's technically a play *inspired* by true events, rather than based on. Dale said this would be more appropriate. But all the important elements are in there.'

'So, who plays me?'

'Obviously a very handsome, charismatic man. His name is Marvin Bell; some of the cast reckon he sounds like the former Supertramp singer, Roger Hodgson.'

He offered her a carefree smile, even though his eyes were sad, hinting that he wasn't keen on the idea of a play derived from such tragedy. 'The character's called Marvin?'

'No, the actor. His character is called Edward Mason.'

'What's Stacey's character called?'

His question threw Jennifer, and she struggled with her response. 'Um, she's... Samantha.'

She was tempted to add that in the musical drama, Samantha wasn't found smoking a cigarette in a dark wood while softly reciting her daughter's poem to her dead husband. She also wasn't apprehended by police officers for slashing her husband's wrists with a broken bottle. Instead, Samantha is arrested in a wheat field before she has a chance to silence her husband and then confesses to framing her grandad for her mother's death.

'Stacey wrote to me from prison,' he said.

'You accepted her letter?'

'I did.'

'I'm guessing she's still begging for your forgiveness. Will you ever be able to forgive her?'

He shrugged. 'I will try.'

'Do you want to talk about it? About what else she said?'

'Another day, perhaps. Another day.'

Jennifer wondered how someone could carry on with life with something so awful hanging over them. How did her sister hide it all away and pretend to the world like she did? How did she bury her anguish, fix a smile on her face, then act like everything wasn't broken and utterly messed up? They'd even put on a little theatre drama of their own when David had pretended to be infuriated with Stacey that she'd been discussing the secret boyfriend at Harriet's party.

'It's your gran's birthday today. She would have loved to see your play. I'll be sure to tell her all about it when I go to her plot.'

'It's a shame she's not still here with us. I wish she'd known the truth.'

He gave her a wry smile and winked. 'Your gran always believed me, Jennifer. From day one.'

'She did?

'Just once, she looked me in the eye and asked me if I did that evil thing to our daughter. I said, "I did not do it, Sally. And you know I didn't." And she nodded, gave me an earnest smile and said she truly believed me. You see, we were soulmates. Still *are* soulmates. We meant everything to each other. Knew each other so well and loved each other unconditionally. My Sally knew I didn't have it in me. She just... *knew*! But we both understood that if she openly took my side, she would have been alienated from the family, and neither of us wanted that.'

'Then why didn't she visit you?'

'Ah, well, you see, she did. Three or four times a year. She kept it a secret because she didn't think anyone would understand.'

Jennifer welled up and had to wipe her eyes. 'Words can't describe how glad I am to hear this, Grandad. I always assumed, like we all did, that you never saw one another ever again.'

'I spoke to my Sally just two months before... before she left this world.' He kissed his wrinkly fingers, lifted his hand up and blew on it. 'I often send her kisses up into heaven. I miss her so much.'

Jennifer kissed her fingers twice and blew the kisses into the sky. 'Those are from me, Gran. I hope they get there safely.'

'They will. They always do.'

Jennifer blew two more kisses into the sky. Those were for her mum.

They sat in silent contemplation for a moment, listening to the birds singing.

'You asked me why I distrust the police so much. Are you aware that there was evidence that an unknown person had handled that length of chain? Some fingerprints that the police never linked to anyone in the family.'

'Yes. David's, I presume. I'm sure that will come out. I bet the detectives have already established this, and the information will soon become public knowledge.'

'They always suspected there was someone else linked to that case. Someone they'd not identified, who wasn't registered on their system. They knew damn well there was. Yet, even with that element of doubt hanging over the trial, they still hung me out to dry.'

Jennifer couldn't find a reply to this. What could you say? It was unfair. A travesty. An epic failing. A monumental miscarriage of justice.

She'd gone over all the old media reports from the past, and the pressure on the police to convict someone for her mum's murder had been immense. But all along, there'd been an element of doubt. Everyone involved must have, at some point during the proceedings, questioned if they'd really got their man. Had they even cared? Had those people who put him in prison for all those years ever lain in bed at night contemplating their actions and decisions? Did they let an element of doubt and guilt creep in? Or was he just another statistic? Just another job ticked off the board.

Surely it mattered if they made the right decisions.

'They justified the existence of the unknown prints by saying that Barren's Lodge was a hive of activity, that anyone could have handled that chain at some point. My lawyer said they were remiss by disregarding this piece of vital evidence. It came up again during my appeal. Again, it didn't help. It was my gold watch being in the water that sealed the deal. I was unable to provide an explanation for that. Nobody could explain that.'

Jennifer imagined a teenage Stacey dropping her grandad's watch into the dark water. She shuddered. It was such a calculated move, and it made her blood run cold thinking about it. Now she knew the truth. She'd witnessed her sister's sly act. She'd seen Stacey remove his watch. That was what this had all been about. That was why they were panicking and trying to stop her from coming to this place. They were convinced she'd remember, and that she'd bring their entire world down when she did. David had ended up so on edge, he'd been prepared to silence her for good.

Jennifer thought this was ironic, because even after being told about this incriminating event she'd witnessed, she couldn't, for the life of her, recall seeing Stacey standing in that room that night. She pictured the glass on the floor, she remembered the potent smell of whisky, and even something about that globe had seemed significant. But as for seeing her sister take that watch – nothing. She had erased the memory from her mind. She'd searched and searched and couldn't find it.

Sometimes even the important stuff simply melts away for ever.

But it didn't matter now. David and Stacey had been convinced that she would have a moment of total recall, which had pitted them against one and other, causing their downfall.

'How are Harriet and Evan doing?' he asked.

'David's folks are taking good care of them. It's going to be so very tough on them.'

'I'd still like to meet them. If they are happy to come here.'

'They will. In time.'

Jennifer had a sudden image of Harriet sobbing and squeezing the life out of her stress unicorn. Then she visualised the girl pinching her little fingers against the material and glaring at her with a screwed-up expression. 'It's your fault Mummy killed Daddy in the woods, Aunty Jennifer! I hate you. I hate you so much.'

Jennifer shook away the angry images of her niece.

'Here he is. Well, you've scrubbed up well, Howard,' said Ernest.

Jennifer gazed up from the bench to find her dad heading over to them. He'd made a decent effort today. His hair was neat, his beard trimmed. He even wore a crisp navy suit. He looked different. Younger. He'd put on a bit of weight, and he appeared so much healthier for it. Ava had said he'd stayed sober for almost two months; having something else to focus on had given the man a new lease of life.

'Hey, Dad. Smart threads.'

Her dad gave her a big smile. 'I'm ready when you are, Jennifer. Let's attend this play of yours, shall we?'

61

J ennifer felt giddy as she sipped her fizz. The pub, situated just across from the theatre, was packed solid. The place exuded a genuine charm with its low oak beams, cosy interior and homely vibe. She lost track of the number of people who had come over and praised her, offered to buy her another drink, or gave her the thumbs-up. It felt like a dream. Like she was in a bubble.

She spotted Dale talking to some of the cast, and they all raised their glasses at her, with Dale offering her a nod and a look that said, *We smashed it.*

'Who's that old mush-malt Dad's gassing to over there?' asked Ava, sitting down on a bar stool. She placed an empty wine glass and what looked like a manuscript on the bar area, using it to slide two empty glasses out of her way.

'Ava, that's horrible. He's chatting with Mary, who works on the scenes. And she's lovely,' said Jennifer tersely, annoyed that Ava had broken her cheerful little bubble.

'Well, she has a grating laugh like an overexcited chimpanzee at feeding time. I noticed she was chugging fizz backstage.'

'She enjoys a tipple. Most of the group do.'

'Except you, hey. Come on, knock that back. You've been sipping that glass for about an hour. I'll order us some prosecco. Or do you want champagne, since your show was such a massive hit?'

'I really don't mind.'

'OK. I'm going to just get this out of the way and say it. The play was fantastic. I don't normally go for all that musical sing-song bollocks, but I must admit, this... this I liked. It was moving, brave and beautiful. Grandad would have been proud. Will be proud. It was filmed, right?'

'Glad you liked it. And yes, someone filmed it.' On reflection, Jennifer wasn't now so sure he should watch it.

'You did bloody well. I liked that song, "Twenty-five Years". Real catchy piece. Musicals normally bore me to death. Apart from *The Nightmare Before Christmas*. How did it go again?' Ava started singing, '*Twenty-five-years... How many days? How many hours?*'

'You don't want to know,' said Jennifer flatly, almost adding, *It's the equivalent of nine thousand, one hundred and twenty-five days, if you're really interested.*

While Ava ordered them two glasses of champagne, still humming the song, Jennifer kept an eye on her dad as he chatted away to Mary. He'd declined any booze today and was drinking coffee instead. He'd told Jennifer he wanted to make a good impression in front of her theatre chums, and she'd decided that was rather sweet of him.

Mary threw back her head and laughed hysterically at something he'd said, and Jennifer caught his eye. He flashed her a soft smile and, with it, an expression that suggested he might have made a big mistake by starting a conversation with Mary. She could be a bit hyper when she'd had a glass or two. She was also renowned for her bullish behaviour towards men while intoxicated, so she'd perhaps save him in ten minutes; they could make their excuses and slip out.

'Let's talk about the elephant in the room,' said Ava, handing her a champagne flute.

'I don't follow.'

'Yes, you do. I can see how everyone is staring at me and wondering – is she *really* like the character she's based on? Lucky I'm thick-skinned, hey?'

'It's *just* a play.'

'I think we both know that whatever this is... whatever your funny little group has just achieved here, it was much, much more than "*just* a play". Is that how you see me? Your antagonist? Am I your lifelong enemy, Jennifer?'

'No, of course I don't see you that way.'

'Ariel Fletcher came across as a bit of a nasty cow, though, right? I felt for Judith... I did. No joke. It got me thinking.'

Jennifer sipped her champagne and felt her cheeks burn. When she'd written the play, she hadn't expected her sister to be first in line to come and watch it. Perhaps she'd not been as subtle as she should have been.

'I am sorry, Jennifer. I haven't always been the best sister to you, and I... I'd say we have some catching up to do. You and me. What do you reckon?'

Jennifer gave her sister a reluctant nod and a thin smile. What did Ava want her to say? OK, she had been jealous of the relationship her older sisters had once shared. She'd always perceived herself as the outcast. The annoying pain in the arse whom they couldn't wait to get rid of. The funny little embarrassment they enjoyed ridiculing in front of others whenever the chance arose. She had been desperate for them to accept her into the fold – and Ava, more so. She'd yearned for the day when they treated her as their equal.

None of that meant she now wanted to be Ava's best buddy. Or that she wanted to have sisterly chats over brunch every week. No, she had no intention of changing things or becoming Stacey's replacement.

Ava swigged back her drink. 'We should do some fun stuff. Go out once a month and get smashed. Have a girly weekend in Italy or Greece. How about that?'

Jennifer smiled. Her sister was plastered already. 'Do some fun stuff.' That was a broad spectrum, she decided. Drinking until you puked or lazing about on a beach in a warm country didn't sound like much fun. Her idea of fun was to consume a cream cake in front of *Never Mind the Buzzcocks*, or to swig chilled wine tucked up in a warm bed, watching a naff film on Netflix on a Friday night.

'What's that there? You've got a copy of the play?' asked Jennifer, pointing at the tatty manuscript on the bar, doing her best to steer the conversation and avoid any more chit-chat about how they needed to go out and start bonding.

'Yeah, I nicked it from backstage. A memento of my little sister's grand achievement. It's even complete with a coffee-ring stain. Might be a collector's item when the show hits Broadway or the West End, right?'

Jennifer nodded, finding Ava's praise disconcerting now. She'd never cared about any of the previous plays she'd been involved in. 'I'm not sure we should get carried away.'

Ava let out a small burp and bumped shoulders with her. 'Don't be so sceptical. Dream big, Jennifer. Oh, here comes your boyfriend. Check out that corduroy blazer. I reckon he pinched it from the local charity shop,' joked Ava.

Dale came sauntering over. 'Hey, you two. Both OK? Drinks?'

'Yeah, cheers,' said Ava, holding up her empty glass.

'Stunning tattoo, Ava. I love the artwork of the lion. It's so detailed,' said Dale.

'Thanks, you got any yourself?' asked Ava with a tepid smile.

Dale nodded. 'I have a huge golden eagle swooping right across my shoulders. He took an epic amount of pain, I can tell you.'

'Seriously? Let's see it, then,' demanded Ava, taking a sudden interest.

'No, I'm just kidding. I don't really have any.' He chuckled.

Ava gave Dale an annoyed grin and started flicking through the manuscript, making it clear she had no desire to talk any further with him.

Jennifer giggled. Both at the idea of Dale having a massive tattoo and at her sister's reaction to his lame attempt at humour.

'What a day, huh?' said Dale, grinning at Jennifer.

'Everyone did such a fantastic job. I can't wait to see it again,' said Jennifer.

'The local paper would like to do an interview about the play. Interested?' said Dale.

'No. I'll let you take the lead on that,' Jennifer replied, half an eye on her sister, who'd stopped flicking through the pages to read something, her long finger tapping her chin.

'Every scheduled show is a sell-out. For the first time in Flair Play's history! How about that? I'll get you two another drink,' said Dale with a thrilled smile, moving further down the bar and waving at the barman.

'He's rather excited. And he likes you, doesn't he? You'd make a good match. You're both a bit...' Ava's voice trailed off as she continued to study the manuscript with a deep frown creasing her forehead. Something had grabbed her attention.

'What's up?' probed Jennifer, now experiencing a slight sense of unease regarding Ava's abrupt change in mood. She didn't like the idea of her sister having a hard copy of the play. She'd guessed she'd only taken it so she could go through it with a scrutinising eye. To see if there was anything she missed. Anything about *Ariel's* character she'd missed.

Ava folded the manuscript over and jabbed a finger at a page. 'What's all this? I don't recall this scene.'

Jennifer studied the page. 'It's the original version. Before we amended it. That's why there are big crosses over the text.' She pointed. 'Here, see. That wasn't in the actual play.'

'Is that so?' said Ava, still reading, a snakelike smile playing on her lips.

Jennifer almost snatched the papers from her. Someone must have kept their original copy so they didn't have to reprint the newer version.

In the scene missing from the final play, it had been insinuated that Judith Fletcher may have been extracting flowers from some foxgloves growing on the grounds of her grandad's home. The scene didn't make it entirely clear what Judith's motives were, and when Dale had questioned Jennifer about this, she had said she wanted to inject a slight element of mystery regarding Judith's intentions. But Dale had said that unless they made it clear why the foxglove was significant, and the intent behind her actions, it would be best to omit that scene. So she'd agreed.

'Fuck, Jennifer, you're a dark horse, you really are,' said Ava, her sharp eyes now fixed on her, like a cat ready to pounce on a clueless sparrow.

'I'm not sure I follow.'

'Don't you bullshit me. I'm not an idiot. I can see why you decided to whip this scene out of the play. A bit too close to the truth, right?'

'No, no, it's just—'

'I know foxglove grows on the grounds of Barren's Lodge. It always has. June to September. Sometimes later.'

'So?'

Ava drummed her fingers on the manuscript's page. 'So, I also know that these plants are used to yield digoxin, which is employed as a heart medication.'

'Oh, is that so? How do you know that?' said Jennifer, trying to sound surprised.

'Because my friend told me all about foxglove after someone she fell out with tried to kill her favourite horse with it. They stuffed the dried leaves into its hay.'

'They did?'

'Yeah, she got lucky. The horse hadn't eaten too much before my friend noticed and stopped it from gobbling it all up.' Ava lowered her voice. 'It's poisonous to humans as well as animals. It can be deadly. If ingested by a person, it can cause vomiting, dizziness, disorientation, convulsions... and even death.'

Jennifer went to sip her drink and realised she'd already finished it. She searched the bar for Dale and spotted him waffling on to another guy. He wasn't looking her way, so she couldn't snatch his attention away.

Ava continued, 'The flowers, seeds, stems or leaves of the plant can all be used. I guess it would be easy enough to slip some into somebody's tea. Or perhaps, say, a bottle of whisky, right?'

'Perhaps.'

Ava closed the manuscript, rubbing her hand over the front cover as she shook her head. 'Yes, you're a dark horse indeed.'

'It could be that Judith Fletcher was merely considering her options. She had a complicated relationship with her grandad.'

'You want my theory?'

Jennifer touched the raised scar near her thumb. She'd often rub this when she was deep in thought. 'If you like.'

'I reckon Judith had loved her mother so much, she was prepared to do the unthinkable. Yes, I'd say our little Judith was ready to act if she deemed it necessary. I think maybe Judith was misunderstood. By everyone. Possibly underestimated, too, right?'

Dale was now heading over with the drinks, and Jennifer realised she felt a tad nauseous.

'If she decided that Ernest Moorby wasn't telling the truth, then she'd intended to take a very different path,' whispered Ava.

'I think you mean the character, Edward Mason,' corrected Jennifer, also whispering.

'Oh, yes, slip of the tongue. Whoops. Or had... *Judith* already started down that sinister path? Was that why her grandad was becoming unwell? Hmm?'

'Here we go, fizz all round,' said Dale in a chirpy tone.

Ava knocked her drink back in one hit. 'Cheers. Right, I'm going to save Dad from that dreadful woman before she drives him back onto the booze. I'll have real champagne next time, thank you very much. Oh, and Dale, isn't it way past time you asked my little sister out on a date? You'd make a... *cute* couple.'

She put down her glass and picked up the play. Then she leaned in close to Jennifer's ear and softly said, 'I'm so proud of you, Jennifer Fincher. So bloody proud, you hear me? You were prepared to undertake what I didn't have the bottle to do. I respect that.' With that, she strutted off to find their dad.

Dale's face was a picture. His cheeks were glowing red enough to match her own. 'Your sister is a bit—'

'Intense.'

'I was going to say scary.'

'I used to be scared of her. Not anymore.'

Dale raised his glass. 'Well... cheers.'

They clinked glasses and sipped their drinks.

Jennifer decided she should sneak out before Dale took her sister's advice, said something stupid and made things awkward between them. Besides, she'd had enough excitement in her life these past few months. She craved some peace and quiet. Wanted nothing more than to be back at home on her own. Back home by herself in her cosy annexe.

What was it Stacey had called her? *A lone wolf...* She'd been right. Being alone was just how she liked it.

Dale was talking to her in an enthusiastic voice, but she wasn't listening. She was peering through the crowds to where Ava stood chatting away to their dad. Mary had gone, no doubt shooed away by her brazen sister.

And now, thinking about her overbearing sister and the foxglove suddenly gave her an idea for her next play. This would be a tale of hatred and revenge. A story so dark it would blow Dale's mind. Blow everyone's mind. But she wouldn't rush into it. There was plenty of time. That play could wait while she got her head straight. There was lots to think about.

Jennifer did rather like the idea of her sister believing she'd planned to poison their grandad. She had no intention of putting her straight and confirming that this *really* had only been a plot point for her play that they'd decided to remove. She could never have done that to him. She cared for him way too much. But Ava respected her now, something that had never happened before, so she felt quite good about herself. In some way, it was a shame she'd found out the things she had, but there could be no going back now. Everything had changed, and it was hard to talk to her sister without losing her cool.

First off, she'd need to reread the letter Stacey had sent her. Especially the part where she apologised for the things she'd done to her all those years ago. The things they'd *both* done to her. The list had been long, though certain things had been hard to take in. Such as her sisters burying Reggie-Hedgy, trashing her beloved hedgehog sanctuary, and dosing her up with sedatives that scrambled her young mind.

But then there had been the hardest part to swallow.

How they'd led her to the copse to find the girl Polly. The girl whose soul they'd told her had been trapped inside that wooden puppet she'd once loved to play with. How they'd hatched a heinous plot to lose her out there... lose her for good. They'd even talked about thumping her with a lump of wood and abandoning her in the wheat field, in the hope a combine harvester would crush her to death.

If their mum hadn't come out there to find them that summer's day, would she even be here now?

Jennifer raised her drink to her lips, and Ava caught her gazing at her. Her sister flashed her a cocky grin, so she looked away and focused back on Dale, who was still rambling on, oblivious to the fact that her mind had drifted miles away.

No, she thought. *This time there will be no story. No play.*

How was it fair that Ava got to walk away from this untouched?

Jennifer would keep her thoughts off the page and lock them inside her head where nobody could ever find them. It would be safer that way if she decided to act on her ideas.

It would need to look like a freak accident, she mused to herself.

Jennifer placed her hand on her heart, feeling it gently thump away.

It's important to just breathe.

Maybe the two sisters should take a short trip away at some point. She'd always fancied Switzerland. A nice mountainous region would be wonderful to explore.

It was a clumsy slip. She plummeted over the side and... vanished. Oh my.

Or a daytrip to a safari park might be another option.

I told her not to get out and check the tyre... God, it's so tragic, because Ava loved lions so much. If you can retrieve her left arm from that huge beast with all those scars on his nose, you'll see the evidence of that love.

In a while she'd sneak out from this place, go home to enjoy a long bath and there imagine all the different ways she could destroy her eldest sister.

Just the mere thought of taking revenge against Ava was giving her goosebumps. She had to fight back the urge not to start laughing like a mad person at all the deliciously dreadful thoughts already spinning in her mind.

She realised that she was a little tipsy now, though. So perhaps she would need to deliberate over her choices when she had a clearer perspective on things.

But at least her feeling of nausea had passed, so she decided she'd stay and have one last drink with Dale and enjoy the buzz for a short while longer.

THANK YOU FOR READING

Did you enjoy reading *Never Forget*? Please consider leaving a review on Amazon. Your review will help other readers to discover the novel.

ABOUT THE AUTHOR

I was born in 1979 and live in Kent with my wife and children. I ran a private investigation agency for over fifteen years, dealing in cases that involved breach of contract claims, commercial debt recovery, and process serving. My agency also specialised in people tracing, so much of my work revolved around tracking down debtors, dealing in adoption matters and locating missing persons. At times, I worked on some pretty bizarre cases and dealt with plenty of interesting and sometimes colourful individuals.

I've had a huge passion for screenwriting for many years and started writing novels in 2021. My first novel, *The Tests,* was based on a spec screenplay that I originally wrote back in 2009. *The Tests* was then republished with Inkubator Books in 2022 under the new title, *The Wrong Girl.*

If you enjoy dark crime fiction and intense psychological thrillers, don't forget to subscribe to the newsletter so you can find out about new releases, book deals, and giveaways. All subscribers receive a free copy of my novella, Survival Weekend. (eBook or Audio version) https://www.robertkirby books.com/subscribe

ALSO BY ROBERT W. KIRBY

The Wrong Girl

The Visit

I Remember Now

Never Forget

Printed in Great Britain
by Amazon